The
Disunited States
of America

Harry Turtledove

TOR®
TEEN

A Tom Doherty Associates Book

New York

THE DISUNITED STATES OF AMERICA

Copyright © 2006 by Harry Turtledove

A Tor Teen Book
Published by Tom Doherty Associates, LLC
175 Fifth Avenue
New York, NY 10010

www.tor-forge.com

Tor® is a registered trademark of Tom Doherty Associates, LLC.

The Library of Congress has cataloged the hardcover edition as follows:

Turtledove, Harry.
   The disunited states of America / Harry Turtledove. — 1st ed.
      p. cm.
   "A Tom Doherty Associates book."
   ISBN 978-0-7653-1485-7
   1. Time travel—Fiction. 2. Virginia—Fiction. 3. Ohio—Fiction. I. Title.
   PS3570.U76D58 2006
   813'.54—dc22

                                          2006044467

ISBN 978-0-7653-2824-3 (trade paperback)

First Edition: September 2006
First Tor Teen Edition: May 2011

The
Disunited States
of America

One

Beckie Royer was running guns from Ohio into Virginia, and she was scared to death. She hadn't intended to be a gun runner. She didn't want to be one. At the moment, she didn't have much choice.

Her grandmother and the man she called Uncle Luke even though he was only a relation by marriage sat in the front seat of his beat-up old white Honda. Beckie had the back seat—what there was of it—to herself. Her feet wouldn't go all the way to the floorboards, and with that cramped back seat she needed all the leg room she could get.

There was a gray blanket down there. When she lifted it to see what it hid, she almost passed out. Half a dozen assault rifles, and heaven only knew how many clips of ammunition.

She didn't say anything. She couldn't say anything. She was too scared—scared not just of the guns but scared that if she opened her mouth Uncle Luke would throw her and Gran out of the car and leave them stuck in the middle of nowhere. He hadn't wanted to drive them to Elizabeth, Virginia, in the first place. If his wife (who really was Gran's sister) hadn't insisted, he never would have done it.

Not for the first time, Beckie wished she were back in California. California had money, and it was at peace with most of its neighbors. Oh, the border squabble with Baja never went away, but it never got too hot, either. Baja knew California would clean its clock if it tried anything real grabby.

Gran had been born in Elizabeth a long time ago, back in the 2020s. Now that she'd turned seventy, she wanted to see her friends and relatives one last time before she died. That was what she said, anyway—Beckie wouldn't have been surprised if she lasted to a hundred.

So Gran took Beckie with her and flew to Columbus. Beckie had been excited then. How many seventeen-year-old girls from Los Angeles got a chance to go to other states, especially states filled with history and blood like Ohio and Virginia?

Everything turned out to be the world's biggest yawn. All Gran wanted to do was visit other old people. The dialects they spoke among themselves were so different from the English Beckie was used to that she hardly understood them. Even the food tasted weird. Nobody'd ever heard of salsa or cilantro. Gran's relatives hardly even used garlic. Boring!

And now the Honda was bouncing through the potholed streets of Belpre, Ohio. The town couldn't have had more than nine people in it. The bridge over the Ohio River looked a million years old. She hoped it wouldn't fall down. Right in the middle of the bridge, in the middle of the river, sat the Virginia border checkpoint.

Uncle Luke stopped the car. Two Virginia border guards in old-fashioned gray uniforms strode up to it. Beckie tried to keep her teeth from chattering. If they found those guns, they would throw her in jail and lose the key. They would figure the rifles were bound for the black guerrillas down in the lowlands. For all Beckie knew, they would be right.

How she wished she were bored now!

"From Ohio, eh?" one of the guards said. "I'm gonna have to see your papers." To Beckie's ear, he spoke with a peculiar nasal twang. *Papers* sounded like *pipers*. She could follow him, but she had to work at it.

"Give me your passports." Uncle Luke—Uncle Luke who wasn't an uncle, Uncle Luke who ran guns—held out his hand, first to Gran, then to Beckie.

She didn't want to give hers up, but what choice did she have? She felt even more naked, even more afraid, without it. She hadn't thought she could.

Uncle Luke's passport got only a brief glance. The guard stamped it and handed it back. But when he saw Gran's and Beckie's, he stiffened like a bird dog coming to point. "Hey, Cloyd! Lookie here!" he called. "These folks're from California!"

"From California?" Cloyd exclaimed. "What in blue blazes are they doin' here?"

"Beats me," the other guard said. "If I lived in California, I sure wouldn't come here, and that's a fact." He let out a wistful sigh, then bent down to speak to Gran and Beckie. Beckie kept her feet very still on the blanket. If she wiggled—and she had a habit of wiggling when she was nervous—the guns might make a noise. That would be dreadful, or whatever was worse than dreadful. "What're you California ladies doin' comin' into Virginia?" he asked.

"I was born in Elizabeth," Gran answered, and the hill-country twang in her voice showed she was telling the truth. "I'm comin' back to visit kinfolk and friends one last time 'fore I die, and I want my granddaughter here to know where her roots are."

"How about that?" the guard said. "If'n I moved away, reckon I'd be prouder I was gone than of where I came from. Ain't that right, Cloyd?"

"Expect it is." Cloyd kept staring at Beckie's passport and Gran's—her real name was Myrtle Bentley, but except when she had to sign something she didn't use it. Beckie wondered if he'd ever seen a California passport before. This was about as no-account a border crossing as the state of Virginia had. Why would a Californian want to come across here? Beckie sure didn't, not with those guns under her feet.

"California," the other guard, the one whose name she didn't know, said with a jealous sigh. California was big and rich and strong, all right. If people in another state tried mistreating its citizens, it could throw rockets all the way across North America. It hadn't needed to for a long time, but it could.

Beckie realized Uncle Luke was using those precious California passports as a shield to make sure his car didn't get searched. Normally, the guards would have looked to see if he was carrying moonshine or grass, trying to sneak them into Virginia without paying duty. That kind of smuggling happened all the time. Guns . . . Guns were a different business.

And Uncle Luke's gamble was going to pay off. "They have the right visas and everything?" the guard by the car asked Cloyd.

"Sure enough do," Cloyd said. He took the California passports over to the kiosk in the middle of the bridge and ran them through a computer terminal. He stamped them, too, as the other guard had stamped Uncle Luke's commonplace Ohio passport—Virginia was an old-fashioned place. Then he brought them back and returned them. "Here y'go, folks. Enjoy your stay."

"Thank you kindly," Gran said. Uncle Luke didn't say anything—he was as sour as an unripe persimmon. He just drove across the bridge, across the river, and into Virginia.

As Beckie stuck her passport into her purse, she let out an enormous sigh of relief. "What's eating you, kid?" Uncle Luke said.

"Nothing." Beckie didn't know if he would get mad that she'd found the guns. She didn't know, and she didn't want to find out. She kept her mouth shut.

"Beckie's just glad to be coming into Virginia," Gran said. "Isn't that right?"

"Sure," Beckie lied. She hadn't got on real well with her grandmother before this trip. Gran wasn't a sweet old lady—her favorite sport was complaining. Traveling with her for so long . . . Well, Beckie didn't like her better now than she had when they set out from Los Angeles.

But she had her precious passport back again, and she was heading for Elizabeth, not wherever Virginia kept the closest maximum-security prison. She wouldn't be a headline—unless Uncle Luke drove off the side of the road. It was narrow and winding, and he seemed to be going much too fast. She almost said something—but the less she said to him, the better, so she kept quiet again.

Parkersburg, the first town on the Virginia side of the border, went by in a blur. Once upon a time, it had been an oil town. Outside of Texas and Russian Alaska, there weren't many of those left in North America any more. Even for California, oil was hard to come by.

Kanawha flew by even faster, because it was smaller. The main highway went south toward Charleston—that was the biggest city in this part of Virginia. If you dropped it on Los Angeles, you wouldn't even notice where it hit. But it was what the locals had to be proud of, and they were.

But that was the main highway. State Route 14 ran southeast towards Elizabeth. Uncle Luke's car seemed to hit every hole in the road, and the road had plenty to hit. Beckie's teeth went together with a sharp click at one of the bad ones—Uncle Luke's shocks were shot, too, if he had any. The rifles under Beckie's feet shifted with a metallic clatter.

"What's that?" Gran ears weren't the greatest, even with a hearing aid, but she noticed the noise.

"It's nothin'," Uncle Luke said.

"I swear I heard a rattle." Gran didn't know when to leave well enough—or bad enough—alone.

"It's nothin', I told you!" This time, Uncle Luke all but shouted it. Gran wasn't much good at taking a hint, but she did now. Beckie breathed a little easier—only a little, but even that felt good. The guns were bad enough. She didn't want a quarrel in the car, too.

They drove past Bloody Hollow—a nice, cheery name for a place, and one that fit too well with what lay under the gray blanket—and Elizabeth Hill before they got to Elizabeth itself. The little town lay on the south bank of a loop of the Kanawha River. A sign at the edge said, WELCOME TO ELIZABETH, SEAT OF WIRT COUNTY. POPULATION (2092)—1,316.

To Beckie, it looked like the smallest, most godforsaken place in the world. Then Gran said, "My goodness, how town has grown! There weren't even a thousand people here when I was born." So it all depended on your point of view.

Uncle Luke gave his: "Lord, what a miserable dump." Beckie didn't like agreeing with him on anything. He was so sour, he made Gran seem sweet by comparison, which wasn't easy. But she would have had a hard time telling him he was wrong.

The county courthouse was smaller and dumpier than a lot of hamburger joints Beckie had seen. It was made of brown bricks that looked a million years old. They would have told her she was a long way from home all by themselves. Because of earthquakes, hardly anybody built with brick in California. The courthouse sat at the corner of Route 14 and a narrow street named—logically enough—Court. Uncle Luke stopped the Honda right by the courthouse. He hit the button that popped the trunk. "You guys get out here," he announced.

"What?" Gran sounded ticked. "I reckoned you'd take me all the way to Ethel's place." She never said *reckoned* in California. Funny words were coming back to her along with her accent.

"Well, then, you reckoned wrong," Uncle Luke said flatly. "You won't get lost, and you won't get tired. This place isn't big enough for that." No matter how snotty he was, he was right again.

"How will we get back?" Beckie asked.

"Not my worry," he said. "Bound to be a bus or something. Come on—hop out. Time's a-wasting."

Beckie almost jumped out of the car. She didn't want to stay near those assault rifles a second longer than she had to. Gran moved slower, not just because she was old but because she was giving Uncle Luke a piece of her mind. Beckie got their suitcases out of the trunk. "The nerve of that man!" Gran fumed as she finally joined Beckie on the sidewalk. The Honda zoomed away. Wherever Uncle Luke was going, he was in a bigger hurry to get there than he had been to come here.

"Gran," Beckie said quietly, "he had guns in the back of the car."

"Maybe he's going hunting after he dropped us off. Maybe that's why he was in such a rush."

"Not unless whatever he's hunting walks on two legs. They weren't just rifles. They were the kind of guns you see on the news, where the person who's got one just did something horrible with it," Beckie said.

"Don't be silly," Gran said. "Luke wouldn't do anything like that."

How do you know? Beckie wouldn't have put anything past the man who wasn't her real relative. But she didn't argue with Gran. She didn't see the point. She wouldn't change her grandmother's mind—nothing this side of a nuke could do that. And she couldn't prove anything now, no matter what she thought.

Gran was looking around with wonder on her usually sour face. "All these places I haven't seen for so long," she murmured. "There's Zollicoffer's drug store. And look." She pointed to a hill off to the southwest, not far out of town. "That there's Jephany Knob."

"Oh, boy," Beckie said in a hollow voice. She was looking around, too. The courthouse had a brass memorial plaque fastened to the side. WIRT COUNTY'S HEROIC DEAD, it said. There were names from the War of 1812, the War of 1833, the First Ohio-Virginia War, the Three States' War, the First Black Insurrection, the Great War, the Second Black Insurrection, the Atlantic War, the Florida Intervention, and all the other fights Virginia had got into over the past three centuries. Wirt County couldn't have a whole lot of people—all of Virginia put together had fewer people than Los Angeles County. But the men here weren't shy about going to war.

While Gran and Beckie looked around, people from Elizabeth were looking at them. Beckie needed a moment to realize that. She needed another moment to realize they weren't friendly looks—not even a little bit. *We're strangers,* she thought. Everybody here knew everybody else. How often did Elizabeth see strangers? And what did it do to them when it did?

In Los Angeles, you were lucky if you knew your neighbors. Your friends were more likely to be the people you went to school with or, if you were a grown-up, worked with. It wasn't like that here. POPULATION—1,316. How long had these people been gos-

siping about one another and feuding with one another? Since
the town was founded, whenever that was. A long time ago—
Beckie was positive of that.

A woman a little younger than Gran came up to them. She was
wearing a frumpy print dress. Well, it would have been frumpy in
California, anyhow. For all Beckie knew, it was the height of style
in western Virginia. Hesitantly, the woman said, "You're Myrtle
Collins, isn't that right?"

"I sure am," Gran answered. Collins had to be her maiden
name. Beckie wasn't sure she'd ever heard it before. Gran went
on, "Are you Violet Brown?"

"No, I'm Daisy," the local woman said. "Daisy Springer nowadays. You went to school with Violet, and you came over to the
house all the time." She smiled. "I was the kid sister who made
trouble."

"Oh, were you ever!" Gran said. She started talking about
stuff that had happened a long, long time ago. She didn't intro-
duce Beckie to Daisy Brown—no, Springer—or anything. She
might have forgotten Beckie was along at all. She'd fallen back
into her own early days, and nothing else mattered.

A man came by sweeping the sidewalk with a push broom.
You wouldn't see anything like that in L.A.—everybody there
used blowers. The man was black, the first black Beckie had
seen in Elizabeth. He had what looked like the crummiest job in
town. Things were like that all over the Southeast—except in
Mississippi, where blacks were on top and persecuted whites instead of the other way around.

"Gran—" Beckie said after a while. Her grandmother stood
right there next to her, but didn't hear a thing. It wasn't just because
Gran was going deaf, either. She was off in another place—no, in
another time. She and Daisy Springer were reliving the days when

they were both kids. They were talking about people Beckie'd never heard of. Even if she had heard of them, she wouldn't have cared about them, not one bit.

"And do you recollect the time Hattie Williamson's dog—" Gran started yet another story.

"Gran—" Beckie tried again. She'd never heard her grandmother say *recollect*, either.

Gran still didn't remember—or recollect—that she was alive. She'd forgotten Beckie existed, or that most of the forty years and more since she moved away from Elizabeth had ever happened. *Will I act that way when I get old?* Beckie wondered. She hoped not, anyway.

Even if Gran had forgotten about her, Daisy Springer still knew she was there. "This'll be your granddaughter, Myrt?" the local woman asked. That made Beckie blink one more time. *Myrt?* She couldn't imagine anybody ever calling Gran by a name like that. It was like calling the Rock of Gibraltar *Rockie*.

But Gran didn't seem to mind. She even kind of smiled. And she finally noticed Beckie was still beside her, and she hadn't fallen back into the 2030s or whenever they were talking about. "Yes, this here's Beckie Royer. She's my daughter Trish's little girl."

"Hello, Beckie." Mrs. Springer smiled, too. She looked nice, even if she did have a face like a horse. "I'm right pleased to meet you."

"Pleased to meet you, too." A handful of words, but they showed how much she was out of place in Elizabeth. In California, she sounded just like everybody else. Here, she showed she was a stranger—a foreigner (*furriner*, they'd say here)—every time she opened her mouth. She didn't like that. Even in Ohio, she'd sounded funny. She sounded more than funny on this side of the border.

"What's your father do?" Daisy Springer asked.

"He's a bioengineer," Beckie said.

"How about that?" Mrs. Springer said. Beckie wondered if she even knew what a bioengineer did. But she must have, because she went on, "There's a fish hatchery over by Palestine, a couple of miles south of here."

"Is there? That might be interesting." Beckie had to think how far two miles was—somewhere around three kilometers. California had been metric for more than 150 years. Some states still clung to the old way of measuring, though. North America was almost as much of a crazy quilt as Europe was.

"Where will y'all be staying?" Mrs. Springer asked Gran. *Y'all.* They really did talk like that! It wasn't just a joke on TV and in the movies.

"With Ted and Ethel Snodgrass," Gran answered. "Ethel's my first cousin, you know."

"Well, I do now that you remind me, but I plumb forgot," Daisy Springer said. She hadn't had to worry about who Gran's relatives were for longer than Beckie's mother was alive. "Down on Prunty Street, then." She didn't make it a question. She knew where the Snodgrasses—what a name!—lived.

Gran nodded. "That's right."

"What's it like in California?" Mrs. Springer sounded wistful. "Is it really as . . . as nice as all the shows make it out to be?"

"Not on your life," Gran said before Beckie could answer. "It's hot like you wouldn't believe in the summertime. People are rude. They don't know their place. You can't grow apples or pears, on account of you never get a frost. You can't imagine how terrible the traffic is. My son-in-law pays me no mind, and my daughter's just about as bad. They—"

Beckie stopped listening. She'd heard all of this a million

times before, even if it was new and fascinating to Mrs. Springer. Would they ever get out of the hot sun and over to the Snodgrasses' house? Beckie wouldn't have bet on it. When Gran started grumbling, she could go on for days.

"Are you ready?" the operator asked as Justin Monroe and his mother got into the transposition chamber.

"Of course not," Mom answered. The operator blinked. Then she decided it was a joke and laughed. Justin smiled himself. His mother liked giving dumb questions crazy answers. She looked at the operator and said, "Are *you* ready?"

"If I have to be," the operator said. *She* didn't seem to have any imagination to speak of. Justin wasn't surprised. You didn't need much in the way of brains to sit in the operator's chair. Crosstime Traffic paid operators to be glorified spare tires. Computers guided transposition chambers from the home timeline to an alternate, or from one alternate to another. If something went wrong (which hardly ever happened), the operator could take over and bring the chamber home with manual controls (if she or he was very, very lucky).

Justin sat down and fastened his seat belt. The seats in the chamber were like the ones in airplanes, all the way down to not giving enough legroom. Justin was tall and lanky—just over one meter, ninety centimeters—so he found that especially annoying.

Six feet three, he reminded himself. *I'm six feet three.* In the alternate where he and his mother were going, Virginia still used the old-fashioned measurements. He'd learned inches and feet and yards and miles and ounces and pounds and pints and quarts and gallons and bushels and the rest of those foolish values. He'd learned them, and he could use them, but they struck him as an enormous waste of time. Why twelve inches to a foot, or 5,280 feet to a mile? How were you supposed to keep track of stuff like that? Counting by tens was so much easier.

"Oh, one more thing," the operator said. "I need your slavery declarations."

"Right." Mom took hers out of her purse and handed it to the woman. Justin had his in a back pocket of his jeans—dungarees, people called them in the alternate where they were headed. The denim was dyed a light brown, not the blue that had been most popular in the home timeline for more than two hundred years.

"Thank you." The operator put them in a manila folder. Crosstime Traffic was supposed to get the most it could from the alternates while exploiting the people in them as little as possible. The year before, though, a scandal had rocked the home timeline's biggest corporation. People, some of them in high places, bought and sold and owned natives of low-tech alternates—not to make money or anything, but just for the thrill of power.

Government regulations came down in a flood. All over the world, governments had been waiting for an excuse to crack down on Crosstime Traffic. Now they had one. The slavery declarations were part of that. Justin and his mother both pledged not to have anything to do with enslaving anybody. That had always been against the rules, of course, but now they had to sign a paper that said they knew it was against the rules. How much good that signed sheet of paper would do. . . . Well, some bureaucrat somewhere thought it was a good idea.

Even though the alternate the Monroes were going to wasn't low-tech, the slavery declarations did matter there more than they would have in some other alternates. Discrimination survived over much of that changed North America, even if slavery was formally against the law everywhere.

"Why didn't they ratify the Constitution in that alternate?" Justin asked.

"They couldn't agree on how to set up the legislature," Mom answered. "The big states wanted it based on population. The little ones wanted each state to have one vote no matter how many people it had. They were too stubborn to split the difference, the way they did here."

"That's right. I remember now. And so they kept the Articles of Confederation instead." Justin made a face. U.S. history went on and on about all the ways the Articles didn't work. This alternate was a history text brought to life.

"They kept them—and then after a while they forgot about them," Mom said. "They still call countries in North America states, and a lot of them have the same names as states in the United States in the home timeline, but they're countries, and there's no United States in that alternate."

"Here we go," the operator said. A few lights glowed and changed color in the instrument panel in front of her. It didn't feel as if the transposition chamber was going anywhere. In one sense, it wasn't. It started out in an underground room in Charleston, West Virginia. It would end up in an underground room in Charleston, too.

But in the alternate where it was going, Charleston was part of Virginia, not of West Virginia. In the home timeline, Virginia seceded from the United States in 1861, as the Civil War was starting. Then West Virginia seceded from Virginia and got admitted to the Union as a separate state. There was no Civil War in that alternate. By the 1860s, the United States had already quietly fallen apart. There were lots of small and medium-sized wars between states, but never one great big one.

"We're going to have to be careful here," Mom warned. "This is a high-tech alternate. Except for traveling crosstime, they know almost as much as we do. We have to make sure we don't draw the wrong kind of attention to ourselves."

"Yeah, yeah." Justin had heard that a million times. "Wouldn't we be smarter to stay away from alternates like that? If they do catch us, they can really use what they squeeze out of us."

"For one thing, we do good business with them," his mother said. He snorted and rolled his eyes. Crosstime Traffic worshiped the bottom line. He didn't, or not so much. Mom went on, "Another reason we're there is to make sure they *don't* find the crosstime secret."

"What do we do? Screw up their computer data?" Justin asked sarcastically.

To his surprise, the operator spoke up: "That's happened in some other alternates. Not in this one, I don't think."

"Oh," he said, some of the wind gone from his sails.

"And another reason we're here is to do what we can to make race relations go better," Mom said. "Things aren't perfect in the home timeline even now. You know that as well as I do. They're a lot better than they used to be, but they sure aren't perfect. Even so, they look like heaven compared to Virginia and the other Southern states in that alternate."

"The other Southern states except Mississippi," Justin said.

Mom shook her head. "No, Mississippi, too. Blacks have no more business lording it over whites than whites do lording it over blacks. Nobody has any business lording it over anybody. It happens, but that doesn't make it right. Right?"

"I guess." Justin hadn't really worried about it one way or the other. His first thought was that the whites in Mississippi had it coming. But the black revolution there was 120 years old now. None of the whites in the miserable state now had ever persecuted anybody black. Why should they be on the receiving end for something they hadn't done themselves?

Before he could find an answer—if there was a good answer to find—the operator said, "We're there."

It felt as if about fifteen minutes had gone by. This alternate's breakpoint wasn't very far from the present, so getting there didn't seem to take very long. But when Justin looked at his watch, it was twenty past four—the same time as it was when he and Mom got into the transposition chamber. He'd seen that before. He still thought it was weird.

Chronophysicists talked about the difference between time and duration. Without the fancy math to back it up, the talk was just talk. Justin accepted it. He believed it because he saw it worked. But he didn't pretend to understand it. He wondered if the chronophysicists did, or if they just parroted what the computers told them.

The door to the transposition chamber slid open. Justin and his mother might not have moved in any physical sense, but they weren't where they had been, either. This concrete box of an underground room had a few bare bulbs glaring down from the ceiling, and that was it.

Mom laughed as she looked around. "Be it ever so humble . . ." she started.

But this wasn't home, even if they'd be living here for a while. This was a different and dangerous place. People here didn't like foreigners, and no one could be more foreign than the Monroes. The locals were racists. They were sexists. And they had a technology not very far behind the home timeline's. If they ever learned the crosstime secret, they could build transposition chambers. Instead of trading, they could go conquering across the alternates. They could—if people from the home timeline didn't stop them.

Even worse, they didn't have to get the crosstime secret from the home timeline. Even if everybody in Crosstime Traffic did everything right, these people might figure out how to travel between alternates all by themselves. Galbraith and Hester had, back in the home timeline. Otherwise, there would be no crosstime travel . . . and the home timeline, with too many people and not enough resources, would be in a lot of trouble.

Justin didn't want to think about that. Behind him, silently and without any fuss, the transposition chamber disappeared. He followed his mother toward the stairs that led up to the business Crosstime Traffic used for cover here.

"Mom," he said, "what *do* we do if they figure out crosstime travel for themselves?"

"Well, it hasn't happened yet," his mother answered. "Not here, not in any of the other high-tech alternates. We've had it for more than fifty years now. Maybe there's something about the home timelines that the alternates can't match for a long time, if they ever do."

"Like what?" Justin asked.

"I don't know." Mom laughed. "Maybe I'm talking through my hat, too. Maybe they're working on it right now in a lab in Richmond or New Orleans or Los Angeles or Fremont." Fremont was an important town here, not far from where Kansas City lay in the home timeline. "Maybe they'll find it tomorrow, and we'll all start going nuts."

"That would be great, wouldn't it?" Justin waited for Mom to climb the stairs so he could take them two at a time. Then he swarmed up after her.

"Hello, hello." That was Randolph Brooks, who ran the Charleston Coin and Stamp Company. Collecting North American stamps and coins was a lot more complicated here than it was in the home timeline. Every state issued its own. Some states had merged with neighbors over the years—there was only one Carolina these days, for instance. Some had broken apart—thanks to the Florida Intervention, that state was divided into three parts, one of which belonged to Cuba.

"How are you?" Mom asked. As far as the locals knew, she was Mr. Brooks' sister, which made Justin his nephew.

"Never a dull moment." Mr. Brooks was in his early middle years, plump, balding, with thick glasses that sat too far down on his nose. He looked like a man who bought and sold coins and stamps, in other words. "You wouldn't believe some of the counterfeits people try to palm off on you."

"I don't think there's ever been an alternate without thieves," Mom said.

"But these are *dumb* thieves." Randolph Brooks sounded annoyed at the stupidity of mankind. "They scan something, they print it on an inkjet, and they bring it in and expect me to believe it's two hundred years old. Ha!"

"How often do you get fooled?" Justin asked.

Mr. Brooks started to answer, then stopped. He tried again: "Well, I don't exactly know. How can I, when getting fooled means I didn't suspect when I should have?"

"Well, did you ever sell something to somebody who brought it back and said it was a fake?" Justin asked.

"No, I never did." Mr. Brooks looked over toward Justin's mother. "He likes to get to the bottom of things, doesn't he?"

"Oh, you might say so." Mom's voice was dry. Justin had an itch to know that he scratched whenever he could.

Right now, he was looking out the window. The buildings across the street looked like . . . buildings. They were made of brick, so they looked like old-fashioned buildings, but plenty of brick buildings still went up every year in the home timeline, too. One was a copy shop, one a shoe-repair place, one a donut house—only they always spelled it *doughnut* in this alternate.

The cars, though—the cars were something else. Quite a few of them still burned gasoline, which was obsolete in the home timeline. Their lines were strange. They *looked* faster than cars from the home timeline. They weren't, but they looked that way. Some of the makes were familiar: Honda, Mercedes, Renault. But Pegasus and Hupmobile and Lancelot and Vance rang no bell for Justin. You saw Vances everywhere. They were the Chevies of this alternate.

And the people seemed different, too. Hardly anybody here had piercings or tattoos. Women didn't wear pants. Their dresses looked like explosions in a florist's shop. Almost all of them were cut below the knee. More men wore suits than in the home timeline, and the four-button jackets with tiny lapels gave them the look of the 1890s. It was only a look, and Justin knew as much. Their technology was a lot closer to the home timeline's than that. The men who weren't in suits mostly had on brown jeans like Justin's.

An amazing number of people smoked. Men and women puffed on cigarettes, cigars, pipes. "Don't they know how bad for them that is?" Justin asked.

"They know. They mostly don't care," Mr. Brooks said. "They say they'd rather enjoy life more, even if that means they don't get quite so much of it." He shrugged. "Not how I see it, but that's what they say."

An African American walked by. He looked like a janitor.

Not many of his race got to be much more than janitors and farm laborers in this Virginia. They weren't called African Americans here, either. Polite whites called them Negroes. Whites who didn't bother being polite used a different name, one that sounded something like the nicer label.

Randolph Brooks saw Justin noticing the black man. "If you aren't racist here, they'll think you're peculiar. Sometimes you have to use those words."

"Won't be easy," Justin said. In the home timeline, people used what had been obscenities in the twentieth century without even thinking about them. What once was bad language turned normal. But if you used a racist or sexist or homophobic word there, most people wouldn't want anything to do with you. It wasn't exactly illegal, but it was like picking your nose in public or wearing fur.

A beat-up white Honda pulled into a parking space in front of the donut house. The middle-aged man who got out looked pretty beat-up himself. He had a narrow, suspicious face and about a day's worth of stubble on his chin. He wore those brown jeans and a T-shirt. Except for the color of his pants, that would have been ordinary enough in the home timeline. Here it said he was a tough guy, or wanted people to think he was.

Whatever he took out of the space between the front and back seats was wrapped in a blanket. It made a heavy, bulky load. His arm muscles bulged as he lugged it into the donut shop.

"Wonder what he's got," Justin said.

"About a month's supply of donut holes," Mr. Brooks said gravely. Justin started to nod, then sent him a sharp look. More to him than met the eye.

A few minutes later, the man came out and started back to his car. A pair of policemen in Smokey the Bear hats walked down the street toward him. When he saw them, he almost jumped out of his skin. If Justin were one of those cops, he would have arrested the man in the T-shirt on general principles.

They could do that here, too, more easily than in the home timeline. Some states in this alternate had bills of rights that limited what their governments could do. Virginia did, but it had lots of exceptions. If the police thought they were putting down a Negro revolt, they could do almost anything they pleased.

These policemen walked past the man in the T-shirt and jeans. They walked past the donut house. They went on down the street, laughing and talking. The man might have been on a sit-com, he acted so relieved. He jumped into the old Honda and drove away as fast as he could.

"Wonder what that was all about," Mom said—she'd noticed, too, then.

"Nothing to do with us," Mr. Brooks said. "All we have to do is sit tight, and everything will be fine." That sounded boring to Justin. He hadn't yet found out that you didn't always want excitement in your life. He hadn't—but he would.

Two

Beckie Royer sat on the back porch of the Snodgrasses' house and watched the grass grow. That was what people in Elizabeth called sitting around and doing nothing. They seemed to spend a lot of time doing it, too.

There sure wasn't much else to do. Beckie yawned. For her, there wasn't anything else to do. Gran sat inside, chattering away with Ethel Snodgrass. The two cousins were trying to catch up on more than half a lifetime apart in a few days. Mrs. Snodgrass seemed nice enough, but she was a lot more interested in Gran than she was in Beckie.

The grass in the back yard needed mowing. Maybe you really could watch it grow. It probably grew faster here than it did in Los Angeles. It rained more here—that was for sure. To Beckie, any rain in the summertime was weird. But these folks took it for granted.

Somewhere not far away, in bushes under some trees, something made a mewing noise. In California, Beckie would have thought it was a cat. Here, it was more likely to be a catbird. Those didn't live in Los Angeles. She thought they were handsome in their little black caps. Robins strutted across the lawn after bugs and worms. They had them in L.A., but you didn't see them every day. You were almost tripping over them here.

She wondered if she'd see a passenger pigeon. Three hundred years ago, just before 1800, they'd probably been the most common birds in the world. By two hundred years ago, they were hunted almost to extinction. But a lot of states banned going after them, and they pulled through. They would never form such huge flocks as they had once upon a time, but they were still around.

Something flew into the trees above the bushes where the catbirds were squawking. Was it a passenger pigeon? For a second, Beckie got excited. Then she saw it was a plain old ordinary pigeon. So much for that.

She looked over toward Jephany Knob. There it was: a knob. In California, it wouldn't have been tall enough to deserve a name. Maybe she would climb it, or go over to the fish hatchery Mrs. Springer had talked about. Or maybe . . . she would just sit here and watch the grass grow.

Little by little, she was starting to understand why places like this seemed to belong to an earlier time. They had modern conveniences. But if you weren't watching TV or using your computer, what could you do? Go to your neighbor's and chat. Go hunting if you were a man, cook if you were a woman. And sit around waiting for something to happen. It was usually a long wait.

She glanced at the sun. It was heading for the horizon, but it was still a couple of hours away. Talk about long waits . . . Some time between now and then, she needed to go back into the house and spray on some mosquito repellent. They had that back in California, but you really needed it here. The bugs would eat you alive if you forgot. They came out when the sun went down.

You almost had to be nuts to sit outside then, even with repellent on. The stuff wasn't perfect. You'd get bitten anyhow. But if you did stay out, if you ignored the buzzes that sounded like tiny dentist's drills whining through the humid air, you got to see fireflies.

Lightning bugs, they called them here most of the time. The locals took them for granted, because they saw them every summer. Beckie didn't—no fireflies in Los Angeles. She hadn't known what she was missing. There you were in the evening twilight, and all at once this little light would blink on in the air. And then it would disappear, and then come back again. Or another one would go on, and another, till you'd think the stars had started to dance.

Fireflies were just bugs. If you saw one in the daytime, when it wasn't glowing, you'd want to swat it or step on it. But when they flew, when they lit up, they weren't *just* bugs. They were marvels.

Gran came out on the porch to watch them, too. She was tight-lipped and disapproving of most of the world, but fireflies made her smile. "I almost forgot about them," she said. "Can you imagine that?"

"How could you forget anything so cool?" Beckie asked.

Her grandmother shrugged. "You just do. I haven't seen lightning bugs for more than forty years."

"Wow." That was more than twice as long as Beckie had been alive. She knew how big the number was, but she didn't understand what it meant. She could feel herself failing whenever she tried. And what was it like to be seventy? She looked at Gran's wrinkled face and gray hair. One day she would probably be that old herself. She knew as much, the same way she knew Saturn had rings. Both were true, but neither seemed to matter to her now.

"I'm glad I came back, in spite of all this silly talk about the border," Gran said.

Beckie hadn't paid any attention to the news since she got to Elizabeth. Nothing outside the little town seemed to matter to her while she was here. But that might not be so. "What silly talk?" she asked.

"Virginia may close it," Gran answered. "They say Ohio is letting too many terrorists and saboteurs across. They say Ohio is stirring up trouble, the way it always does." Raised here, she was a Virginia patriot.

Beckie didn't care one way or the other. She just wanted to make sure she could get home when she needed to. And . . . . "Terrorists and saboteurs? You mean like Uncle Luke?" She still remembered—she would never forget—the feel of assault rifles under the soles of her shoes.

"Don't talk silly talk," Gran said impatiently.

"I'm not," Beckie answered. "He was running guns."

"Oh, look at that one." Gran pointed at a firefly. She *was* hard of hearing. Maybe she missed what Beckie said. But she was hard of listening, too. Maybe she didn't want to hear it.

"How will we get out if we can't go back into Ohio?" Beckie asked. They were supposed to fly back from Columbus.

"Go down to Charleston, I suppose." Gran made a sour face. "That will be expensive. Changing flight plans always is."

"Can we do it?" Beckie didn't care about the money. She just wanted to make sure they could get home all right. "Or will some of the other states start shooting down airplanes from Virginia?"

"I hope not!" Gran heard that, all right. She'd lived through— how many little wars was it? They were just history lessons to Beckie, but they seemed a lot more than that when Gran started talking about them. Now she said, "I don't *think* they would do anything so terrible, especially if California stays neutral. But I reckon you never can tell."

"Maybe we ought to get out now, while we still can," Beckie said. "Nobody's shooting at anybody yet, right?"

"Well, no," Gran said. "But I hate to just up and leave. I haven't been home in so long, and seeing my cousin again. . . . It's almost like being young again, not that I expect you'll know what I mean. People your age just don't have any respect for their elders. You don't understand what I went through. When I was young, we didn't have it so easy, let me tell you."

"Sure, Gran." Beckie stopped listening. When Gran started grumbling, she didn't know how to stop. And she didn't want to think about anything else while she was doing it, either.

She might not want to do a whole lot of thinking about it anyway. How much would she mind if they got stuck in Elizabeth for however long the fighting lasted? As long as no one dropped any bombs here—and why would anybody in his right mind?—she'd be safe enough, and happy enough, too. She'd grown up here. This felt like home to her.

It didn't feel like home to Beckie. Every day she spent here seemed to last three weeks. If she got started, she could . . . *I could complain as well as Gran,* Beckie thought. The very idea was enough to make her clap a hand over her mouth. She couldn't imagine anything worse.

Justin Monroe was walking along minding his own business when he got caught in a police spot check. The cops were good at what they did. They sealed off a whole block at both ends in nothing flat. "Come forward for a paper check!" they shouted through bullhorns. To make sure people did as they were told, the Virginia State Police carried assault rifles.

This kind of thing couldn't happen in the United States in

the home timeline. Things here seemed similar on the surface to what Justin was used to, so the differences hit him harder.

This wasn't a small difference. If the cops didn't like his papers, or if they thought he was carrying a false set, they would . . . do what? *Whatever they want to,* he thought uneasily. The papers he carried were supposed to be perfect forgeries. Had they ever been tested like this? He didn't know. No, he didn't know, but he was going to find out.

Somebody who didn't want the State Police looking at his papers ducked into a secondhand bookstore. They saw him do it, though, and dragged him out. They also dragged out the little old woman who ran the store. Her documents passed muster, and they let her go. His made red lights go off. Either he wasn't who the papers said he was or he was somebody the cops wanted. They threw him into a paddy wagon—actually, it looked more like an armored car.

Men and women formed two lines, one for whites, the other for blacks. There were only three or four African Americans in that line. If Justin hadn't been briefed, he might have got into it himself because it was shorter. But that would have made him an object of suspicion here. He stayed in the longer line.

He might not have moved any faster in the shorter one. The police questioned the Negroes much more thoroughly than they did the whites. If a white person's papers didn't set off their machines, they passed him or her through. The blacks weren't so lucky.

When Justin got to the front of the line, a burly cop looked at his papers. "Says you're from Fredericksburg," he remarked.

"That's right," Justin said. "My mom and I are here to give Mr. Brooks a hand at his coin and stamp place. He's my uncle."

"Well, I've known Randolph a while. He's square clean

through," the policeman said. In this alternate, that was a compliment. The officer fed Justin's identity card into a reader. Then he said, "Hold out your arm."

Justin did. The cop ran a blunt scraper across the skin of his forearm. Then he put the scraper into another window in the reader. The electronics inside compared the DNA from the few cells on the scraper to the data on the identity card. A light turned green. The reader spat out the card. "Everything okay?" Justin asked.

"You're you, all right." The policeman returned the card. "Go on, now. Enjoy your stay in Charleston."

"Thanks." Justin put the identity card in his wallet again. It *was* good enough to fool the locals, and the readings on it were from his own DNA. He hoped he didn't sound sarcastic, even if he felt that way. In the home timeline, you needed a search warrant to go after DNA information. Not here. Here, you could just go fishing. That wasn't the only way the Virginia State Police and the rest of the government kept people in line, either.

Not far past the police checkpoint was a newsstand. The headline on the *Charleston Courier* read OHIO BANDITS MUST BE STOPPED! Every paper in Virginia would carry a headline like that today. All the TV and radio newsmen would say the same thing. Qualified representatives of opposing groups . . . kept their mouths shut, or had their mouths shut for them.

Charleston was close enough to Ohio and the state of Boone—which was Kentucky and about half of Tennessee—to pick up TV and radio signals from them. But Virginia jammed those signals, and Ohio and Boone jammed the ones from Virginia. If not for cable systems (which didn't cross borders), most people would have had no TV or radio at all.

The Web was in the same sort of shape. There was no World

Wide Web in this alternate. There were national Webs—mostly called state Webs on this side of the Atlantic. They didn't connect with one another, and local governments kept a much closer eye on them than in the home timeline. That was probably one reason why this alternate's technology had fallen behind the home timeline's.

But the Web, national, World Wide, or deep-fried, wasn't the first thing on Justin's mind. Getting out of the trap was. But he couldn't even talk about it when he got to the coin and stamp shop. Mr. Brooks was dickering with a local over a threepenny Virginia green from 1851, a rare and famous stamp in this alternate.

After going back and forth for twenty minutes, they settled on 550 pounds. The customer walked out with his tiny prize, a happy man.

Randolph Brooks looked happy, too. "That'll keep me eating for a while," he said.

"Sure," Justin said. Money here was a lot more complicated than in the home timeline. Virginia used pounds and shillings and pence, the old kind—twelve pence to a shilling, twenty shillings to a pound. In the home timeline, even Britain's money went decimal more than 120 years earlier.

Pennsylvania used pounds, too, but a Pennsylvania pound was worth more than a Virginia pound, and was divided into a hundred pence. Other kinds of pounds and dollars and reals and pesos and francs were scattered across the continent. Every computer had a money-conversion program, and every one of those programs needed updating at least once a week.

"How are you?" Mr. Brooks asked. "Am I wrong, or do you look a little green around the gills?" Nobody said anything like that in the home timeline, but old-fashioned phrases hung on here. Mr. Brooks had been here quite a while, so they fell from his lips as naturally as if he were a local.

Justin didn't have much trouble figuring out what this one meant. "Yeah, I guess I do," he said. "I got caught in one of the paperwork checks the State Police are running."

"Oh!" Mr. Brooks said. "Well, you must have passed, or they'd have you in a back room somewhere."

"Uh-huh." Justin nodded. "They scraped my arm for DNA and everything. But the stuff on the card really does come from my DNA, so I got the green light and they let me go. It was still scary. In a high-tech alternate like this one, you never know for sure if our forgeries are good enough."

"That's true." The older man didn't look happy about admitting it. "There are a couple of alternates where we have to be even more careful than we are here, because they're ahead of us in everything except knowing how to travel crosstime."

"What *will* we do if somebody else ever finds out?" It was on Justin's mind. He knew he couldn't be the only person from the home timeline who worried about stuff like that, either. If you sat down and thought about it for a little while, you had to worry . . . didn't you?

"What will we do?" The coin and stamp dealer gave him a crooked smile. "We'll sweat, that's what."

He wasn't likely to be wrong. The home timeline had been on the point of collapse when Galbraith and Hester discovered crosstime travel. Thanks to Crosstime Traffic, there was enough to go around again, and then some. Because the home timeline didn't take much from any one alternate, the worlds of if that it traded with weren't much affected.

None of the other high-tech alternates had that luxury. Some of them rigidly limited population, to make the most of what they did have. A couple took much more from the oceans than people in the home timeline ever did. And others exploited the rest of the Solar System. Nobody'd ever quite taken space travel seriously in the home timeline. Oh, weather and communications satellites were nice, but the real estate beyond Earth turned out to be much harder to use than early generations of science-fiction writers thought it would. People in the home timeline were still talking about making the first manned flight to Mars.

A couple of alternates, though, were already terraforming it. They were talking about doing the same thing with Venus. This alternate wasn't that far along, but even here astronauts from California and Prussia had gone to Mars and come back again. It was expensive, but people said it was worth it. Justin thought so. Riding a rocket was a lot more exciting that sitting in a transposition chamber.

"How long do you think we've got before someone else does start traveling crosstime?" Justin asked. "It's bound to happen sooner or later, isn't it?"

"Probably," Mr. Brooks said. "The bigwigs at Crosstime Traffic say it won't, but they have to say stuff like that. If they don't, the stock will fall. One of the reasons we come to high-tech alternates even though it's dangerous is to keep an eye on them."

"On the way over here, the chamber operator said we've messed up other alternates' work when they were getting close," Justin said. "Messed up their computer data or whatever, so they never found out how close they were."

"I've heard the same thing," Randolph Brooks said. "Ask anybody official and she'll tell you no. But that's just the official word, what you've got to say if you're in that kind of job."

"Yeah? What else have you heard?" Justin asked eagerly. Sometimes—often—gossip was a lot more interesting than the official word. Sometimes—often—it was more likely to be true, too. "What do we do if they make the experiments again anyway, see if their computers were maybe wrong?"

"I don't know. What if they do?" Mr. Brooks said. "Either we have to sabotage them one more time—blow up their lab or something—or else we've got something brand new to worry about."

He sounded calm and collected. In a way, that made sense. If some other alternate found the crosstime secret, it wasn't his worry, not particularly, anyhow. But it sure was the home time-line's worry—the biggest worry anybody would have had since people found out how to travel from one alternate to another.

"A crosstime war . . ." Justin murmured.

"Bite your tongue," Mr. Brooks said. "Bite it hard. You thought the slavery scandal was bad?"

"It *was*," Justin said. "People from the company never should have done anything like that."

"I know," Mr. Brooks said patiently. "But you've seen pictures from some of the alternates that went through atomic wars, right?"

"Sure. Who hasn't?" Justin said. Those pictures reminded you why counting your blessings was always a good idea.

But Mr. Brooks didn't let him down easy. "Okay. Imagine things like that in the home timeline. Imagine them in the alternate that figures out how to go crosstime. And imagine them in all the alternates where we bump together."

Justin tried. He tried, yes, and felt himself failing. He knew how bad a war like that would be. Knowing didn't help, because he could feel that his imagination wasn't big enough to take in all the different disasters in that kind of war. "We can't let it happen!" he said.

"Of course not," Mr. Brooks said. "But what if we can't stop it, either?"

The fish hatchery down by Palestine was less exciting than Beckie hoped it would be. There was the Kanawha River. There were ponds next to the river where they raised the baby fish. They had nets that lifted the fish from the ponds and put them into the river. The people who worked with the fish were excited about what they did. They wouldn't have done it if they weren't. Beckie could see that.

But she didn't care if they were excited. So they were going to put trout and bluegills and crappies—she didn't bust up at the name, but keeping her face straight wasn't easy—into the Kanawha? Big deal. They were doing it so people farther downstream could catch them and eat them. Beckie wasn't a vegetarian, but the idea of catching her own fish didn't thrill her.

So she listened to the enthusiastic people in the tan uniforms, and then she started back to Elizabeth. Maybe the uniforms were part of what turned her off, too. Lots of people in Virginia wore them. You didn't have to work for the government, though the fishery people did. The man who fixed the Snodgrasses' air conditioner wore a uniform. So did the servers who sold stuff at Elizabeth's one diner. If you came from California, it was pretty funny.

In California, nobody but soldiers and sailors and cops wore uniforms. In California, a uniform meant somebody else got to tell you what to do. Californians liked that no more than anyone else, and less than most people. In Virginia, though, a uniform seemed to mean you got to tell other people what to do. It was weird.

It's not weird. It's just foreign, Beckie thought as she followed the loop of the Kanawha back toward Elizabeth. The river was foreign, too. You couldn't walk alongside a rippling river in Los Angeles. Most of the time, there wasn't enough water in L.A. Every few winters, there was too much.

Down by the stream, under the trees a lot of the time, it didn't seem so hot and sticky. The fishery people didn't just have uniforms. They had bow ties! Back in California, her father said he wore ties at weddings, funerals, and gunpoint. He was kidding, but he was kidding on the square. And most men in California felt the same way. Oh, the prime minister would put on a tie when a foreign dignitary showed up. A few conservative businessmen still wore them, and the jackets that went with them, but that only proved how conservative they were. Why be uncomfortable when you didn't have to?

That was how people in California looked at things, anyway. Here in the eastern part of the continent, they had different ideas. They dressed up for the sake of dressing up, the way people out West had up into the middle of the twentieth century. Beckie wondered what had made them change their minds there. Whatever it was, she liked it.

Up in a tree, a little gray bird with a black cap hung upside down from a branch and said, "Chickadee-dee-dee!" in between pecks at bugs. Beckie had already found she liked chickadees. They didn't live around Los Angeles. Too bad.

A highway ran right by the Kanawha. In California, the road would have leaped over the river so it could go straight. People did things differently here. Where the river looped, the road looped, too. You needed more time to get where you were going, but the highway didn't take such a big bite out of the landscape.

Oh, people here did what they had to do. Beckie had looked

at the Charleston airport on the Virginia computer network. If she and Gran needed to fly out of here, she wanted to know what it would be like. The Virginians had had to hack the tops off a couple of mountains so planes could take off and land there. Flat space in this part of the state was mighty hard to come by.

A car roared past on the highway. Signs warned drivers to slow down and be careful. Nobody paid much attention to those signs. People drove as if the roads were as wide and straight as the ones in California. They drove that way—and they paid for it. On the way to the fish hatchery, Beckie had walked past a couple of wrecks. She was coming up to one of them now. She shook her head. The car hadn't made a curve. It went off the road and straight into a tree. The flat tires and the rust on the fenders said it had been there a long time.

She wondered what had happened to the driver. By the way the windshield was scarred, nothing good. She hoped he'd lived, anyhow.

Why do I think it was a he? she wondered. Women could also crash cars. But guys were more likely to, here or in California or, for that matter, in Europe. *Testosterone poisoning,* Beckie thought with a scornful sniff. Women didn't usually do things like tromp on the gas to see how fast the car would go. She'd been in a car with a guy who did that, just for the fun of it. Nothing bad happened that time—it didn't always, or even most of the time. But she tried not to ride with him any more.

There was Jephany Knob, now due north of her and about as close as she could get unless she felt like crossing the highway and picking her way to it through the woods. She didn't. It stuck up and it had a funny name, and that was about it.

Or so she thought, till she noticed a couple of people up near the top of the knob. What were they doing up there? Why would you want to climb the knob, anyhow? To watch birds? People here didn't seem to do that, or not so much as they did in California.

But they did hunt. Hunting struck her as even stranger than fishing. Wild turkeys and grouse and squirrels and deer were a lot smarter than fish. Maybe that was why she felt wronger—was that a word?—about killing them.

Here, though, people didn't hunt just for the sport of it, if there was such a thing. They hunted for the pot. Beckie'd liked Brunswick stew till Mrs. Snodgrass told her the meat in it was squirrel. Then she almost lost dinner. Gran never turned a hair. All she said was, "Goodness, I don't remember the last time I ate squirrel."

It wasn't bad, if you didn't think about what it was. It didn't taste like rabbit, which Beckie had had before. It didn't taste like anything but itself, not really. If she and Gran stayed at the Snodgrasses' a while longer, they would probably have it again. *I can eat it,* Beckie thought. *I guess I can, anyway.*

One of the people on Jephany Knob saw her, too. He pointed her way. His friend stopped whatever he was doing and looked at her, too. The first man raised a rifle to his shoulder. He fired— once, twice. The bullets cracked past Beckie's head, much too close for comfort.

With a small shriek, she scurried behind a tree. *He was trying to kill me,* she thought. *He was. What's he doing? Did he think I was a deer? Or did he know I was a person? Is that why he aimed at me?* She had no answers. She wished she had no questions. Now she knew what was worse than being bored: being scared to death.

No more shots came. Peering out ever so cautiously, she saw that the other man was yelling at the one with the gun. It wasn't aimed her way any more. She hoped it was all just a crazy mistake. Even so, she crawled away from there and stayed under cover as much as she could all the way back to Elizabeth.

When Justin heard that Virginia and Ohio really had declared war on each other, he waited for missiles to start flying or guns to start going off or computers to start catching viruses or . . . something. When nothing happened—and when nothing went right on happening—he almost felt cheated.

"Chances are not much *will* happen," his mother said. "Virginia declared war on Ohio to make a lot of people farther east happy."

"But those aren't the people who border Ohio," Justin said.

"I know," Mom answered. "But they're the white people in the parts of Virginia with lots of African Americans. They're the ones who think Ohio is giving African Americans guns. So they're the ones who want to do something about their neighbors." She set a bone down on her plate. "This is good chicken, Randy."

"Thanks," Mr. Brooks answered. "I'd take more credit for it if I didn't buy it around the corner."

"It's good anyhow," Justin said. It was hot and greasy and salty—what more could you want from fried chicken? His plate already held enough bones to build a fair-sized dinosaur. But he didn't want to talk chicken—he wanted to talk politics. "Why did Ohio declare war on Virginia, then?"

"If somebody pokes you, won't you poke him back?" Mom answered. That made the two squabbling states sound like a couple of six-year-olds.

"Besides, Ohio really is running guns," Mr. Brooks added.

"It is?" That wasn't Justin—it was his mother. She sounded astonished.

"Sure," Mr. Brooks said calmly. "The more trouble Virginia has, the better off Ohio is. The folks in Ohio can see that as well as anybody."

"How long have you been running this shop?" Mom asked slowly.

For a second, Justin thought Mom was changing the subject. Then he realized she wasn't. She'd found a polite way to ask, *Have you been here so long, you're starting to think like a Virginian?*

Mr. Brooks understood her. "It's a fact, Cyndi," he said. "I don't have anything good to say about segregation. Who could? Black people here . . . Well, who'd blame them for feeling the way they do about whites? But a race war won't make things better. Besides, they're bound to lose—a lot more whites here than blacks. And even if they win, what do they get? Another Mississippi." He grimaced. "That's no good, either."

"But why would Ohio want to touch off a civil war in Virginia?" Justin asked.

"A lot of it has to do with the coal trade," Mr. Brooks answered. "There's coal on both sides of the border here, but Ohio started mining it before Virginia did. Virginia works cheaper than Ohio, and she's taking away some of the markets Ohio's had for a while. Ohio doesn't like that."

"It would be nice if Ohio were giving the African Americans guns because it wanted them to get their rights," Justin said.

Mr. Brooks nodded. "Yeah, it would be nice, but don't hold your breath. The people in Ohio don't like Negroes much better than the people in Virginia do. Oh, they don't have laws holding them down in Ohio, but that's mostly because Ohio hasn't got enough Negroes to make laws like that worth bothering about. There aren't a lot of Negroes in this alternate except in the old South."

"How come?" That wasn't Justin—he knew the answer. It was Mom.

"In the home timeline, blacks moved north and west in the twentieth century. They did factory work in the World Wars, things like that," Randolph Brooks said. "That didn't happen here. They would have had to cross state lines, and the states that didn't have many didn't want any more."

Justin decided to show off a little: "And a lot of states were on the Prussian side in the First World War—the Great War, they still call it here. They had lots of German settlers, and they didn't like the way England was pushing them around. So here they fought the war on both sides of the Atlantic, and it was almost twice as bad as it was in the home timeline."

"That's how it worked, all right." Mr. Brooks eyed him for a minute, then glanced over at Mom. "He's a smart fellow."

"He must get it from his father." Mom's voice had a brittle edge. She and Justin's dad were divorced a couple of years earlier. Mom wasn't over it yet, and neither was Justin. Neither was Dad, come to that. Whenever Justin saw him, he said things like, *I sure wish your mother and I could have got along.*

Every time Justin heard that, he wanted to scream, *Then why didn't you?* He'd asked Dad once (carefully not screaming). All he got back was a shrug and, *Sometimes things don't work out the way you want them to.* Mom said almost the same thing in different words. What it boiled down to was that they couldn't stand each other any more, even if they both wished they still could. That didn't do Justin any good. He'd needed a long time to see that, no matter how hard *he* wished they would, they weren't going to get back together again.

"Wherever he gets it from, it's a good thing to have." Mr. Brooks didn't notice how Mom sounded. Or maybe he did, and just didn't let on. A lot of politeness boiled down to not saying anything you could be sorry for later.

Mom said something along those lines: "Brains are like anything else. What you do with them matters more than how many you've got."

"That's a fact," Mr. Brooks agreed. Grown-ups always said stuff like that. They could afford to. They'd already gone through college and got themselves settled in life. When you were getting ready for SATs and wishing you hadn't ended up with a B- in sophomore English, you wanted all the brains in the world. But then Mr. Brooks added, "I will say one thing for being smart—it lasts longer than being strong or being good-looking . . . most of the time, anyway."

He was looking at Mom when he tacked on the last few words. She kind of snorted, but Justin could see she was pleased. As for Justin, he found himself nodding. Oh, a handful, a tiny handful, of guys got rich playing sports. But even the very best of them were washed up at forty—and wasn't that a sorry fate, with the rest of your life still ahead of you? And time turned the homecoming queen and her court ordinary, too.

If you were sharp, though, you stayed sharp your whole life long. Sooner or later, you'd pass a lot of people who got off to faster starts than you did. If you could stand being the tortoise and not the hare . . .

There was the rub. Shakespeare was almost five hundred years dead now, but he still had a word for it. Who wanted to wait for a payoff if there was a chance of getting a big one right away? Justin knew he wasn't good-looking enough for that to matter to him. Oh, he wasn't bad, but you had to be better than not bad if you were going to make it on looks.

He was big and he was strong. He was a backup tight end on

his high-school football team, a backup guard on the basketball team, and the right-handed half of a platoon at first base on the baseball team. He did okay at all his sports, no more than okay at any. He wasn't in line for an athletic scholarship, let alone a pro career.

It would have to be brains, then. When he got back to the home timeline after this stretch at Crosstime Traffic, he was heading for Stanford. Comparative history was a subject that hadn't existed before transposition chambers were invented. These days, you could either use it for the company or teach once you got your degree. You weren't likely to get movie-star rich, but you were pretty sure to do all right.

Mr. Brooks said something. Woolgathering the way Justin was, he missed it. "I'm sorry?" he said.

"I said, how would you like to go out into the boonies with me tomorrow?" Mr. Brooks repeated. "I've got a customer for an 1861 Oregon goldpiece, only he's got car trouble and he can't get down to Charleston. We've been doing business ever since I opened up here, so I don't mind getting in the car for him. There's always a lot of handselling in coins and stamps, even in the home timeline."

"Sure, I'll come. Why not?" Justin said. "Be nice to see a little more of this alternate than what's across the street from the shop."

"Okay, then—we'll do that," Mr. Brooks said. To Justin's mother, he added, "Most of the trip's on the state highway. Hardly any on the little back roads."

"The state highway is bad enough," Mom said. Roads in this part of Virginia had to wiggle and twist and double back on themselves. Otherwise, the mountain country wouldn't have any roads at all. From what Justin had seen in West Virginia in the home timeline, the roads there were all twisty, too. Mom looked at him. "I don't know. . . ."

"It'll be all right," Justin said.

"Should be," Mr. Brooks agreed. "I've made the trip a few times. As long as you pay attention, there's nothing to worry about."

"I always worry," Mom said. "That's what mothers are for." But she didn't tell them no.

Three

Beckie paced around the Snodgrasses' back yard, looking for the spot that gave her the best cell-phone reception. It wasn't good anywhere in this back-of-beyond little town, but there was one place. . . .

She found it. Her mother's voice came in loud and clear. Beckie wished it didn't, because Mom was saying, "I want you to get out of there and come home as soon as you can. The war—"

"Everything's fine, Mom," Beckie said. "Nobody's shooting, nobody's dropping bombs, nobody's doing anything but yelling."

"I never would have let you go if I'd known the trouble would blow up like this," Mom said.

"There isn't any real trouble," Beckie said again. "It's all in the papers and on TV, mostly. Nothing's going on, honest."

Her mother didn't want to listen to her. "You should head for home as soon as you can."

"Why are you telling me?" Beckie asked, starting to lose patience. "I can't do anything about it by myself—I won't be of legal age for another year. Do you want me to get Gran?"

She figured that would nip the idea in the bud, and she was right. "I can't talk to my mother! She won't pay any attention to me," Mom said. From everything Beckie had seen, that was true. Beckie wondered if, when she was all grown up herself, she would say the same kind of thing about Mom. She hoped not. She really didn't think so, either. Mom wasn't *quite* so boneheaded stubborn as Gran—most of the time, anyhow.

For now . . . "If I can't fix that stuff myself and you don't want to try to talk Gran into doing it, what other choices are there? Pitching a fit is silly. Why don't you settle down and relax?"

"Because you're in the middle of a war, and I'm worried about you!" Mom exclaimed.

"I'm not in the middle of a war. I'm in the middle of nowhere." Beckie wasn't about to tell her mother about whoever'd almost taken a shot at her from Jephany Knob. She hadn't told anybody about that. It might have been a dumb mistake. She thought it probably was. And even if it wasn't, it couldn't have anything to do with the war . . . could it? To keep from worrying about that, she went on, "You wouldn't believe how tiny and dead this place is."

"Sure I would. I know what my own mother's like," Mom said. That might not be very nice, which didn't mean it wasn't so.

"Mr. Snodgrass showed me his coin collection," Beckie said. "That's the kind of thing people do for fun around here." She did lower her voice when she said that, because she didn't want Mr. Snodgrass hearing her. He was nice enough to put up with having Gran in the house for a lot longer than he'd planned on. He was also nice enough to put up with having Beckie there, but that didn't cross her mind.

"Oh, boy. Such excitement." Mom yawned into the telephone.

Beckie laughed, but she said, "It was kind of interesting, actually. More than I thought it would be, anyway. He turns out to know a lot about history. I guess you have to, to understand why the coins are the way they are."

"Well, how else would they be?" Mom said.

"I don't know. I suppose there'd be different ones if Deseret had lost the Rocky Mountain War—things like that," Beckie said. "And he has to know which ones are real and which ones are counterfeit, too, so he doesn't get cheated."

"If you say so." Mom didn't yawn again. If she had, she wouldn't have been joking this time. She really did sound bored.

"Anyway, though, I'm fine, and there's nothing to worry about," Beckie said. "If we get a chance to come home that seems safer than staying here, we'll do that, I guess. But sitting tight looks best right now."

"All right." By the way Mom said it, it wasn't even close to all right. But she couldn't do anything about it. She was on the wrong side of the continent even to try. "I always did think you acted older than you really were," she said. "Now's your chance to prove it."

"Shall I act like Gran, then?" Beckie said. "They roll up the sidewalks at six o'clock. The food is funny. Half the time, I can't understand them when they talk. The computer net is stupid." She did her best to grumble like her grandmother.

Her best was good enough to set Mom giggling helplessly. "I ought to spank you, but I'm too far away and I'm laughing too hard," Mom said. "Be careful, that's all. I love you."

"Love you, too," Beckie said. A lot of the time, those were just words. Maybe separation made her feel them more than usual. "'Bye," she added reluctantly, and broke the connection.

She went back into the Snodgrasses' house. Mr. Snodgrass wore a handlebar mustache that had been red once upon a time— pictures of him in his younger days were all over the house. Now it was the color of vanilla ice cream with a little strawberry mixed in. Beckie thought it made him look like a hick no matter what color it was. Nobody in California wore a handlebar mustache. Nobody in Ohio did, either, not even someone like Uncle Luke.

But if he was a hick, he was a nice hick. He nodded and said, "Mornin', Rebecca." He didn't call her Beckie, the way almost everybody did. She'd almost told him to a couple of times, but she always held back. This was a more formal kind of place than California. She didn't hate her full name or anything. She just didn't use it very often.

"Good morning, Mr. Snodgrass," she said. Even though his name sounded funny to her, she didn't feel comfortable calling him Ted. He was old enough to be her grandfather, after all. "You've got your coin stuff out."

He nodded again. "Got a dealer fella comin' up from the city." In Elizabeth, Charleston was *the* city. It wasn't anything next to Los Angeles. Compared to this little place, though, it had to seem like L.A., New York City, and Riverton all rolled into one. He went on, "He's got a goldpiece I want to buy if I like it when I see it with my own eyes and not just online. If he wants cash money for it, I'll pull out my credit card. But if he wants to work a swap— well, that's part of the fun of this."

"It is?" Beckie couldn't see why.

He plainly meant it, though. "He's got somethin' I want—or I expect he does, 'cause he plays straight about his coins. Seeing what I've got that'd interest him . . . It's not all what the catalogues say a piece is worth. It's what he's interested in, and what he reckons he can sell down there, and stuff like that."

"Okay." Beckie had a friend who collected stuffed animals, but they were almost like pets to her. She didn't care about what they were worth.

Mr. Snodgrass smiled over the tops of his glasses. "Some card games—hearts, for instance—are fun just to play. But poker's not interesting without money on the table."

"I don't know anybody who plays poker," Beckie confessed.

He blinked. His glasses magnified his eyes, which made his expressions look strange sometimes. "What *do* they do to pass the time out there?" he murmured. For a second, he made Beckie feel as if she were the hick. That was ridiculous, but it happened anyway. Then he poked a thumb at his own chest. "You do so know somebody like that—me."

"Sure." She laughed. "I didn't till now, though."

"That's a different story." Mr. Snodgrass looked at his watch. "He ought to be here any minute now."

Justin Monroe had his driver's license. All the same, he wasn't sorry Mr. Brooks was behind the wheel. "I know why they build the roads like this," he said as the car went around another hairpin bend. There was no guard rail on the curve. There wasn't anything off the road but a lot of straight down.

"Why's that?" Mr. Brooks asked, hauling the Mercedes into another turn, just as tight, that went left instead of right.

"Because of wars, that's why," Justin said, glad he wasn't the sort who got carsick easily. "If anybody tried to invade, he'd have about three tanks and six soldiers left by the time he made it down to Charleston."

He waited for the older man to laugh, but Mr. Brooks nodded instead. "Wouldn't be surprised if you're right. Pretty rugged country around here."

"Oh, just a little." Justin tried to stay cool about how rugged it was. Watching the vultures circle overhead didn't help.

"Buzzards," Mr. Brooks said when he remarked on them. "They mostly call 'em buzzards here. Black buzzards and turkey buzzards."

"Buzzards. Right." Justin hoped he would remember that.

People would understand him if he said *vultures* instead. They would understand, yes, but they would decide he wasn't from around these parts. He wasn't, of course, but he was supposed to be.

"Besides, things could be worse," Mr. Brooks went on. "We could have headed east instead of north. We're coming down into the lowlands here—well, the lower lands, anyhow. If we were going up into the mountains . . ."

Justin didn't want to think about that. Because he didn't want to, he didn't—much. They left the state highway at a little town called Ripley. *Believe it or not,* Justin thought. The cartoonist was a century and a half dead, but his name and the phrase stayed tied together—in the home timeline. Here, if Ripley had lived, he never got famous. Forgetting *believe it or not* was as important as remembering *buzzards.* More important, probably: some people in this alternate did say *vultures,* but there was no connection here at all between Ripley and the phrase.

The road that went east to Elizabeth was barely wide enough for two cars. That didn't keep the few people who used it from driving like maniacs. Justin saw some wrecked cars by the side of the road. He wasn't surprised—the only surprise was that he didn't see more.

"Here we are," Mr. Brooks said when they drove into Elizabeth.

"Oh, boy." Justin could hardly hide his enthusiasm. It looked like the same sort of little town as Ripley. It also looked as if the twenty-first century, and a good deal of the twentieth, had passed it by. Even the bricks seemed old and faded. Nothing had gone up anytime lately—that was plain enough. Justin wondered if there was a fasarta in the whole town. They had them down in Charleston—not the fancy subflexive kind people used in the home timeline, but fasartas even so. Here? He wouldn't have bet on it.

When he said as much, the coin and stamp dealer looked surprised. "You know, I never noticed one way or the other. Maybe you'll get the chance to see for yourself."

Justin did notice one thing: houses here didn't have satellite dishes on the roof. It made them seem incomplete, like people without ears. California might have sent men to Mars, but there was no continent-wide entertainment market in this alternate. English was the dominant language of this North America, yes. But the dialects were much more pronounced, and the social differences between states were much wider than in the home timeline. What was funny in California might be offensive in Virginia, and the other way around. (What was funny in Alabama might touch off terrorism in Mississippi, and the other way around.)

Except for the missing dish, the house in front of which Mr. Brooks stopped his car seemed nice enough. The front lawn was neatly trimmed. It didn't have any cars parked on it, which a lot of lawns here did. All the trim had been painted not very long before.

Before Mr. Brooks got out of the car, he looked carefully in all directions. He carried a briefcase in one hand. The other didn't go far from the waistband of his trousers. Did he have a gun there?

He noticed Justin looking at him. "I'm a stranger here," he said. "I'm a stranger, and my stock in trade is small and valuable. That might make me fair game. Why take chances?"

"I didn't say anything," Justin answered. How often *did* a town like this see strangers? Did they ever come in and not go out again? Once Justin started stephenkinging, he had a hard time stopping.

"Okay." Mr. Brooks went up the walk. Justin followed. The older man rang the bell.

The door opened right away. "Hello, Mr. Brooks," said the man who stood there. He scratched at his almost-white mustache as he eyed Justin. "Who's your accomplice here?"

"My sister's son—his name's Justin Monroe," Mr. Brooks answered. "They're over from Fredericksburg for a bit. I brought him along to see some of this side of the state. Justin, this is Ted Snodgrass."

"Nice to meet you, Mr. Snodgrass." Justin stuck out his hand.

"Pleased to meet you, too, Justin—mighty pleased." Mr. Snodgrass shook hands. He still had a pretty good grip. His accent held the same sort of twang as Mr. Brooks', only more of it. "Are you a collector yourself?"

"Not really," Justin said. "I'm interested, but I don't know a whole lot." This alternate's North American coins and stamps, like the history of the continent, were much more complicated than they were in the home timeline.

"Everybody starts that way. If you *are* interested, you'll learn." Ted Snodgrass stepped aside. "In the meantime, why don't you come on in?" One of his eyelids went down and then up again. Was that a wink? It sure looked like one. He went on, "Matter of fact, I'm right glad you came."

"How's that?" Mr. Brooks asked. The house wasn't real big, but it looked comfortable, even if it also seemed old-fashioned to Justin. The furniture could have come out of the twentieth century, or maybe the nineteenth. And nobody, but nobody, used maroon velvet upholstery in the home timeline these days. That didn't mean the chair to which Mr. Snodgrass waved Justin felt bad to sit in, though.

"How's that?" Mr. Snodgrass echoed, and he winked again. Justin wondered what in the world was going on. Then Mr. Snodgrass raised his voice a little: "Rebecca! Come out here a minute, would you?"

The girl who stepped into the front room was about Justin's age—maybe a year younger, he thought. She was blond and cute—not gorgeous, but definitely cute—and the last thing he'd expected to meet here. Was she Mr. Snodgrass' granddaughter?

"Beckie, this is the coin dealer I was telling you about, Mr. Randolph Brooks," Ted Snodgrass said. "And this tall young fellow is his nephew, Justin, uh, Monroe. Friends, this is Rebecca Royer. My wife's cousin went out to California to live, and she's back here for the first time in a coon's age. Rebecca here is her grandchild."

"Hello," Justin said. "I'm glad I decided to come along for the ride." Mr. Brooks laughed. So did Mr. Snodgrass.

"Good to meet you," Rebecca—Beckie?—Royer said. Her accent was nothing like Mr. Snodgrass'. She sounded more as if she came from the home timeline, but not quite. Something else was there. Justin tried to figure out what it was.

"Why don't the two of you grab fizzes from the icebox and get to know each other while Mr. Brooks and I break out the skinning knives?" Ted Snodgrass said.

"Oh, I don't aim to skin you—much," Mr. Brooks said. He and Mr. Snodgrass laughed again, this time on a different note.

The icebox was a refrigerator that looked almost the same as the one at Justin's house back in the home timeline, except that one wasn't pink. Fizzes were sodas. "Thanks," he said when she handed him one.

"You're welcome," she said. "Did I hear your uncle say you were from Fredericksburg?"

"That's right." Justin had to remember not to talk about the Civil War battle there. In this timeline, it never happened. Neither did that war. Others, yes. Which reminded him . . . "Are you stuck here in Virginia because of the trouble with Ohio?"

Her mouth twisted. "It sure looks that way. Gran didn't think this would happen when she decided to come back here."

"That must be fun," he said.

She smiled a little. "But of course," she said. Someone from the home timeline would have said *Yeah, right* or *And then you wake up,* but it amounted to the same thing. And he worked out what was odd—to his ear—about the way she talked. Ever so slightly, she rolled her r's. California in this alternate had even more connections with the Mexico of which it had once been a part than it did in the home timeline. Spanish had rubbed off on the English the local Californians spoke.

"Good heavens, but you're a thief!" Mr. Snodgrass said to Mr. Brooks. Justin felt alarmed. Rebecca Royer looked alarmed. What was going on in the other room?

Then Mr. Brooks answered, "I thank you for the compliment," and he and Mr. Snodgrass both laughed some more. Whatever was going on, it didn't seem serious.

"Do you want to see the back yard?" Rebecca asked. "That way, they can yell at each other as much as they want." She might have been a mother talking about two little boys.

"Sure." Justin nodded. They went outside. "Nice trees," he said. He meant that. This alternate had missed out on both chestnut blight and Dutch elm disease. Genetic engineering had finally got ahead of both of those in the home timeline. But the resistant trees were still scarce, and hadn't had time to grow tall. Some of the ones Justin could see in the distance were probably older than the Revolution.

"They are, aren't they?" Rebecca Royer sipped her fizz. It was lemon-limey, on the order of Sprite, and called 6+. It wasn't bad, but Justin didn't think it was anything to get excited about.

She went on, "Everything is so green here compared to what I'm used to."

"Where in California are you from, Rebecca?" Justin asked. "I know it's a big place."

"Call me Beckie—almost everybody does. I'm from Los Angeles." Beckie made a face, then grinned. "I'm not one of those San Francisco people." Wherever both towns existed, they were rivals.

He tried to think of something else to say. He found one obvious question: "What do you think of Virginia?"

"It's very pretty. Like I said, things are a lot greener than they are back home. The people seem nice." She wrinkled her nose. "They put up with Gran, so they must be nice. But this is an awful small town when you come from the big city."

"I guess," Justin said. Los Angeles here wasn't the enormous sprawl that it was back home. They didn't have so many of the irrigation projects that let the basin fill up with people. But Elizabeth, Virginia, could disappear in it and never get noticed.

"Some things here are different," Beckie said. "Can I tell you something without making you mad?"

"Huh? Sure," Justin said. He'd taken a shower in the morning. He'd brushed his teeth. His fly wasn't open—he glanced down to check. What could she say that might make him angry, then?

He found out. "In California, we try to treat everybody the same, no matter what people look like," Beckie said. "We don't always do it, but we try. It's . . . really strange being in a place where people don't even try to do that."

"Oh," Justin said, and then, before he thought about it, "I feel the same way."

Beckie stared at him. "You do?" she said. "Really? You're the first person here who ever said anything like that to me."

That meant he'd made a mistake. Virginians in this alternate were convinced they were doing the right thing by lording it over the African Americans in the state. And if those African Americans ever grabbed power, they wouldn't give whites a big smile. No—they would do what the blacks in Mississippi had done, and rule the roost themselves.

"Don't tell anybody," he said. "It would ruin my reputation." He wasn't kidding, either. Mr. Brooks would want to skin him alive if he heard about his falling out of character like that. And any white Virginian from this alternate would think he'd gone round the bend. Black Virginians were liable to think he was crazy, too.

Beckie looked at him—looked through him, he thought miserably. "All right," she said. "But it's too bad you have to be ashamed of a decent thought."

"Things are different here." Justin didn't just mean different from California, though Beckie couldn't know that. He also meant different from the home timeline.

"Are they?" she said. "Some things are decent and right no matter where you go, seems to me."

That could have been the start of a lovely argument. But Justin had to act like what he wasn't. "Things aren't as simple as they look, you know," he said. "There really are black terrorists here. People in places like Ohio really do run guns to them. Is that decent and right?"

She turned white. No—she turned green. The only time he'd ever seen people turn that color before was on a tour boat that went out into the Pacific from San Francisco Bay. The waves then were a lot heavier than the captain expected. What Justin said now hit a lot harder than he thought it would, too.

"Well, you're right," she said, and he didn't expect that, either. "I wish you weren't, but you are." She sounded like someone who knew what she was talking about.

"How come you're so sure?" he asked. Maybe they'd had a TV show that convinced her, or something.

Instead of answering, she turned even greener. He hadn't thought she could. She gulped a couple of times, and he wondered if she was going to be sick all over her shoes. "I don't want to talk about that," she said in a muffled voice. "I'm sorry, but I really don't."

"Okay. Whatever." Justin didn't know what kind of nerve he'd poked, but it was a sensitive one. He could see that.

He was trying to figure out what to say next when Ted Snodgrass stepped out onto the back porch and said, "I reckon you kids better come inside a minute."

Justin looked at Beckie. She was looking at Mr. Snodgrass, and seemed just as surprised and confused as Justin felt. He didn't know whether that was good or bad. He could try to find out—and he did, asking, "What's up?"

"Well, I turned on the noon news for a minute, and there's something you need to see," Mr. Snodgrass said.

In one way, Justin was glad to hear that. It meant Mr. Snodgrass and Mr. Brooks weren't quarreling. In another way . . . He hurried inside, Beckie right behind him.

In the home timeline, the newscaster's tie would have been too short and too wide and too loud. His jacket, with its little lapels and broad pinstripes, would have been almost too fashionable to stand in 1891. But his handsome, sober face and deep, smooth voice would have marked him as a TV performer anywhere.

"To repeat," he said, "outbreaks of this illness have been

reported here at Richmond, at Newport News, and at Roanoke in the south-central part of the state. Doctors have declared that it is a genetically engineered disease. It seems to be highly contagious. Because of this, Consul Pendleton has ordered all unnecessary travel suspended until further notice. He has vowed that shipments of food and fuel will go through. Stay tuned for further bulletins."

The TV cut to a commercial. Justin stared at Mr. Brooks. Beckie was staring at Mr. Snodgrass. They both said the same thing at the same time: "Oh, my God! Does that mean we're stuck here?"

Sheriff Chester Cochrane was one of the biggest men Beckie had ever seen. He was several centimeters—no, they said two or three inches here—taller than Justin Monroe. He was wide-shouldered and narrow-waisted, and had a long, sad face that showed very little of what he thought. "Is this about where they were at?" he asked as he and Beckie paused near the top of Jephany Knob.

She looked down toward the road by the river. "I think so," she said. "Somewhere close, anyway." She pointed that way. "I was right about there when the shots went off."

"Okay." The sheriff had a metal detector. He swung it this way and that. After a moment, he grunted and swung it in a narrower arc. Then he walked over and bent down near a tree trunk. He reached out. When he straightened, he held a couple of cartridge cases. "These are new brass, Miss Royer, sure enough."

"I wasn't making it up," she said.

"Well, I didn't really reckon you were, but you never can tell." His voice was like a rumble from the bottom of a cave. "Even so, this doesn't *prove* anything. Folks could have been up here hunting or just to get some plinking in."

"I told you, I can't prove they were shooting at me—at me as a person, I mean," Beckie said, and Sheriff Cochrane nodded. She went on, "That's why I didn't come to you right away. But I *think* they were, so I figured I'd better tell *somebody*."

"Not the best marksmen in the world if they missed you at this range," Cochrane remarked. That wasn't what Beckie wanted to hear. She wanted sympathy, not scorn for the fools who couldn't shoot straight.

One look at Chester Cochrane told her he didn't care what she wanted. He was doing his job—that was all. She wondered how big a job he had to do most of the time. "Why would they shoot at me at all?" she asked.

"Don't rightly know," he answered. "Maybe they didn't get a good look at you. Maybe they reckoned you were a deer." He eyed her, then muttered to himself. "You're not built like any deer I ever saw. Still and all, you'd be amazed at the dumb things people can do."

A sheriff probably saw more of those dumb things than ten ordinary people put together. "I guess so," Beckie said.

"Let me ask you one other thing," Cochrane said. "These people who took those shots at you—were they white?"

Even hearing the question made Beckie want to go down to the Kanawha and wash herself off. She understood why Sheriff Cochrane asked it. She knew there was a lot of nasty history between whites and blacks in Virginia. She knew blacks had caused some of the nastiness, too, even if, in her judgment, they were provoked.

"I'm not sure," she answered, which was the truth. "It was a long way to tell something like that, and I wasn't paying a whole lot of attention."

"You what? How could you *not* be?" Chester Cochrane

stopped. Then he gave her a long, measuring look, nothing like the one he'd used when he said she wasn't built like a deer. There wasn't even a hint of a twinkle in his eye as he went on, "That's right, you're from California. Furriners have some funny notions, don't they?"

Beckie wasn't about to let him get away with that. "I think some of the notions you've got here are the funny ones."

"Oh, you do, do you?" he growled. "We've been doing things our way here in Virginia for almost five hundred years. We aren't a bunch of johnny-come-latelies like some folks."

"Would you rather do things your way or the right way?" Beckie asked.

Try as she would, she couldn't faze Sheriff Cochrane. "We don't reckon there's any difference," he said—actually, it sounded more like *ary difference*. They headed back to town together. After a while, the sheriff went on, "You want to be careful what you say and do around these parts. Some folks don't cotton to furrin ways."

"Well, I didn't exactly like almost getting my head blown off, either," Beckie said.

"I believe that," Cochrane said. "For now, I'm going to hope it was just an accident—some fool of a hunter getting careless."

"What if it wasn't?" Beckie asked.

"If it wasn't . . ." Chester Cochrane's long face got even longer. "If it wasn't, then it seems to me the war's come to Elizabeth, and that's not so good." He paused. "You know those strangers who came to visit Ted Snodgrass?"

"Sure. What about them?" Beckie said. Randolph Brooks and Justin Monroe were staying in Elizabeth's one and only motel. It wasn't called the Dismal Swamp, but from the look of the place it should have been. Justin had some interesting things to say about the food at the diner across the street. Beckie had eaten there a couple of times. If anything, she thought Justin was too nice.

"Do you suppose they were the people you saw up on Jephany Knob, the people who took a shot at you?" the sheriff asked.

"They didn't get here till the day after that happened, so I don't see how they could be," Beckie said, wondering if he'd gone nuts.

He sighed. "No, I don't reckon so," he admitted. "But we don't get a whole lot of strangers around here. Now we've got two lots in town. I just kind of wondered if there was any connection."

"I don't think so." Beckie did think he wanted the people with a gun handed to him on a silver platter. If he could do things the easy way, he wouldn't have to try to figure out what really happened. *Beats working,* she thought. *Beats trying to discover who* did *shoot at me, too.*

Sheriff Cochrane sighed again as they tramped up State Highway 14 into Elizabeth. They could walk on the asphalt—you'd hear a car coming in plenty of time to move out of the way. "Sooner or later, I'll get to the bottom of it," the sheriff said. "Somebody who knows something'll blab where he shouldn't, and word'll get back to me. People can't keep their fool mouths shut a lot of the time, even when they ought to."

"I guess so," Beckie said. They walked past Clay Street, and up to Prunty. "Can I ask you something?"

His big head went up and down. "Sure. What is it?"

"What's it like trying to be a sheriff when you already know all the people you're trying to ride herd on?"

"Well, it's interesting sometimes." Even the sheriff's smile looked mournful. Maybe he had some bloodhound on his mother's side. "Sometimes you have to do your job in spite of knowing people. If somebody punches somebody else in the nose, it doesn't matter if you went fishing with him day before yesterday. You've got to see that it doesn't happen again. I've lost friends on account of that, I'm afraid."

"I bet you have," Beckie said. She liked Cochrane better, or at least respected him more, for knowing he would come down on his friends if he had to. She turned onto Prunty to go back to the Snodgrasses' house. Would the sheriff follow her?

He didn't. He just tipped his broad-brimmed hat and ambled up 14 toward the county courthouse. When he got there, he'd probably fill out a form. Chances were it would stay buried on his computer's hard drive till the end of time. Or would he have to put it down on paper instead? He might have a couple of hundred years' worth of arrest reports in one file drawer. How much ever happened in Elizabeth? How much ever happened in this whole county?

When Beckie got back to the Snodgrasses' house, she wasn't surprised to find Mr. Brooks and his nephew there. Mr. Snodgrass was the only person in town Mr. Brooks knew. As long as the coin and stamp dealer was here, he could do some more business— and he could pass the time with someone who was interested in the same things he was. It beat the stuffing out of sitting in that grim-looking motel staring at the TV—or at the wall.

As for Justin . . . Beckie smiled to herself. Plainly, he knew a good bit about coins and stamps. But she didn't think that was the only reason he'd come over. She didn't mind. He was interesting to talk to—more interesting, and more complicated, than she'd expected someone from Virginia to be. And they both had to know nothing that happened here was likely to matter much. When they could, they'd go back to where they lived and get on with their real lives.

Gran was there, too. She was talking with her cousin—and

shooting suspicious glances at Justin. Disapproval stuck out all over her, like quills on a porcupine. Beckie couldn't see why. Justin wasn't doing anything rude. He was just listening to his uncle and Mr. Snodgrass talk about coins, and putting in something himself every once in a while.

He did brighten up when Beckie came through the door. "Hi," he said.

"Hi, Justin," Beckie said. Gran's quills got longer and pointier. But then, Gran disapproved of everybody and everything. Beckie went on, "Want to grab a fizz and go out back and talk?"

"Sure," Justin said, and then, politely, "If that's okay, Mr. Snodgrass?"

"Don't see why not." Mr. Snodgrass chuckled. "When I was your age, I was more interested in pretty girls than in nineteenth-century silver, too."

Mrs. Snodgrass clucked. "Watch yourself, Ted. You'll embarrass him."

"I think it's terrible that—" Gran started.

Beckie didn't wait to find out what Gran thought was terrible this time. What Gran *didn't* think was terrible made a much shorter list. Beckie grabbed a couple of fizzes from the refrigerator. Justin followed her outside. Once he'd closed the door behind him, he said, "I'm afraid your grandmother doesn't like me much."

"Don't worry about it," Beckie told him. "You don't have to be special or anything for Gran not to like you."

"She seems nice," Justin said, which proved how polite he was.

"That only shows you don't know her very well," Beckie said cheerfully. "Have you heard any news lately? Do they know when they're going to lift this stupid quarantine? People must be going crazy."

"I bet they are," Justin said. "I talked to my mom down in Charleston. She says it hasn't got there yet."

"That's good, anyhow." Beckie made a face that reminded her more of Gran's usual expression than she wished it did. "You know what a mess this is when the best news you have is that a stupid disease hasn't got somewhere."

"Have they figured out what it is yet?" Justin asked.

"Modified measles—that was on the news last night," Beckie answered. "No word when they'll have a vaccine, though."

"Measles." Justin sounded worried. "That's not so good."

"I know. The regular kind will kill you if you get it and you don't have a lot of immunity." Beckie thought about American Indians and Pacific Islanders, then wished she hadn't.

Maybe Justin was thinking along with her, because he said, "Nobody's likely to have a lot of immunity to this strain." Beckie nodded. He added, "What a great thing to talk about on a nice summer afternoon." She nodded again, even more unhappily.

Four

Justin was as thrilled about going back to the motel as he would have been about getting his wisdom teeth yanked. At least dentists knocked you out when you lost your wisdom teeth, and they gave you pain pills afterwards. Bioengineers said they were only a few years away from taking wisdom teeth out of the gene pool so no one had to worry about them any more. They'd been saying that for as long as he could remember, though, so maybe they weren't so close as they thought.

As for the motel . . . It was clean, anyhow. *Why not?* Justin thought. *They would have had plenty of time to wash things since the last time anybody stayed here.* Clean or not, there'd been a lot of dust on top of the TV set.

"How do you suppose they stay in business?" he asked Mr. Brooks.

"Beats me," the older man answered. "They must live in one of the units themselves—"

"Poor devils," Justin said. People talked about fates worse than death. If spending all your time in a place like this wasn't one of them . . . "Do you have any idea when we'll be able to get out of here?"

"Sure don't," Mr. Brooks said. "A mutated measles virus would be bad news in the home timeline—they used one of those against

Crosstime Traffic in Romania a couple of years ago. Do you remember?"

"I didn't, not till you reminded me," Justin said. "They aren't as good at fighting them here as we are, either."

"They also aren't as good at making them," Mr. Brooks said. "I can hope our immunity shots will hold up."

That made Justin feel better, but only for a little while. There were no guarantees, and he knew it too well. Making viruses was easier than fighting them. Making them just took selective breeding, picking the strongest strains from each generation. People had been using selective breeding ever since they first tamed dogs. Controlling viruses once they got loose, though—that was another story.

Mr. Brooks' eyes sparked. "You're probably happy as a clam here," he said. How happy were clams? Some of the slang this alternate used was downright weird. The coin and stamp dealer went on, "You've met a pretty girl—and I think she's a nice girl, too. Don't get me wrong. But anyway, you may not care whether you get back to Charleston or not."

"Yes, I do. Beckie *is* nice, but I'm even more foreign here than she is," Justin said. "I showed it the day I met her, too." He told Mr. Brooks how he hadn't acted like a proper Virginian when it came to the way whites and blacks dealt with each other. "I know I should have sounded like everybody else, but I couldn't stand it."

"Well, I ought to get mad at you, because you did goof," Mr. Brooks told him. "And in a way I *am* mad at you. But I know how you feel. Everybody who comes here from the home timeline feels that way. Well, maybe not everybody, but the people who don't at least know they'd better act like they do when they're back home."

Justin nodded. Racism wasn't dead in the home timeline. Neither was sexism. Neither was homophobia. He wondered if they ever would be. But, even if they weren't dead, they were rude. You couldn't make people love all their neighbors all the time—that wasn't in the cards. But if you made them lose points for showing they didn't, that worked almost as well.

"I told her not to tell anybody what I said," Justin said. "Here, a white person's rude if he shows he *doesn't* think African Americans are inferior."

"All the states with lots of blacks in them are independent," Mr. Brooks said with a sigh. "Nobody can tell the people in them what to do. That's almost everybody's motto in this North America. 'Nobody can tell me what to do,' people say. And they're right. If they want to act like a bunch of idiots, no one can stop them."

"I don't mind that so much," Justin said. "But now I have to act like an idiot, too, because I'm supposed to come from a state where people do. That, I don't like."

Mr. Brooks sighed again. "Sometimes you're stuck with it, that's all. It's protective coloration. If you were in an alternate where the Roman Empire didn't fall, you'd have to make offerings to the Emperor's spirit."

"That wouldn't be as bad as this," Justin said. "That's just strange—and people always say, 'When in Rome, do as the Romans.'" Mr. Brooks winced. Justin grinned, but the smile slipped as he went on, "Making like a Virginian just hurts, because it feels like everything I grew up with is all twisted here. They say they believe in freedom, but they only mean it for people who look like them. Anybody else better watch himself."

"We try to reform them, but we can only do so much. We're mostly here to do business with them and keep an eye on them,"

Mr. Brooks said. "And we're here to try to stop them if they look like they're working on crosstime travel."

"I know," Justin said. "But there are states in this North America where Negroes have the same rights as anybody else. California's one of them. That's what made me slip up with Beckie."

"You're right. There are—and California *is* one of them." Mr. Brooks sounded grim. A moment later, Justin found out why: "Do you know one of the big reasons those states give Negroes those rights?" He held up a hand. "Wait. I know you do, because you told your mom about it."

"Uh-huh," Justin said unhappily. "Those states can afford to give African Americans equal rights because they've only got a few of them."

"That's it," Mr. Brooks agreed.

"It's the end of the twenty-first century," Justin said. "This alternate's got a technology that's close to ours. They know what freedom's all about—they have the Declaration of Independence even if they don't have the Constitution. There are free countries in Europe. Why don't they get it here?"

"You might as well ask why terrorists in the home timeline don't get it," Mr. Brooks replied. "They've got free countries for examples, too. But they worry more about being on top than being free."

"I guess." Justin whistled between his teeth—not a cheerful noise. "But have you seen the African American who's the town janitor here?" He waited for Mr. Brooks to nod, then went on, "Well, I wish I didn't have to be embarrassed I'm white every time I set eyes on him."

"I don't know what to tell you about that—except not to let him know you're embarrassed. It could blow your cover," the older man said. "I've talked with him a little. He's not a bright man—he might be a janitor even in an alternate that didn't discriminate so much."

"Maybe. Or maybe he just doesn't want to let a white man know he's got a working brain," Justin said. "That might be dangerous. It probably is."

It was Mr. Brooks' turn to let out a couple of mournful notes. "You've got a point."

Justin turned on the TV. Again, the newsman wore a tie nobody in the home timeline would have been caught dead in. "Welcome to the five o'clock news. Casualties from the disease launched by Ohio continue to mount. Here is a hospital scene in Richmond."

A tired-looking doctor walked from patient to patient. He wore a real gas mask, not just a surgical mask. An ambulance screamed up to the emergency room with another victim—no, with two. Ambulances here had snakes twined around a staff on the door, not the Red Cross.

"In spite of travel limits, the disease continues to spread." The newsman pointed to a map of Virginia. More than half of it was red. He went on, "In Richmond, the consul is vowing revenge against Ohio."

A statue of Washington stood in Capitol Square in this Richmond, as one did in the home timeline. But this wasn't the same statue, and hadn't gone up at the same time. From the statue, the camera went to the consul's office inside the Capitol. Most states in this alternate had a consul instead of a president or a governor. It all added up to the same thing, though—this was the man in charge.

He didn't look like George Washington. He was a round little man with a bland face. But when he said, "Ohio will pay for the misery she is causing. She will pay more than we do, so help me God," you had to believe him. He wasn't the kind of man who kidded around or made jokes.

A jet plane—no, several jet planes—flew by over the motel, low enough to make the windows rattle, and Justin's teeth, too. At the same time, the consul said, "As a first step, I have ordered the VAF to strike targets in eastern Ohio. Further countermeasures will be taken in due course."

More slowly than Justin should have, he realized the VAF was the Virginia Air Force. More slowly still, he realized he'd just heard it heading into action. "They're going to blow things up!" he exclaimed.

"They sure are," Mr. Brooks said grimly. "And Lord only knows what happens next. Both these states have the bomb." Lots of states had the bomb in this alternate. So did lots of countries in Europe and Asia. It didn't get used very often, for the same reason it didn't get used very often in the home timeline. Once you let that genie out of the bottle, how did you put it back?

But what this alternate didn't have were superpowers. Nobody was strong enough to tell anybody else not to do something or else and make the *or else* stick. Every time a squabble started here, people worried. Caught in the middle of a war, Justin was one of those worried people.

When the bombers flew over Elizabeth, Beckie didn't know what was going on. The Snodgrasses didn't have the TV on. Mr. Snodgrass was looking at some of his coins. Mrs. Snodgrass and Gran were going back and forth about something that had happened when they were both much younger than Beckie was now. They remembered it two different ways.

Beckie didn't think it mattered which of them was right, but they both seemed to. Not even the roar in the sky slowed them down. It made Beckie jam her fingers in her ears. When it was over, she said, "Don't you have laws against low-flying planes here? We sure do back home." She wished *she* were back home.

Her grandmother and Mrs. Snodgrass went on arguing with each other. They didn't care about jets landing on the roof, let alone flying over it. Mr. Snodgrass looked up from the silver florin he was examining. He spoke in a soft, sad voice: "All the rules go out the window in a war, Rebecca."

"In a—? Oh!" She hadn't even thought of that. California hadn't been in a real war since more than twenty years before she was born. And that one was fought more with software than with germs or bombs. "Do you really think those were . . . warplanes?"

"I don't know what else they could have been," Ted Snodgrass answered.

"And that was when the cat threw up the hairball in his lap," Gran said triumphantly.

"It was no such thing," Ethel Snodgrass said. "How could it be, when he didn't come over till two days later?"

Mr. Snodgrass looked from one of them to the other. "Good thing they don't have bombers, I reckon," he said to Beckie.

That held so much truth, it hurt. Beckie started laughing so she wouldn't start to cry. Gran looked bewildered—she hadn't heard what Mr. Snodgrass said. Her cousin had. Husbands and wives often listened to each other out of the corner of their ear, as it were. "That's not funny, Ted," Ethel Snodgrass said.

"Well, maybe it isn't," he said. He wasn't the kind of man who got in a fight for the sake of getting in a fight. But he wasn't the kind of man who backed away when he thought he was right, either. "Don't you reckon you're being silly, going on and on about how things happened when Hector was a pup? What difference does it make now?"

"It makes a difference, all right," his wife answered, though she didn't say what sort of difference it made.

"It sure does," Gran said. Then she kind of blinked and scratched her head. She wasn't used to agreeing with anybody about anything.

The phone rang. "Saved by the bell," Mr. Snodgrass said, and pulled it out of his pocket. "Hello? . . . Oh, hello, Mr. Brooks. . . . Yes, tomorrow morning would be fine. . . . Ten o'clock? Sure, that'll work. See you then. Will your nephew be along? . . . All right. 'Bye now." He hung up. "That was the coin fella," he announced.

"I never would have guessed." Mrs. Snodgrass could sound a lot like Gran. Anybody would have figured they were related. Mrs. Snodgrass seemed to have a little more style with her sarcasm, though.

"The young man'll be along to pass the time of day," Mr. Snodgrass added to Beckie. His wife might not have spoken, as far as he was concerned. She might not even have been in the same county. He went on, "I expect he's more interesting than old folks going on about what happened a long time ago. I expect he may even be more interesting than these Georgia shillings from the 1920s."

Beckie had no idea how to answer that, so she didn't try. Gran and Ethel Snodgrass went back to arguing about what had happened a long time ago. Mrs. Snodgrass didn't stop arguing even when she served up ham and corn on the cob for supper.

The food was terrific. It didn't taste as if it was made in a factory and frozen and came off a supermarket shelf. It tasted as if somebody down the street had raised the hog and smoked the ham and grown the corn. And somebody down the street probably had. Lots of people in Elizabeth had little gardens and kept a few pigs and chickens.

Dessert was a cherry pie that also never saw the inside of a freezer. Beckie was just finishing up when jets flew over again, this time from west to east. "I hope those are our planes coming home again," Mr. Snodgrass said. "If they aren't . . . Well, if they aren't we've got even more trouble than I was afraid we did."

"How will we know if they're not?" Beckie asked.

"If you hear things go boom, that's a pretty good clue," he answered. He got off zingers even more readily than his wife did, but in a nicer tone of voice.

And what he said usually had the ring of truth behind it. For the next half hour, Beckie kept cocking her head to one side and listening for bombs going off. She was relieved when she didn't hear any. Then she wondered if she ought to be relieved. Virginia wasn't a very free place. But Ohio wasn't her state, either. She just wished they would have held off on their stupid war till she got home. No doubt that was a selfish attitude, but it was how she felt.

"Mr. Snodgrass!" she said suddenly.

"What is it?"

"Do you have any coins from the days of the old United States?"

"Yes, I think so. A few. That's a long time ago now—almost three hundred years since things fell apart."

"Could I look at them?" Beckie asked.

"Well, let me see where I've got 'em stashed." Mr. Snodgrass flipped through an album and took a plastic mount off a page. "Here's what they call a quarter dollar from 1801, not long before states started breaking away and going off on their own."

One side of the silver coin showed a woman with flowing hair—Liberty, she was supposed to be. On the other side, an eagle spread its wings. Beckie sighed. "I was just thinking—it might have been neat if the United States stayed united. We wouldn't have all these quarrels and wars in that case."

"We'd probably have something even worse. Things happen for the best—I'm sure of it," Mr. Snodgrass said. "Besides, holding that mess together just wasn't in the cards. The little states wouldn't admit that they weren't as important as places like Virginia and Pennsylvania. Imagine—there was a place called Rhode Island. It's part of Massachusetts now, of course, but in those days you could spit from one side of it to the other, near enough. And it said it had to be as strong in Congress—that's what they called the United States legislature—as anybody else."

"I remember reading about how it got founded—they teach us that even on the West Coast," Beckie said. "And I know it's not a state any more. Was that the Second Northeastern War or the Third?"

"The Second, I think, but don't hold me to it." Ted Snodgrass chuckled. "I haven't studied that stuff in a lot longer than you." He paused. "I haven't studied it in school, I should say, but you learn some history if you collect coins, too." After he got out another album, he showed Beckie a stout silver coin, as big as a five-peso piece back home. "See? It's a commemorative from 1837, and that means it's from after the Second Northeastern War."

She looked at the coin. COMMONWEALTH OF MASSACHUSETTS,

it said, and 2 FLORINS. A bald man with sideburns was identified as John Quincy Adams. On the other side, the coin showed a cannon and the words LIBERATION OF PROVIDENCE. "Did the people who lived in Providence think they were liberated?" she asked, handing it back.

"Don't bet on it," Mr. Snodgrass answered. "If I recollect right, somebody from Rhode Island took a shot at old Adams not long after that."

"You're right!" Beckie exclaimed. "They made a movie about it—I've seen it on TV. If the movie has things straight, Adams deserved it."

"How often do movies have things straight?" Mr. Snodgrass asked, which was a good question. The answer was, *Not very often.* He went on, "If that's so, I'm not surprised we've never seen it here. The courts wouldn't let in a film that showed somebody shooting at a consul or whatever Adams called himself—too likely to give folks nasty ideas, and they get too many already as is."

In some states, you could print anything you wanted or say whatever you pleased in movies or on TV or on the radio or on-line. In others, the censors would land on you with both feet if you tried. Virginia was one of *those.* What would happen to somebody here who tried to say on the air that Negroes ought to have equal rights? Nothing good—Beckie was sure of that.

Where you couldn't publish different ideas, almost every-body had the same ones. But Justin didn't. Beckie reminded herself of that. He was nervous about admitting it, but he didn't. He seemed embarrassed to come from this state at all.

Beckie took a last look at the United States quarter dollar. If you had one government stretching from coast to coast, you wouldn't need to be embarrassed about where you came from. Maybe a state like that would have fought wars with Quebec and

Ontario and Monterrey, but would it have fought as many wars as the real North America had seen? Beckie didn't think so.

"Not much point in driving," Mr. Brooks said. "It's only a few blocks. Come on—the walk will do you good."

"What if somebody knocks us over the head and steals your coins?" Justin asked.

"I'm a big boy now. I can take care of myself. Besides, even if I can't, everybody here knows everybody else. Everyone would know who did it as soon as it happened."

"But you said before that we're not from here, so would they tell?"

"Well, I hope they're starting to get used to us. I don't intend to get them mad or anything. I'm not going to rip off Ted Snodgrass, and I don't expect you to bang the drum for Negro rights where you'll tick folks here off." Mr. Brooks eyed Justin over his glasses. "What you say to the young lady from California . . . Well, be careful about that, too, okay?"

Justin's ears heated. "Okay. I'll try, anyhow."

"I suppose that'll do." Mr. Brooks grinned, which took a lot of tension out of the air. "Come on. Let's go."

As they walked down to Prunty, they passed three or four people out walking dogs or just walking for exercise. Everyone said hello. Nobody tried to knock the strangers from the big city over the head. Justin felt foolish. He felt even more foolish when one of the dogs licked his hand as he was petting it. "Ollie right likes you," said the woman who had the mutt on the leash.

"Uh, I guess he does," Justin answered. Ollie's frantically wagging tail said it was a good guess. So did the dog spit on Justin's fingers.

Mr. Snodgrass let them in when Mr. Brooks rang the bell. "Mornin', gents," he said. "I've got the coffee on, and there's fizzes in the icebox if you don't care for that."

"I'll have a fizz, thanks," said Justin, who wasn't much of a coffee drinker.

"I'll get it for you," Ted Snodgrass said. Beckie walked into the front room then. Mr. Snodgrass chuckled. "No, I'll let the spry young legs do the job. Rebecca, seems like Mr. Monroe here is perishin' of thirst. You suppose you might lend him a hand?"

"Well, I know you've got a garden hose . . ." Beckie said. Mr. Snodgrass snorted.

"Helpful," Justin said.

"That's me," Beckie agreed. She went into the kitchen and came back with two fizzes.

"Thanks," Justin said when she handed him one. Mr. Snodgrass poured coffee for Mr. Brooks. They started talking about coins. Beckie raised an eyebrow. Justin nodded. The two of them went out into the back yard. "Where's your grandmother?" Justin asked.

"She and Mrs. Snodgrass went down to Palestine to shop," Beckie answered.

"You didn't want to go along?" he said.

She shook her head. "Nope. All they'll want to look at is clothes for old ladies, and that's so exciting I can't stand it." She yawned. Justin laughed. She went on, "Besides, the less I have to do with Gran, the happier I am, and you can take that to the bank. I've been traveling with her for seventy-four days now, and that's about seventy-five too many."

"Oh," Justin said, which seemed safe enough.

Beckie nodded as if he'd said something more. "Yeah, that's about the size of it," she said. "I don't think I'll ever get along with Gran again. I mean, I can still put up with her and every-thing, but that's not the same as liking her. She's . . . sour."

Justin didn't say anything this time. People could talk about their own relatives as if they were swindlers and bank robbers and grouches. If anybody else said the smallest bad thing about the same people, though, they'd rise up like tigers in their de-fense. Even if Justin thought he was right—no, especially if he thought she was right—keeping quiet about it looked like a good idea.

"Ever wonder how things might have been?" Beckie asked out of the blue.

"Huh?" Justin said. *Brilliant,* he thought. *Now she won't think you're an idiot. Now she'll be sure of it.*

But she wasn't—or it didn't show if she was, which was good enough. "If things were different," she said again.

"What kind of things?" Justin asked. At least that was a bet-ter question.

"All kinds of things," Beckie answered. "Things from way back when. Last night, Mr. Snodgrass showed me a coin from the United States. I asked him to, because I was thinking about that stuff."

"Were you?" Justin said. What he was thinking now was, *Uh-oh.* It worried him a lot more than *Huh?* had.

Beckie nodded seriously. "I sure was. I wondered what it would have been like if all of this were one state—one country, I guess I mean—and not a whole bunch of them." She waved her arms to show *all of this* meant everything from sea to shining sea. Except it didn't mean *exactly* that here, because nobody ever wrote "America the Beautiful" in this alternate. It came along in 1893, and by then this North America was chopped into more pieces than the chicken in a Chinese chicken salad.

"I don't see how that could have happened," he said—a lie he had to tell. In the home timeline, it *had* happened. The big states and the little ones compromised, and they all agreed to the Constitution, and it worked. But he couldn't let on that he knew anything about that. He'd already talked too much once.

Beckie didn't point her finger at him and go, *Oh, yes, you do!* She couldn't know he didn't belong in this alternate. All she knew was that he made kind of a peculiar Virginian. And even Virginians were entitled to be peculiar. It was a free state—as long as you weren't an African American, and as long as you didn't push it too hard.

Instead of pointing a finger, Beckie said, "Mr. Snodgrass told me the same thing. I suppose he's right—I suppose you're right, too. It's interesting to think about, though, isn't it? What might have been, I mean."

"Sure," Justin said. "There isn't any way to tell for sure what would have happened after that, though." He knew how true that was, where Beckie didn't. One alternate where the South won the Civil War had racial problems that made the ones here look like a walk in the park. Another alternate U.S.A. was a nasty tyranny that ran most of its world because it could squash anybody else. Yet another, in a world where the Germans won World War I and all the wars afterwards, remained under occupation by the Kaiser's soldiers even now. Endless possibilities . . .

Beckie, who didn't know about any of those alternates or the home timeline, was thinking along different lines. "Not being able to know makes it more interesting, not less. It isn't like some math problem in school, where there's only one right answer. You can just talk about it and see how it might have gone this way, or that one, or even the other one."

Or it might have gone all those different ways—only you'd

need a transposition chamber to see how they worked out. Justin couldn't talk about that, either. He was just glad his face didn't give him away. For all practical purposes, Beckie had figured out the crosstime secret.

He made his thumb and forefinger into a pretend gun and aimed it at her. "If you come up with the one true answer, I'll have to kill you," he said, doing his best to sound like a spy.

His best must have been good enough, because she giggled. "You really are out of your mind, aren't you?"

"I try," he said modestly.

"Well, good, because it's working," she told him.

There was a low, deep rumble, like thunder far away. That was a pretty good comparison, because this part of the continent got some ferocious thunderstorms. Only one trouble: the sun blazed down out of a bright blue sky. Not a cloud anywhere to be seen. But there was a cloud on Justin's hopes as he said, "What's that?" because he feared he knew the answer. Beckie said the same thing at the same time, and he thought he heard the same fear in her voice.

Then she said, "That was something blowing up, wasn't it?" Sometimes naming your fear could drive it away. Other times, naming it made it worse. This felt like one of those.

Justin breathed in a big lungful of warm, muggy air and then sighed it out. "I don't know of anything else it's likely to be."

Her hands folded into fists, so tight that her knuckles turned pale under her California tan. "These people are crazy. What is there to fight about?"

That was a pretty good question in most wars, and a really good question in this one. Justin had to remind himself that he was supposed to come from Virginia, which meant he was supposed to be a Virginia patriot. "Ohio wants to hurt our coal business," he said, which was true. "Ohio wants to stir up trouble between our whites and Negroes, too, to keep us hopping." That was also true. "We can't just let them get away with it." Was *that* true? Anybody from Virginia would naturally think so. Someone from Ohio? That was likely to be a different story.

"It's all stupid, if you ask me," Beckie said. "Isn't there enough coal business for Ohio and Virginia to share it?"

"There's Pennsylvania, too, and Boone," Justin said. "They think Virginia and Ohio both have too big a share already." If he were a real Virginian, he would know that. Coming from the other side of the continent, Beckie might not.

She said something rude about Pennsylvania and Boone—and about Ohio and Virginia, too. A Virginia girl wouldn't have said it the same way, but people from California seemed less restrained. Some things didn't change much across timelines. Then she added, "Don't get mad, but it seems to me that your Negroes could use somebody on their side, even if it is somebody foreign."

It seemed that way to Justin, too. And people from Ohio really were foreigners in this alternate's Virginia. People from California were more foreign still—otherwise, she never would have said such a thing. Justin picked his words with care: "Maybe it wouldn't be so bad if Ohio were on the Negroes' side because they're getting a raw deal here. But that's not how it works. People—white people—in Ohio don't like blacks any better than Virginians do. You don't see them letting Negroes immigrate into their state or anything. They just want to use ours to hurt us."

He watched her chew on that. Finally, even though he could tell she didn't like it, she nodded. "Okay. You're right. I was in

Ohio before I came here, and I saw some of what you're talking about. But it doesn't make what you're doing here any better."

"I didn't say it did," Justin answered.

A robin hopping on the grass cocked its head to one side and looked at him and Beckie. It was only three meters away—ten feet, people said here. Once it decided they didn't want robin stew, it plunged its beak into the ground and pulled out a fat worm. The worm wriggled, but not for long.

If worms could talk, they would make angry speeches about robins. And talking robins would complain that worms didn't play fair when they hid. But neither side there knew any better. Virginians and Ohioans . . . were supposed to, anyhow.

"Your mother's in Charleston, isn't she?" Beckie said. "Is everything all right there?"

"So far." Instead of knocking on wood, Justin banged his knuckles off the side of his head. Beckie must have understood what he meant, because she smiled. He went on, "I guess we're lucky we came west, because there sure are cases of this thing back in Fredericksburg."

"Some luck," Beckie said. "When do you suppose Virginia will start a plague in Ohio?"

If he were a good state patriot, he would have said something like, *Well, Ohio has it coming after what she did to us.* He knew that, but he couldn't make himself bring the words out. Instead, he said, "I wish they'd find some way to end the war before it comes to that."

Beckie didn't answer for most of a minute. She was studying him as if he were a rare animal in the zoo, one she might not see again for a long time. At last, she said, "You're all right, Justin." He couldn't have felt prouder if . . . he didn't know what. He couldn't have felt prouder, period. Exclamation point, even.

Disaster crews fought fires in the center of Parkersburg. Buildings were flattened for blocks around. Ambulance crews raced to get injured people to hospitals. "A fuel-air explosive is the next most powerful weapon after a nuclear bomb," the announcer said indignantly. "That the barbarians in Ohio would use this device against us shows what vicious, unscrupulous enemies they are. The consul has vowed to take revenge once more."

Mr. Snodgrass sighed. "That's what we heard earlier today, all right. If we lived in the big city, we could've wound up in one of those ambulances."

Beckie didn't show what she was thinking. Only somebody who lived in Elizabeth or someplace like it could imagine that Parkersburg was a big city. But he wasn't altogether wrong, either. Parkersburg was big enough to be worth bombing. She couldn't see anyone wasting a fuel-air explosive on this tiny place.

Gran, meanwhile, was mad about something else. "They didn't want to let us go shopping in Palestine," she said irately. "They didn't want to let us, do you hear? They thought we might have a disease, just on account of we came down from Elizabeth. Can you believe such a thing?"

Since Beckie could, she didn't say anything. The no-travel order, along with everything else that was going on, was plenty to make anybody nervous. She might have pointed that out if she thought her grandmother would listen. *Fat chance,* she thought. Gran wasn't too hard of hearing, not for somebody her age, but that didn't mean she'd pay any attention.

Mrs. Snodgrass had her nose out of joint, too. "The nerve of those Palestine people," she said. "The nerve! They're nothing but trash down there, not like the good stock that lives here. Well, they'll get what's coming to them—see if they don't."

"I should hope so," Gran said.

"I'm going to put a flea in Hank Meadows' ear, I am," Mrs. Snodgrass said. "You see if I don't. When those people come up here looking for lamps, they'll get what's coming to them."

"I hope we don't have another feud like the one thirty years ago," Mr. Snodgrass said. "That was more trouble than it was worth."

"Oh, I don't know," his wife said. "They learned their place, didn't they?"

"A couple miles south of here, right?" he said.

"Now don't you be difficult, Ted," Mrs. Snodgrass said. "I hate it when you're difficult." By that, she seemed to mean doing or saying anything she didn't approve of.

"Well, you've put up with me this long," he replied. "I reckon we'll last a bit longer."

Mrs. Snodgrass gave him a kind of indulgent smile. She might have been saying she put up with him even when he didn't deserve it. She probably was saying just that. Gran looked from one of them to the other as if they'd stopped speaking English, or even what passed for English in this western corner of Virginia. Her own marriage hadn't lasted. Her husband, a sailor who drank, lit out for parts unknown not long after her daughter—Beckie's mother—was born. Having put up with Gran for going on three months herself now, in a certain sense Beckie had no trouble blaming him.

But when she listened to the Snodgrasses going back and forth, she had all she could do to keep from breaking into a great big grin. They reminded her of her own mom and dad. People who lived together for a long time and made it work found ways to talk about things. They could tease each other without wounding, and they had a pretty good notion of when to let up.

No wonder Gran doesn't get it, Beckie thought sadly. Her grandmother wounded people almost every time she opened her mouth. Had she been the same way with her husband the sailor? Beckie wouldn't have been surprised. *No wonder he drank.* That hadn't crossed her mind before. She wished she weren't thinking it now.

Five

"Mornin', gents," said the waitress in Elizabeth's one and only diner, across the street from the one and only motel. "What'll it be?" By now, she was used to them coming in for breakfast every day.

"Ham and eggs today, I think, Irma," Mr. Brooks answered.

"Sausage and eggs for me," Justin said.

"Potatoes or grits?" Irma asked.

"Potatoes," they said together. Mr. Brooks added, "See? We sing in hominy."

The waitress started to nod, then stopped, did a double take good enough to go on TV, and sent him a dirty look. Justin gave him another one. "Did you *have* to do that, Uncle Randy?"

"No," Mr. Brooks admitted. "But I enjoyed it."

"That makes one of us," Justin said. This time, Irma did nod.

She set coffee in front of Mr. Brooks and ice water in front of Justin. He still couldn't get stoked about coffee, and it was too early in the day for a soda. *A fizz*, he reminded himself. *I've got to think of them as fizzes, or I'll call 'em by the wrong name one of these days. That wouldn't be so good.*

A local came in and sat down at the counter a few stools away from Justin and Mr. Brooks. He gave them a polite nod and spent a couple of minutes chatting with Irma before he ordered ham and eggs for himself. He chose grits to go with them. Chances were he'd been eating them all his life. If you got used to something when you were little, you'd go on liking it once you grew up.

Justin hadn't eaten grits when he was little. He feared he would never get used to them. In states like Georgia and Alabama, potatoes were hard to come by. There, most of the time, it was grits or nothing. That made Justin glad he at least had a choice.

"Terrible thing about Parkersburg," the local remarked when Irma gave him his coffee.

"Good Lord, wasn't it!" she exclaimed. "The front window rattled when that boom got near. I was afraid it'd break to pieces. Don't know what we would've done if it did. That's a big old piece of plate glass."

"Mighty dear," the man said, by which he meant expensive.

"Isn't it just?" Irma said. "Isn't everything nowadays? I had to have a tooth filled last week, and it cost me twenty pounds. *Twenty* pounds, can you believe it?" She paused and looked startled. "I had to go to Parkersburg to do it. I hope my dentist's office is still there. I hope my *dentist* is still there."

"How did you get them to let you into town with the travel ban on?" Justin asked.

"Sweetheart, I told the cops at the checkpoint I was from Elizabeth, and they let me by," Irma answered. "Nothing ever happens here, so they knew I wasn't carrying any stupid disease."

"Have there been any cases *in* Parkersburg?" Mr. Brooks didn't say any more than that. He didn't want to come right out and ask if the waitress had brought the sickness back with her.

And she didn't seem to catch the drift of the question. "My dentist didn't talk about any," she said. Then she went back to the tall counter between the kitchen and the outer part of the diner. She plucked two plates off it and set one in front of Justin and the other in front of Mr. Brooks. "Here you go. Enjoy your breakfasts, now."

Justin dug in. The diner would never win any prizes, but it wasn't bad, either. Irma went on shooting the breeze with the other customer till his food was ready. After she gave him his plate, she came over and refilled Justin's water and Mr. Brooks' coffee. Justin felt her breath on the hairs of his arm. After the question Mr. Brooks asked, he wished he didn't.

The older man was thinking along with him. "Well, we'll find out, won't we?" Mr. Brooks murmured. "Find out how good our shots really are too."

"I'm afraid we will." As soon as Justin heard what he'd said, he wished he hadn't put it like that. He didn't believe in omens and bad luck—not in the top part of his head he didn't. Believe or not, he knocked wood. He hoped it was wood, anyhow, not some synthetic. He didn't knock loudly, but Mr. Brooks noticed. "It can't hurt," Justin whispered. The older man nodded.

They both left the little diner as soon as they finished. Would that do any good? Justin had his doubts. By Mr. Brooks' somber expression, so did he. Again, though, it couldn't hurt.

"What now?" Justin asked.

"Now we hope," the coin and stamp dealer answered. "Hope we have some immunity. And Irma's not sick, so chances are we'll be all right. Of course, who knows how long the virus takes to incubate?"

"Yeah," Justin said, and then, "That isn't really what I meant. What are we going to do today?"

"Oh. That." The way Mr. Brooks said it, it didn't sound very important. He had a point, too. He had to think for a moment before he went on, "Well, laundry would probably be a good idea."

"Yeah," Justin said, more happily. They were washing their clothes at the Snodgrasses'. Elizabeth didn't boast a washeteria, which was what they called laundromats here. They'd also had to go down to Palestine to buy more for themselves after they got stuck here. Now they had three or four days' worth of outfits, not just what they'd worn when they got here.

Mr. Brooks smiled at him. "You won't be sorry to see Beckie again, will you?"

"Why should I be?" Justin answered. "She's nice. I'm not going to bring her back to the home timeline or anything, but she's nice." He suddenly wondered when—and if—he'd be able to get back to the home timeline himself. Crosstime Traffic wouldn't be eager to let people who might have been exposed to a genetically engineered disease bring it back with them. Diseases from other alternates had ripped through the home timeline more than once. People were a lot more careful now.

"Okay." Mr. Brooks set a hand on his shoulder. "Why not? Let's go deal with the laundry, then."

Beckie listened to Justin with rising horror. The more she tried to fight it down, the more it rose. Even the waitress' name somehow fueled it. Irma? Nobody in California would carry such an old-fashioned handle. "She came back from Parkersburg, and there's sickness there?" she said.

"She came back from there, anyhow," Justin told her. "She said her dentist didn't talk about any cases. That proves nothing one way or the other. But Parkersburg's a fair-sized town, and it's close to the Ohio border, and it's on a main road, so. . . ."

"Yeah. So," Beckie echoed unhappily. "Well, I don't think I'll get a whole lot of sleep tonight. Thanks a lot."

"I'm sorry. Would you rather I didn't tell you?" Justin sounded unhappy, too.

"I don't know." Beckie had to think about that. She finally shook her head. "No, I guess not. I'd rather be up on what's going on. Then I know what to worry about, anyhow."

"Good. I didn't think you'd want to be a mushroom," Justin said.

"A mushroom?" Beckie frowned. "What do you mean?"

"Sure. You know—they keep you in the dark and they feed you, uh, horse manure."

"Oh." The more she thought about it, the wider she grinned. "I like that. I *really* like it. Did you make it up yourself?"

He shook his head. For a split second, he looked—worried? The expression disappeared before Beckie was sure she saw it. "Not me," he said. "I deny everything. They say it in school back home, that's all."

"Oh," Beckie said again. She didn't have any particular reason not to believe him. She wasn't sure she did, though. He brought it out too pat—maybe that was what bothered her. And she couldn't imagine that kids in a place like Fredericksburg, a place that was Nowhere with a capital N, could come up with something so neat all by themselves. Maybe she wasn't giving them enough credit. Maybe . . . but she didn't think so.

"Do you know where the closest doctor lives, just in case?" Justin asked. "I don't think there's one here, and I don't think there's one in Palestine, either."

"If I were a doctor, I wouldn't live in a place like this," Beckie said. Justin nodded, and this time she had no trouble believing he really agreed with her. She went on, "I bet I know where the nearest doctor is." He raised an eyebrow. She told him: "Parkersburg."

He winced. "I bet you're right. If the disease shows up there, they'll be busy enough so they won't want to come out here, too."

"I know," Beckie said. "But look on the bright side. Even if they did come out, how much could they do?"

"Is that the bright side?" Justin asked. "If it is, what's the dark side?"

We all die. Beckie wished that hadn't gone through her head. She didn't want to say it. Saying things made them seem realer. She knew that was foolish, which didn't make it any less true. So she said, "Something worse," and let it go at that.

She watched Justin as he nodded. Watching him, listening to him, made her want to scratch her head. She knew what she wanted to ask him: something like, *Where are you* really *from?* Everybody else she'd met in Virginia made her feel as if she'd stepped back in time here, as if California were years and years ahead of this place. Maybe that was right, maybe it was wrong, but it was how she felt.

With Justin, it was different. It was as if he thought she was the one who was out of it. He didn't make a big deal out of that, but she felt it was true. And she wanted to know why.

Was it just that he was stuck up? With some people, she would have said yes right away. But he didn't act like that. He went out of his way not to act like that, as a matter of fact. He wanted to fit in as well as he could. It was as if he couldn't help thinking the way he thought, even if he didn't mean to show it.

Since she didn't want to ask him about himself and why he thought the way he did, she decided to ask about what he'd said instead. That seemed less likely to spook him. "I do like that thing about mushrooms," she told him. "What else do they say at your school?"

He turned red. She might have thought she wouldn't make

him nervous, but she turned out to be wrong. "I don't know," he mumbled. "We talk, that's all."

"I can't believe it," Beckie said. "I bet that line will go all over the continent. Has it been on TV here?"

"I've never noticed it," Justin answered.

"Only goes to show that TV writers don't listen to people," Beckie said. For some reason, that made Justin turn red all over again. She went on, "What are some of your favorite shows?"

"I don't watch a whole lot," he said. "News and sports, mostly." He yawned. "Boring, right?"

He sounded as if he wanted to be boring, as if he hoped it would be boring. But Beckie said, "I like football, too. I like rounders, but I like football better."

"Oh, yeah?" Justin said. Now Beckie knew exactly what he was thinking. Guys always had trouble believing it when they found a girl who was interested in sports.

"Yeah," Beckie said. "Which kind of football do you like better, rugby or association?"

"Uh, rugby," Justin answered, now sounding like somebody who was in over his head. But Beckie hadn't expected anything else. They played games where you could throw the ball more in the eastern states than they did in California.

"We play association most of the time in California," Beckie said. "Some of our sides go down to the Mexican states and take on their best clubs. We win a lot of the time, too."

"That's . . . impressive," Justin said. "Uh, I think maybe I ought to go in now. See if the laundry's dry." He almost fled into the house.

The laundry wasn't dry. Mr. Brooks and Mr. Snodgrass sat hunched over a chessboard. Mr. Brooks pushed a pawn. Mr. Snodgrass said, "You'll pay for that."

Justin looked at them in what seemed like real dismay. Beckie said, "Hey, I've got a rounders question for you, since you live on the East Coast. Was George Herman really as good as people say he was?"

"Uh . . ." Justin blinked. Beckie would have sworn he'd never heard of George Herman. But if you paid any attention to sports, that was impossible . . . wasn't it?

Mr. Snodgrass looked up from his game. "He wasn't as good as that, Rebecca—he was *better*," he said. "He could hit a ball farther than any man who's played the game since, even if he is a hundred and fifty years dead. That season he had stomach trouble, the Highlanders finished next to last. And he really did aim his club out toward the sign, like people say, and then smack the ball over it."

"Oh, my. The called shot," Mr. Brooks murmured. So he knew something about George Herman, too.

"I've heard that," Beckie said. "Is it really true? Is there video to prove it? I've never seen any in California."

"Well, I don't reckon I have, either." Mr. Snodgrass sounded as if he didn't want to admit it. "But everybody says it's so."

Beckie started to laugh. Everybody else looked at her— everybody except Gran. That only made it funnier, as far as she was concerned. *They say* was an article of faith with her grandmother. *They* said this, that, and the other thing. Gran never quite knew who *they* were, but *they* said it, and she believed it, no matter how dumb it was.

"George Herman must have been one ruthless player, all right." Now Justin sounded like somebody trying to make up for lost time.

Mr. Snodgrass nodded politely. As for Mr. Brooks . . . Mr. Brooks turned red and wheezed and choked, for all the world as if he was trying so hard not to laugh that he was hurting himself. Beckie wanted to scratch her head. Justin hadn't made a joke—or not one she got, anyway.

In the laundry room, the drier beeped to show the clothes in it were finally done. Mr. Brooks went in and loaded them into a duffel bag. He said, "We can pick up the game tomorrow, Ted, if that's all right with you."

"I suppose," Mr. Snodgrass said. "You just want to wait a spell before you see what I'm going to do to you, that's all."

"In your dreams," Mr. Brooks said sweetly. They both laughed.

After Mr. Brooks and Justin left, Beckie said, "I'd swear Justin never heard of George Herman."

"How could you not have?" Mr. Snodgrass said. "It's like not hearing of Stephen Douglas or Franklin Delano Truman. You'd have to come from Mars not to."

"Mars," Beckie echoed. "A couple of things he said make me wonder if he's from even farther away than that."

Justin kicked at a pebble on the sidewalk as he and Mr. Brooks walked back to the motel with their clean laundry. "Well, I blew it again," he said, angry at himself. "Who'd figure that a girl would like sports? I mean really like sports, so she knows more about 'em than most guys do."

"Life is full of surprises," Mr. Brooks said, which didn't make Justin feel any better.

He kicked at another pebble. "She made me look like a jerk. She made me sound like a jerk," he said. "People I never heard of—but I'm supposed to, if I'm a proper fan."

"Ruthless," Mr. Brooks muttered. "I ought to punt you for that, except it's the wrong game."

They turned the corner onto State Route 14, then both stopped in their tracks. Red lights flashing, an ambulance was parked in front of the diner across from the motel. Justin's stomach did a slow lurch, the way it would have when an intercontinental shuttle went weightless.

He glanced over at Mr. Brooks. The older man licked his lips. Was he paler than he had been a moment before? Justin thought so. But then, he was probably paler than he had been himself. "That doesn't look so great," he said.

"No, it doesn't." Mr. Brooks tried not to sound worried. That only made him sound more so.

"Maybe it doesn't have anything to do with . . . stuff like that," Justin said. "Maybe somebody got burned or something."

"Maybe." Mr. Brooks didn't sound as if he believed it. Justin bit his lip. He didn't believe it, either, no matter how much he wanted to.

The paramedics or whatever they called them here brought somebody out on a wheeled cart. Justin bit his lip harder. That was Irma, all right. And the men taking care of her wore gas masks and orange rubber gloves.

Mr. Brooks and Justin both took half a step back before they knew they'd done it. Justin laughed at himself, not that it was really funny. As if half a step could make any difference in whether they came down with whatever it was.

"She always seemed fine," Mr. Brooks said. "I thought we were worrying over nothing."

"I hoped we were worrying over nothing," Justin said. Amazing how changing one word in a sentence could change the whole meaning.

Siren wailing, the ambulance zoomed away—back up Highway 14 toward Parkersburg. Justin and Mr. Brooks both watched and listened till the flashing lights vanished in the distance and the siren dopplered away into silence. Then the coin and stamp dealer kicked a pebble of his own. "Well, not much use pretending we haven't been exposed," he said. "Now we see what happens next."

"Yeah." Justin didn't see what else he could say. He took his phone off his belt. "I'd better let Mom know what's going on."

"She won't be happy," Mr. Brooks said.

"I'm not real happy myself," Justin said. "I'm especially not real happy 'cause we're stuck here." Any of the locals who overheard him would think he meant stuck in Elizabeth. And he did. But he also meant stuck in this whole alternate. And he and Mr. Brooks *were* stuck, because no transposition chamber would take them back to the home timeline, not with a genetically engineered disease loose here.

He punched in Mom's number. The phone rang—once, twice. "Hello?" Mom said.

"Hi. It's me."

"Hi, you. What's up?"

"An ambulance just took Irma the waitress away. She may have it." There. Justin had said it. He waited for his mother to pitch a fit.

She just said, "Oh," in a strange, flat voice. Then she said, "I was hoping you'd miss it in a little town where nothing ever happens. It's here in Charleston, too."

"It is?" Justin said in dismay. But he wasn't only dismayed—he was angry, too. "They haven't said anything about it on TV or anything."

"They wouldn't," Mom answered. "They don't want to make people jump up and down and worry or anything. But it's here, all right."

"That's . . . too bad," Justin said, which would do for an under-statement till a bigger one came along. Mr. Brooks raised a questioning eyebrow. He pointed south, toward Charleston. Justin nodded. The older man clapped a hand to his forehead.

"Stay well, you hear me?" Mom said.

"I'll try." Justin didn't want to tell her that someone who'd come down with it had been breathing into his face every morning for the past week. "You stay well, too," he said. What kind of things was Mom not telling him? Did he really want to know? He didn't think so.

"I'll do my best. The doctors say they're getting close to a cure." Mom spoiled that by adding, "Of course, they've been saying the same thing since it broke out, and there's no cure yet. Dummies." Anyone who overheard her would think she was complaining that the local doctors weren't as smart as they thought they were. And she was. But she was also complaining that they knew less than their counterparts in the home timeline. She was right about that, too.

Sometimes being right did you no good at all. This felt like one of those times. "Love you, Mom," Justin said. Some things you didn't want to leave unsaid, not when you might not get another chance to say them.

"Love you, too," she answered. "Be careful."

"Sure," he said. "You do the same."

They were both whistling in the dark. Justin knew it. No doubt his mother did, too. They both did it anyhow, to make each other feel better. Justin didn't feel much better. He hoped Mom did.

"It's really in Charleston?" Mr. Brooks asked as Justin put his phone away.

"Uh-huh." Justin nodded. No, he didn't feel very good about the way things were going, not even a little bit. He glanced over at Mr. Brooks, hoping the older man would do or say something to cheer him up.

Mr. Brooks was looking south, toward the city where he lived and worked. His face usually wore a smile, but now his mouth was set in a thin, hard, grim line. "A lot of nice people down there," he said. "Oh, plenty who aren't so nice, too, but I can't think of anybody who deserves to come down with a mutated virus."

Justin, by contrast, was looking around Elizabeth. By now, it was more familiar to him than Charleston ever got the chance to be. "I can't think of anybody here who does, either," he said. "Including you and me."

Mr. Brooks managed a smile for that, but it was a halfhearted one, not one his face really meant. The corners of his mouth curled up and he showed his teeth, but his eyes. . . . Behind his glasses, his eyes didn't brighten at all. "Well," he said, "if you're going to fuss about every little thing . . ."

"I don't think you ought to let them in the house any more," Gran said to Mrs. Snodgrass. "That woman has it, and they've been eating where she works."

"You know the saying about locking the barn door after the horse is gone?" Mr. Snodgrass said. "Well, Myrtle, you're trying to lock the horse out after he's already got his nose in the barn."

"Are you sure, Ted?" Mrs. Snodgrass said. "Maybe they weren't catching yet, and now they are."

"Maybe." In Mr. Snodgrass' mouth, it came out, *Mebbe*. "Don't reckon it's what you'd call likely, though."

Beckie didn't reckon it was, either. She laughed at herself for even including the word in her thoughts. She didn't think she'd ever heard it in California, even if it seemed natural as could be

here. She almost said what she thought, but at the last minute
kept quiet. These people were four times her age. They wouldn't
pay any attention to her no matter what she said. The only people
Gran ever paid attention to were her mysterious *they*.

"I don't want to turn them away," Mr. Snodgrass said firmly.
"I just don't. It wouldn't be neighborly. How could I do business
with Randolph Brooks again if I told him he wasn't welcome inside my house? I'd be ashamed to, I would."

That got through to his wife. "Well, you're right," she said.
She didn't sound happy about it, but she didn't argue any more,
either.

Neighborly, Beckie thought. That was another word you didn't
hear much in California—certainly not in enormous Los Angeles. In little towns in the mountains or the desert? She supposed
so, but she wasn't from one. She'd never stayed in one till now.

She'd never stayed anywhere with a tailored virus loose, either. She could have done without the honor. Only trouble was, it
didn't look as if she had a choice.

"How is the woman, anyway?" Gran asked. "Does anybody
know?"

"The hospital in Parkersburg doesn't want to say anything,"
Mrs. Snodgrass said. "You know how hospitals are."

"But we need to find out," Gran said, as if that made all the
difference.

"Good luck," Mrs. Snodgrass said. You could tell she and
Gran were cousins, all right—she was ready to argue about anything, too.

"Maybe somebody could call and say they're a relative."
Gran actually had an idea. Beckie blinked. She couldn't remember the last time that happened. It wasn't even a bad idea.

Mrs. Snodgrass turned to her husband. "Take care of it, Ted," she said in tones that brooked no argument. "Tell 'em you're Irma's husband."

He didn't look thrilled about getting drafted—or maybe about the idea of being Irma's husband. "And what'll I tell 'em when they ask how come I'm not there with her?" he asked.

Mrs. Snodgrass had all the answers. "Tell 'em you weren't with her when she came down sick. Tell 'em you're hoping you don't catch it yourself. Heaven knows *that's* true."

"I don't reckon they'll talk to me," Mr. Snodgrass said dolefully. But he looked up the number and called the hospital. The longer he talked, the less happy he looked. He clicked off the phone with more force than he really needed. "They said I'm the fifth different husband she's had, by the phone numbers from incoming calls. She's had two mothers, three sisters, and five daughters, too—oh, and two sons."

"Okay, you tried," his wife said, unabashed. "So they wouldn't tell you anything, then?"

"Oh, I didn't say that," Mr. Snodgrass answered.

"*Well?*" Mrs. Snodgrass and Gran and even Beckie all said the same thing at the same time.

By the way Mr. Snodgrass shook his head, it wasn't well or okay or anything like that. "She died last night, a little before midnight."

The diner had a sign on the door: SORRY, WE'RE CLOSED. PLEASE COME BACK SOON. Justin and Mr. Brooks eyed it in identical dismay. "Is there any other place to eat in Elizabeth?" Justin asked.

"If there is, they've hidden it someplace where I haven't found it," the coin and stamp dealer answered. "And I don't reckon this town is big enough to have any places like that."

Justin didn't think so, either. "What are we going to do?" he asked.

"We could go down to Palestine." As soon as the words were out of Mr. Brooks' mouth, he shook his head. "No, by now they'll have heard Irma's sick. Anybody from Elizabeth will be as welcome as ants at a picnic. I think we'll have to go to the grocery store and pick up whatever we can find that we don't have to cook much."

"Oh, boy," Justin said in a hollow voice. "Junk food and sandwiches and frozen dinners. Yum, yum." Some of what this alternate's Virginia used for junk food grossed him out. Mr. Brooks had had to explain where pork rinds came from. Once Justin knew, he didn't want to eat them any more, even if he didn't think they were bad before. Mr. Brooks said people in the home timeline ate them once upon a time. People in the home timeline had done all kinds of disgusting things once upon a time. They'd kept slaves. They'd worn furs. Pork rinds probably weren't that bad, but they weren't good, either.

Mr. Brooks understood his expression perfectly. "If you see something in the deli section called 'head cheese,' chances are you don't want that, either," he said.

Even the name was enough to make Justin gulp. "You're so helpful," he said.

The grocery was a mom-and-pop. Even in Charleston, there weren't many chain stores here. Because this North America was split up into so many states, corporations couldn't get enormous the way they did in the home timeline. Things were more expensive than in the home timeline, but there was more variety here.

"Mornin'," the grocer said when they walked in. He knew who they were. Everybody in Elizabeth knew who they were by now.

"Mornin'," Justin and Mr. Brooks answered together.

"You'll have heard Irma passed on day before yesterday?" The man's voice held a certain amount of doubt. They were strangers, so who could say for sure what they'd heard?

"Yes," Mr. Brooks said. "We heard that." Justin nodded. You didn't just walk in and buy what you wanted in a place like this, the way you would in the home timeline. Oh, you could, but that would mark you as not just a stranger but a foreigner. People from states like Ohio and Pennsylvania and New York did abrupt, rude things like that. If you were a Virginian, you chatted with the storekeeper for a while.

"Hope you gents are doing all right," the grocer said.

"Well, now that you mention it, so do we," Mr. Brooks said dryly.

"Just a little, yeah," Justin added.

"I believe it," the grocer said, chuckling. "I ate over at the diner a couple of times myself the last two weeks, and Irma's been in and out of here, too."

Why was he laughing, then? Justin had trouble understanding it. The only thing that occurred to him was that laughing at fear was better than giving in to it. Not needing to fear would have been better still.

"You know what's worst about the whole thing?" Mr. Brooks said. "What with the travel ban and the worry about getting crowds together, there are no games on TV. If you're stuck in a motel the way we are, they help make the time go by."

"Or even if you're not stuck in a room," said the man behind the counter. "I was a pretty fair rounders player in the old days, if I say so myself." Justin judged that would have been forty years, thirty kilos, and three chins ago. The grocer went on, "I know how the game's supposed to be played, and I like watching it when it's played right."

"Sometimes, I bet, you like watching it when it's played wrong," Mr. Brooks said. "Then you can tell them what a bunch of fools they are, and how they don't deserve to wear the uniform."

The grocer laughed again. "There is that. Yes, sir, there is that."

Now that the social rituals were satisfied, Justin and Mr. Brooks could go on into the store and get what they wanted. They had an old microwave oven, a gift from the Snodgrasses, in their room so they could nuke frozen dinners. (Here, though, it was a radio range, and you zapped things instead of nuking them.) Frozen dinners in this alternate were even less exciting than they were in the home timeline, but they did give the illusion of sitting down to something cooked instead of eating sandwiches all the time.

Mr. Brooks was buying some bread and Justin was getting some canned chicken and canned fruit when another customer walked into the store. "Mornin', Charlie," the grocer said.

"Mornin', Mr. Kerfeld," answered the janitor who was, as far as Justin knew, the head of the one and only black family in Elizabeth.

"How are you today?" the grocer said.

"Not too bad, sir. Not too bad," the black man answered.

"Wife and kids doing well?"

"Yes, sir. Thank you. Terrible thing, this sickness, isn't it?"

"It really and truly is, Charlie. You heard Miss Davis died?"

"I did. It's a shame, Mr. Kerfeld, and that's the truth. She was a nice lady, a mighty nice lady."

"That's a fact."

Their chat was almost the same as the chitchat Justin and Mr. Brooks had had with the grocer—almost, but not quite. Yes, there was the ritual of gabbing a while before getting down to business. But Mr. Kerfeld had spoken with Mr. Brooks and Justin as equals. They were whites, the same as he was. The janitor, by contrast, called him *mister* and *sir*, while the grocer used the African American's first name. The waitress was Irma to whites, but Miss Davis to Charlie.

In the home timeline, racism lingered even after more than two centuries had passed since the Civil War. It didn't just linger here—it was alive and well. In most of the Southern states, whites still oppressed blacks, even if blacks were legally free. In Mississippi, where the black majority had risen in revolt, it was the other way around. And most of the states that had only a few Negroes didn't want any more. It seemed sad and scary to someone who'd grown up knowing better.

Charlie seemed to accept things. But what else could he do? If he fussed, the law would land on him like a ton of bricks. Under his politeness, though, what was he thinking? In his shoes, Justin would have hated Mr. Kerfeld and every other white person he saw. If the janitor didn't, why not?

If he did, on the other hand, what could he do about it? Blacks had rebelled in several states besides Mississippi, and got crushed every time. If they tried it again in Virginia, weren't they bound to fail again? Of course they were . . . unless, perhaps, Ohio gave them a hand. Ohio wouldn't do that from the goodness of its heart—oh, no. But Ohio might do it to give an enemy a hard time.

One thing that hadn't happened in this alternate was a peaceful civil-rights movement. Negroes here hadn't set out to persuade whites that they were as good as anybody else. Justin wondered why not. Maybe their being crammed into the Southern states and not spread across the continent had something to do with it. And maybe the history of uprisings left whites and blacks too distrustful of each other to look for common ground.

More questions than answers, Justin thought unhappily. Things often worked that way out among the alternates. Crosstime Traffic tried to keep an eye on so many of them, it hadn't had the chance to study them all as well as it might have.

"You ready, Justin?" Mr. Brooks asked. He couldn't know what Justin was worrying about.

"Yeah," Justin said. "I guess so."

They talked with the grocer a little more as they paid for their food. "Take care, now," Mr. Kerfeld said when they walked out.

The air felt hot and sticky. Clouds built up in the west. "Rain coming," Mr. Brooks remarked.

"I guess so," Justin said, and then, softly, "Do you suppose anyone here but Charlie knows what his last name is?"

"People know," Mr. Brooks answered. "They just don't care. There's a difference." Justin nodded. But didn't that make it worse, not better?

Six

Lightning flashed, not far enough away. Beckie counted vampire bats. She'd barely counted two of them before thunder boomed, loud as a cannon's roar. Rain came down in buckets.

"Wow!" she said. "You hardly ever see this in California."

"This isn't anything special," Gran said. "Why, when I was a little girl . . . When was that storm, Ethel? You know the one I mean—the *bad* one. Was that in '36? Or was it '37?"

"It was '37, I think," Mrs. Snodgrass answered, so of course Gran decided it must have happened in 2036. They went back and forth, back and forth. Either way, it was more than forty years before Beckie was born, so she didn't worry about it a whole lot. Another flash of lightning strobed across the sky. This time, the thunder came even sooner. The Snodgrasses' house shook.

"You don't want to see the lightning and hear the thunder at the same time. That's real bad news," Mr. Snodgrass said. He glanced at his wife and Gran. One of his gingery eyebrows rose a little. Was he thinking they were the lightning and the thunder? Beckie wouldn't have been surprised.

Water drummed on the roof. No, you didn't get rain like this in Los Angeles. It came down, and it kept on coming. Nine zillion raindrops danced on the growing puddles in the back yard. Beckie wondered how often the Snodgrasses' house got flooded. They didn't seem antsy, so maybe it didn't happen as much as she guessed it might.

Mr. Snodgrass had other worries on his mind. "Hope we don't get tornadoes," he said.

"Bite your tongue, Ted!" his wife exclaimed. Mr. Snodgrass really did stick out his tongue and make as if to chomp down on it. Mrs. Snodgrass rolled her eyes before she went on, "We haven't had a twister tear through Elizabeth for as long as anybody can recollect. But remember the one that got Palestine? What year was that, Ted? Was it '71? Or '72?"

"Well, I reckoned it was '73 myself, but I'm not gonna get all hot and bothered about it," Mr. Snodgrass answered, a dig plainly aimed at his wife and Gran. Mrs. Snodgrass rolled her eyes again. Gran didn't even notice she'd been zinged. Beckie might have known—*had* known—she wouldn't. *None so blind as those who will not see*, Beckie thought.

More thunder boomed and rumbled, this time a little longer after the lightning that lit up the front room with a white-purple flash. Beckie could imagine funnels forming in weather like this. "What do we do if there is one?" she asked.

"We go down cellar and say our prayers," Mrs. Snodgrass answered. "If God is listening, it'll stay away from us. If He's not . . ." She screwed up her face into what was meant for a smile. "If He's not, I expect He's got somebody else He needs to save more than us. His will be done."

She sounded as if she meant it. People here took their religion more seriously than they did in California. Back home, Gran went to church but Mom and Dad didn't, or not very often. In Elizabeth, almost everybody seemed to. Beckie had gone since she came here—with the Snodgrasses and her grandmother going, staying away would have made her seem rude and weird. At seventeen, she felt the need to fit in. She didn't think she was getting much out of going—the preacher was a bore. But people smiled and nodded just to see her there. That counted, too.

Another flash of lightning lit everything up for a moment. As Beckie blinked, she counted bats again. Halfway between five and six of them, the thunder crashed. "That's more like it," she said. "A mile away, or pretty close."

"About what I figured myself," Mr. Snodgrass said. "I bet that one came down on Jephany Knob. A lot of times after a thunderstorm you'll see trees knocked down up there. It draws lightning, sure enough."

High ground did. Beckie knew that. She'd seen pictures of trees blasted during thunderstorms. She tried to imagine what they'd smell like. What was the odor of hot sap? She didn't know, but she wanted to find out. "After the rain stops—if the rain ever stops—I'd like to have a look up there," she said. *Look* wasn't all of what she meant, but saying something like *I want to have a sniff up there* would only make everybody think she was strange.

"Well, you can do that," Mr. Snodgrass said.

"I don't want you going up there by yourself," Gran said.

Beckie started to say everything would be fine. What she wanted to say was that Gran was an old foof who belonged back in the twentieth century, or maybe the nineteenth. Before she could get the words out, Mr. Snodgrass said, "Myrtle's right, Rebecca. There may be snags up there. There may be rattlers, too—there usually are."

And there may be people with guns, Beckie remembered. She swallowed whatever protest she might have made and nodded instead. "Okay, I won't," she said. "Maybe Justin will want to go up there with me."

That didn't make Gran any happier—but then, what did? "I don't know what that boy has in mind," she said, but that wasn't what she meant. She meant she knew just what Justin had in mind, and she didn't like it one bit.

"Don't be silly, Gran," Beckie said.

"I'm not being silly. Don't you wish you could say the same?" The look Gran gave her meant her grandmother thought she had the same thing in mind as Justin did. The only thing Beckie had in mind right then was picking up a lamp and bashing Gran over the head with it. She didn't, but it sure was tempting.

"Justin's a nice enough fella," Mr. Snodgrass said.

"Yes, and a whole lot you know about it," Gran said.

"Oh, I recollect, I do," he answered. "I may not be young any more, but I'm not dead yet, either, not by a long chalk. Isn't that right, sweetie?" He turned to his wife for support.

"Men," Mrs. Snodgrass sniffed. By the way she made it sound, half the human race was in big trouble if she had anything to say about it. Mr. Snodgrass mimed being cut to the quick. His wife laughed, but she wasn't kidding—or not much, anyhow.

The high-topped running shoes Justin had worn when he came up to Elizabeth were good enough for almost anything. Oh, he'd get stares if he went to a fancy dinner in them, but he doubted anybody in Elizabeth had ever set out that fancy a dinner. They weren't hiking boots or anything, but he felt more than sure-footed enough in them to climb Jephany Knob.

"How you doing?" he asked Beckie.

"I'm fine," she answered. Just then, her foot came down on some slick mud. She almost took a pratfall, but a wild flail of her arms and a helping hand from Justin kept her upright. "Thanks," she said.

"Sure," he said. "You helped keep me from landing on my can a couple of minutes ago." He didn't much want to let go of her hand, but he did. Right now, she was a girl he knew, not a girl-friend. He knew Mr. Brooks wouldn't want her to turn into a girlfriend. Romances between Crosstime Traffic people and locals almost always turned out badly.

"It's nice, isn't it?" she said. "The air feels . . . washed clean."

Justin nodded. Now that the rain had moved through, the nasty humidity was down. Everything smelled green—almost like spring but not quite so sweet, because fewer flowers were in bloom.

No sooner had that thought crossed Justin's mind than a wisp of breeze brought a new odor with it. His nose wrinkled. So did Beckie's. That sickly-sweet smell was unmistakable. They both said the same thing at the same time: "Something's dead!"

It had to be something good-sized, too, or the stink wouldn't have been so obvious. Feeling a little—a very little—like Daniel Boone, Justin followed the breeze up the knob.

"Look!" Beckie pointed. "There's a tree down." Her laugh sounded shaky. "When the storm was bad a couple of days ago, I wondered if a tree would get hit, and what hot sap smelled like. But that's not sap."

"No." Now Justin shook his head. "It's a dead bear or . . ." His voice trailed away. He saw what he'd hoped he wouldn't see. "Are you sure you want to look? It's a dead man."

"It's Charlie!" Beckie said. In and around Elizabeth, the

black man stood out, all right. "He must have run over by the tree when the lightning started coming close, and. . . ."

"That's the worst thing you can do," Justin said. "People are supposed to know it is, too, but they do it anyway."

"What's that by him?" Beckie asked.

Justin took a closer look. However much he wished it would, that didn't change a thing. "It's a gun," he answered.

"It's not just an ordinary gun, is it?" Like him, Beckie seemed to be doing her best not to say what desperately needed saying. She went on, "I mean, it's not a squirrel gun or a deer gun on. . . ."

"No, it's not any of those." Then, because he had no choice, Justin said the thing he had to say: "It's an assault rifle." Guns made for shooting game could be works of art in their own right. Guns made for shooting people were ugly and functional. This one, of metal and plastic with a big, fat magazine, was no exception. It was an infantryman's weapon, not the kind a janitor out hunting had any business carrying.

And why would Charlie have gone hunting in the middle of a thunderstorm that had everything in it but the crack of doom? Justin couldn't think of any good reason. He had no trouble coming up with piles of bad ones, though.

"What are we going to do?" Beckie said in a small voice.

"Why are you asking me?" Justin snapped. He wasn't angry at Beckie—he was angry at himself. The question had several obvious answers, and he didn't want to think about any of them.

Beckie sent him a hurt look. "You're the Virginian. You know what you're supposed to do when something like this happens."

"Something like this?" He laughed harshly. "Nobody ever wants to run into something like this."

That was true. It was also one of the biggest understatements of all time. He especially didn't want to have to deal with this mess, because he wasn't a real Virginian—not from this alternate, anyhow. If he were, he would have reacted without even thinking. He was sure of that. A black man with an assault rifle? What could that mean but an uprising against the whites who'd ruled this Virginia as long as there'd been a Virginia here? And what else could you do about it but report it to the authorities and turn them loose on all the African Americans for kilometers— no, for miles—around?

Because he was from the home timeline, Justin didn't see things the way a local would have. He knew the blacks here were oppressed. He sympathized with them for wanting to do something about it. He didn't want to get shot himself, though, any more than an ordinary white Virginian here would have.

"We need to call the police, don't we?" Beckie said.

"The sheriff, you mean," Justin said. Elizabeth wasn't big enough to have a police department. But it was a county seat, and the sheriff's office and the county jail were in the same building as the county courthouse.

"That's right. I've talked with him before," Beckie said. She took her phone off her belt. "Do you want to call, or shall I?"

"I'll do it," he said. "We're both strangers, but at least I come from Virginia." One more lie he had to tell.

He didn't have the Wirt County sheriff's number, but a call to information took care of that. "This here is Sheriff Cochrane," said a deep voice on the other end of the line. "Who am I talking to?" Justin gave his name. He told Sheriff Cochrane where he was, and what he and Beckie had found there. "Good God in the foothills!" the sheriff burst out. "Charlie? Are you sure?"

Before Justin answered, he breathed in another lungful of that foul odor. "I'm sure, all right," he answered grimly.

"Okay. I'm on my way—top of Jephany Knob, you said? Don't touch anything before I get there, you hear?" Without waiting for an answer, Cochrane hung up.

"Well?" Beckie asked when Justin gave her phone back.

"He's coming," Justin said. "He says not to touch anything."

That made her mad, which Justin thought was funny. "How dumb does he think we are?" she demanded.

"He probably doesn't think we are. He probably said it just in case," Justin answered. "He probably says it every time anything happens." How often did things happen in Wirt County? Justin had no idea.

Sheriff Cochrane wasted no time. Red lights flashing, his car pulled to a stop at the bottom of the knob inside of five minutes. He wore brown boots, a khaki uniform, and what Justin thought of as a Smokey the Bear hat, though nobody in this alternate had ever dreamed up Smokey. He climbed Jephany Knob with the air of a man who knew the ground as well as he knew his own office— and with a pistol in his right hand.

"You two," he muttered when he saw Justin and Beckie. "Strangers." By the way he said it, that was almost a crime in itself. He didn't quite aim the pistol at them, but he sure had it ready.

Justin pointed to the lightning-blasted tree. "There's the body."

"Uh-huh." As soon as Cochrane turned towards it, his long face got even longer. "Yeah, that's Charlie, sure as the devil." His nostrils twitched. He grimaced. "And he's been here a couple days, hasn't he?" He did some more muttering, then walked over and crouched next to the dead man—and next to the assault rifle by his right hand. Cochrane pointed to it. "You kids touch this piece? At all? I won't get mad—well, I won't get real mad—if you tell me yes. But if you tell me no and your prints show up, you don't even want to think about how much trouble you're in, not in wartime you don't. So—did you?"

"No, sir," Justin and Beckie said together.

"Okay." The sheriff put on rubber gloves. He picked up the assault rifle, holding it by the barrel, and put it in a plastic evidence bag. Then he looked down at Charlie and shook his head. "I hadn't seen him around, but I didn't think anything of it, you know? His wife didn't call him in missing, either. I don't like that a bit. I don't want to believe any of this. If Charlie's not to be trusted, there's not a colored fellow in the whole blamed state who is."

He was likely to be right. Why would blacks in Virginia stay loyal to the government that didn't give them the rights whites took for granted? The only reason Justin could see for their staying quiet was that they were afraid to rise up. If they lost that fear . . . Well, there Charlie lay.

"Strangers," Sheriff Cochrane muttered again. He eyed Justin and Beckie. "What were you two doing up here, anyway?"

"Just taking a walk," Justin answered.

"We were glad to get out after the rain cooped us up," Beckie added.

"Uh-*huh*," the sheriff said. That might have meant he wondered if they'd come up here to fool around. Rules or no rules, Justin wouldn't have minded. But Cochrane was also thinking of something else. "You weren't by any chance up here *while* it was raining, were you?"

They were white. He had to be careful how he questioned

them. But Justin knew what he meant. He wanted to know if they had anything to do with the Negro and the assault rifle. That was what they got for being strangers. They both shook their heads at the same time. "You can ask my grandmother and Mr. and Mrs. Snodgrass," Beckie said. "Besides, I would have drowned if I went out in that."

"My uncle will tell you I was with him all the time," Justin said.

"Another stranger," Sheriff Cochrane said. But he went on, "Well, I've known the Snodgrasses since dirt. They wouldn't have any truck with a thing like this, that's a fact." He got to his feet. "You kids come on back to the car with me. I'll take you into town."

"What about Charlie?" Justin asked.

Sheriff Cochrane looked back at the janitor's body. "He's not going anywhere," he said, and Justin couldn't very well argue with that. The sheriff's voice took on the snap of command: "Come on, I told you."

Down Jephany Knob they went, all of them skidding when they hit slick patches of mud. Nobody fell, which Justin took for a minor miracle. The sheriff started to open the back door to the bright red car, then changed his mind and opened the front door instead.

"Crowd in beside me," he said. "If I put you in back, everybody who sees you in there'll figure I've jugged you, and I've got no call to do that." As with most police cars, this one had a fine metal grill between front seat and back to make sure prisoners didn't kick up any trouble.

The front seat was crowded with three people in it. Justin, in the middle, didn't mind getting squeezed against Beckie. Sheriff Cochrane was a different story. He smelled of tobacco, and the pistol on his right hip was an uncomfortable lump. Justin was glad it wasn't more than a couple of minutes' ride back to Elizabeth.

Cochrane stopped the car at the corner of Route 14 and Prunty. "Guess I'll let the two of you out right here, if that's okay," he said.

"Sure," Beckie said, and got out in a hurry. Justin slid out after her. The sheriff's car headed on up toward the courthouse. "Shall we go back to the Snodgrasses'?" Beckie asked.

Justin shook his head. "Let's just wait here for a little bit." She looked puzzled, but she didn't say no.

Inside of ten minutes, the sheriff's car raced down Route 14 toward Jephany Knob again. This time, Sheriff Cochrane had his deputy along with him. "Oh," Beckie said. "Is that what you were looking for?"

"Yeah," he answered. "Weren't you?"

"I guess," she said. "I'm not from here, so I don't know for sure—how much trouble is what we found going to cause?"

Even though Justin wasn't really from this alternate's Virginia, either, answering that was easy as pie. "Lots," he said.

"Charlie?" Mrs. Snodgrass said. "Charlie up there on the knob with a rifle? I don't believe it."

"I don't want to believe it," Mr. Snodgrass said, which wasn't the same thing at all. "If Charlie could do a thing like that . . ."

"Ungrateful, is what it is," his wife said. "Everybody in town treated him almost like he was one of us."

That *almost* was the problem. Beckie could hear it, and could hear that it was wrong. By all the signs, nobody born and raised in Virginia could. She thought about saying something, but she was sure nobody would listen to her. She'd hoped her grandmother might, but Gran was nodding along with what Mrs. Snodgrass said—for once, she'd found something she agreed with. You could take the young woman out of Virginia, but taking Virginia out of the young woman was much harder. Virginia's attitudes stayed in Gran even though she wasn't young any more.

"If things are like that here," Mr. Snodgrass said, "what's it like places where they have lots of colored people?"

"The TV hasn't talked about anything bad," his wife said.

"It wouldn't, not unless things are so bad it can't pretend they're good," he said darkly.

"Maybe the sickness has something to do with keeping everything else quiet," Beckie said.

"Maybe it does. I wouldn't be surprised," Mr. Snodgrass said. "And when you've got to go and thank a disease for something, you know you're in a pile of trouble." Beckie wished she could think that was wrong, too, but she feared it was much too right.

Late that afternoon, somebody rang the doorbell. When Mrs. Snodgrass opened the door, she exclaimed in surprise—it wasn't Mr. Brooks and Justin, and it wasn't any of her neighbors, either. "Who are you?" she asked, her voice a startled squeak.

"We're from the Virginia Bureau of Investigation," one of the men at the door said in a hard, flat voice. "Here is my identification."

"And mine," another man said.

"We're here to see a Miss, uh, Rebecca Royer. Is she staying at this address?" yet another man added.

"Yes, she is," Mrs. Snodgrass answered. She turned and raised her voice: "Beckie! Three men from the VBI to see you!"

Beckie wanted to see men from the VBI, or even one man from the VBI, about as much as she wanted to lose her appendix without anesthetics. Nobody cared what she wanted, though. She was just a foreigner here, and Virginia, as Sheriff Cochrane had reminded her and Justin, was at war. If she gave these people trouble, they could give her more and worse. "Here I am," she said.

In came the men from the Virginia Bureau of Investigation. They weren't quite so alike as three peas in a pod, but they came close. They wore sober suits, two of gray, one of navy. Their hair was cut short, military style. They were about the same size, and they all had serious expressions. The one in the blue suit said, "Miss Royer, I am Senior Agent Jefferson. With me are Agent Madison and Agent Tyler." They all flashed badges. Jefferson's was gold, the other two silver. The senior agent went on, "May I see your passport, please?"

"Here." Beckie pulled it out of her purse. When you were in a foreign state, you always had to have it with you. She knew that.

Senior Agent Jefferson didn't just examine the passport. He took a jeweler's loupe from his pocket and stuck the magnifier in front of his eye. Even that didn't satisfy him. He used some kind of handheld electronic sniffer on the passport, too. Only after a green light came on did he grudgingly hand the booklet back. "This does appear to be genuine," he said. "What is the purpose of your visit to Virginia?"

"My grandmother grew up in Elizabeth," Beckie answered. "She and Mrs. Snodgrass are cousins."

"That checks out," Agent Tyler said—Beckie thought the one on Jefferson's left was Tyler, anyhow.

"Well, it would, whether or not. The other side isn't about to miss that kind of trick," the senior agent said.

"What other side?" Beckie asked.

Jefferson didn't answer her, or maybe he did: "What was the purpose of your stops in Ohio prior to entering Virginia?"

They think I'm a spy. The certainty she was right filled Beckie with fear. *They even think* Gran's *a spy.* If that didn't prove they'd never had thing one to do with Beckie's grandmother, nothing ever would. "Two of Gran's sisters live in Ohio," she said, as calmly as she could. "We stayed with them before we came here."

"That also checks," Agent Madison said.

"I told you—it would." Senior Agent Jefferson seemed to make a career out of not letting anything impress him. He turned back to Beckie. "And by chance you were one of the people involved in the discovery of Charles Clark's body?"

"If that's what his last name was. I never knew. Nobody here ever used it." Beckie couldn't resist the little sarcastic dig.

She might have done better to let it go. Jefferson looked at her with no expression at all on his face. "What is your opinion of Virginia's social structure, Miss Royer?"

That one had teeth and claws and spines. She didn't need to be a secret agent to see as much. "In California, we treat everybody pretty much the same way," she said carefully. "We try to, anyhow. It seems to work for us."

"And so you would be opposed to our forms of social control?" Senior Agent Jefferson pounced.

If she said no, he'd think she was lying. He'd be right, too. If she said yes, he'd think she was some kind of subversive. What to do? What to do? "Well, if I were black, I sure wouldn't want to live under them," she answered. "But that doesn't mean I want to pick up a gun and start shooting people."

"Would you give other people guns so they could pick them up and start shooting with them?" the VBI man asked.

"No!" There was real horror in her voice, horror and terror enough to make all three agents blink. Tyler stepped back a pace.

They didn't know—she hoped to heaven they didn't know—about Uncle Luke and about the rifles she'd helped smuggle into Virginia.

The agents put their heads together. They plainly believed her. How could they not believe her after she let out a yelp like that? If they did believe her, they also had to believe she had nothing to do with the assault rifle poor Charlie Clark was carrying when lightning and the toppling tree did him in.

"Why were you up on Jephany Knob when you discovered the dead man's body?" Agent Madison asked.

"It felt nice to get out and about. It felt nice to be able to get out and about," Beckie said. "We'd had two days of thunderstorms like you wouldn't believe—like I wouldn't believe, anyway. We don't get that kind of weather in Los Angeles."

"You were with"—Madison paused to check his notes—"Justin Monroe on the knob. What is your relationship with Justin Monroe?"

"We're friends," Beckie said.

"Are you . . . more than friends?"

"No," she said. "We both got stuck here in Elizabeth. Gran and I couldn't get out after the war started, and he and his uncle couldn't leave after the disease broke out." Justin and Mr. Brooks had been exposed to it, too. She tried not to think about that, because it might mean she'd also been exposed.

"Why did you make friends with him and not with some of the young men from Elizabeth?" Madison asked. "And how did it happen that two strangers found the body, not any of the locals?"

"He's been over here a lot because his uncle does business with Mr. Snodgrass," Beckie answered. "He's nice enough, and he's from a city, too. We have more in common than I do with people in Elizabeth." She had less in common with people from

Elizabeth than she did with anyone this side of men from the moon, but she didn't want to say that.

Agent Madison was stubborn. "You only answered the first half of my question," he reminded her.

"Oh. Why were we the ones who found the body? I don't know what to tell you. Dumb luck is the only thing I can think of. It wasn't good luck, either."

"We think it was," Senior Agent Jefferson said. "It shows that treason has reached even out-of-the-way places like this. Treason is a disease worse than the one Ohio turned loose on us, but we'll fix it." He sounded grim and determined. But then he eased—just a little. "I don't believe you were personally involved in it, even if you are from California. Thank you for your time." He and the other two agents left.

Even if you are from California. They assumed she was a radical just because she'd grown up in L.A. By their standards, they were right, too. California and Virginia weren't only two different states. They were two different worlds. But she was stuck in this one now, no matter how much she wished she weren't. She'd got through this first grilling. What was coming up next?

In movies and on TV, the knock on the door always came in the middle of the night. Justin and Mr. Brooks were getting ready to go the the grocery when it came in Elizabeth. They both jumped. They weren't used to company in their motel room.

Justin was closer to the door, so he opened it. He didn't expect to see three somber men in this alternate's somber business suits. "Who are you?" he said foolishly.

"Senior Agent Jefferson, VBI." The one in the middle flashed a gold badge. "With me are Agents Tyler and Madison." The other two men showed silver badges. Jefferson went on, "You would be Justin Monroe, correct?"

"That's right."

"And your uncle is Randolph Brooks? Is he here now?"

"I'm here," Mr. Brooks said from behind Justin. "What's this all about?"

"We have some questions for your nephew, Mr. Brooks, regarding his discovery of the body of Charles Clark," Jefferson answered. He gave his attention back to Justin. "May I see your identification, please?"

They were in a state called Virginia. It was a democracy of sorts. They spoke an English not much different from that of the home timeline. Even so, Justin couldn't tell them to get lost, not unless he wanted to see the inside of a cell in nothing flat. He'd already found that his forged documents were good enough to pass muster. All the same, his heart thumped as he handed them over. Senior Agent Jefferson examined them with a lens and with an electronic gadget, then nodded and passed them back. Justin tried not to show how relieved he was as he stuck them in his wallet and put the wallet in his pocket.

"Thank you," Jefferson said, plainly not meaning it in the least. "Please describe how you found Charles Clark's body. You were not alone on Jephany Knob when you did—is that correct?"

"Yes, uh, sir," Justin answered. Jefferson had to know that. He would have talked with Sheriff Cochrane. If he hadn't, he wouldn't be in Elizabeth at all. Had he already talked to Beckie? Justin wouldn't have been surprised. He said, "Do you people want to come in instead of standing in the doorway?"

"Thank you," the senior agent said again, this time with a little more warmth in his voice. The three VBI men walked into the motel room and sat down on the ratty couch. Without missing a beat, Jefferson continued, "Who was with you?"

"Beckie Royer," Justin said.

"From California." That was Agent Tyler. In the home time-line, people from states like Virginia sometimes looked down their noses at Californians—and vice versa. It seemed all the more true here, where the two states really were separate countries instead of just acting that way.

Justin only nodded. He couldn't very well deny that Beckie was from California. "Nice-looking girl," Agent Madison remarked, as if cutting him some slack. He nodded again. Madison asked, "Why did you go up onto the knob?"

"Just to have something to do. It was nice to get out after the rain." Justin made a face. "If I knew we'd find a body up there, we would have gone somewhere else, believe me."

He got a thin smile from Madison, a stony stare from Jefferson, and a dirty look from Tyler. "How did you find the body?"

"We smelled it." Justin would never forget that odor for the rest of his life. "He must have been dead a couple of days by then. The smell led me to the body, and I saw the gun by it. That's when I called the sheriff." They couldn't think there was anything wrong with that . . . could they?

"You were not on Jephany Knob while the thunderstorm was at its peak?" Senior Agent Jefferson asked.

"You'd have to be nuts to go up there then," Justin said. "It wasn't just raining cats and dogs—it was raining cougars and wolves."

That got him another smile from Agent Madison. But Agent Tyler said, "Clark didn't care about the weather."

"No, sir," Justin agreed, "but he should have, shouldn't he?"

The VBI men only grunted. In the background, Mr. Brooks coughed once or twice. Justin supposed that meant he shouldn't rattle the agents' cages. Part of him knew the coin and stamp dealer was giving him good advice. Part of him insisted their cages needed rattling—after all, they were trying to rattle his.

"How do you feel about Virginia's social system?" Senior Agent Jefferson asked.

I hate it. I think you deserve every pound's worth of trouble you've brought on yourselves, Justin thought. Sometimes the truth wasn't the best answer. If he told the truth here, they would haul him off to an unpleasant jail and do even more unpleasant things to him. He didn't like being a hypocrite, now or any other time. But the question rubbed his nose in the fact that you couldn't always say what you thought.

And so he gave what he thought was a casual response: "The same as anybody else does, I guess." It wasn't even completely a lie. Anybody else from the home timeline was likely to feel the same way he did.

Jefferson's face showed none of what he thought. He probably made a dangerous poker player. "Doesn't it bother you that Rebecca Royer plainly believes in the pernicious doctrine of Negro equality?" he asked.

No, it doesn't bother me, because I do, too. Again, Justin didn't say what he thought. Instead, he just shrugged. "She's from California. What can you expect?"

That was the right answer. All three VBI agents nodded. "Kid's got some sense," Agent Madison muttered.

"Why do you hang around with her, then?" Agent Tyler asked.

Now Justin looked at him as if he wasn't very bright. "We don't spend a whole lot of time talking about politics," he said.

Let them use their imagination to figure out what he and Beckie did talk about.

Agent Madison snickered, then tried to pretend he hadn't. Agent Tyler turned a dull red. Senior Agent Jefferson, grinning as a glacier, said, "Miss Royer states that the two of you are just friends."

"Well, yeah," Justin admitted, and his sorrowful tone of voice made Madison snicker again. Justin went on, "But there's no law that says I can't keep trying, is there?"

"Maybe California has one—I don't know." Jefferson tried a smile himself. It didn't look quite natural on his face. He changed the subject: "Are you acquainted with Irma Davis?"

"Not any more—she's dead," Justin blurted.

"Well, yes. But were you acquainted with her?"

"Sure. She was the waitress at the diner across the street. Uncle Randy and I would eat breakfast over there all the time till she, uh, got sick."

"So you have been exposed to the biological agent Ohio wickedly unleashed on our innocent population?" Jefferson sounded as if he'd listened to too many Virginia newscasts.

"We hope we haven't," Mr. Brooks said before Justin could reply. No matter which of them said it, that was no lie.

"So do we," Agent Madison said. They weren't wearing gas masks and protective gear, the way the paramedics who put Irma in the ambulance had been. Maybe they had nostril filters that didn't show, but those could do only so much. Getting ordered to Elizabeth wouldn't have made the agents jump up and down with glee. Justin wondered if they'd have to get decontaminated after they drove away. He also wondered if that would help.

"What will you do in case of Negro unrest?" Jefferson asked.

"Hope things settle down before too many people get hurt,"

Justin answered. That seemed to satisfy the VBI men. Justin was afraid he knew why: when they thought about people, they didn't include African Americans. And the blacks in Virginia were as ready to hate him because he was white as whites would have been if he were black. Did that have any good answers? If it did, he couldn't see them.

Seven

The first time Mrs. Snodgrass sneezed, Beckie didn't pay much attention. But when she did it four or five times in a row, each sneeze more ferocious than the one before, Beckie said, "Good heavens! Bless you! Are you all right?"

"I . . . *a-choo!* . . . think so." Mrs. Snodgrass made a liar out of herself by sneezing three more times. She pulled a tissue from a box on the end table and blew her nose. Then she sank down onto the couch. "I hope I'm all right, anyway. All that sneezing kind of takes it out of you."

"I guess it would." Beckie looked at her. Was she flushed? Beckie thought so, but she wasn't sure—or maybe she just didn't want to dwell on what her being flushed might mean.

Mr. Snodgrass came into the room. "You trying to blow your head off, Ethel?" he asked. That made Beckie smile—her father and mother teased each other the same way. But he stopped teasing when he got a look at his wife's face. "You okay, sweetie?" Sudden worry roughened his voice.

"I think so," Mrs. Snodgrass said again, but she didn't sound so sure this time.

Mr. Snodgrass walked over, stooped, and pressed his lips to her forehead. Beckie's mom would do that when she or one of her brothers or her sister wasn't feeling well. The lines between Mr.

Snodgrass' eyebrows and the ones that bracketed the sides of his mouth got deeper and harsher. All at once, he looked like an old man. "You're warm," he said. It sounded like an accusation.

"Well, maybe I do feel a little peaked." Mrs. Snodgrass screwed up her face and started sneezing again.

"You reckon I ought to call the doctor?" Ted Snodgrass asked.

"Now how would you get him to come out to Elizabeth with things the way they are?" His wife blew her nose again, as if to say how silly the idea was.

Gran walked in gnawing on a roll. She took one look at her cousin and said, "Ethel Snodgrass, are you coming down sick with that stupid plague?" There never was a situation that Gran couldn't make worse with a few ill-chosen words.

"Of course not," Mrs. Snodgrass, and started sneezing again as if it were going out of style.

"I reckon maybe I will call the doctor," Mr. Snodgrass said. "Just to stay on the safe side." He gave Gran a dirty look. Beckie didn't blame him a bit. He walked into the other room to use the phone. Beckie didn't blame him for that. He couldn't want his wife to hear how worried he had to be.

Beckie couldn't make out what he was saying, either. She could make out his tone of voice, though. If he wasn't scared to death, she'd never heard anybody who was.

She thought of Charlie Clark, and wished she hadn't. Talking about death wasn't the same when you'd seen the real thing. And then she thought about the waitress at the diner. What was her name? Irma, that was it. She was dead, too. Beckie looked at Mrs. Snodgrass, then looked away in a hurry. She didn't care for any of the directions her mind was going in right now.

Mr. Snodgrass walked into the front room again. He said,

"Well, hon, they're going to send an ambulance from Parkersburg. Be here in twenty minutes, a half hour, they told me."

"That's silly," Mrs. Snodgrass said. "It's nothing but a summer cold."

Gran started to say something about that. Beckie kicked her in the ankle, accidentally on purpose. Gran jumped. "You be careful!" she said. "What in the world do you think you're doing?"

"I'm sorry, Gran," Beckie said, meek as you please. If Gran got mad at her . . . well, so what? Gran had got mad at her lots of times, and this wouldn't be the last one—not even close. However much Gran fussed and fumed, Beckie could deal with it. Poor Mrs. Snodgrass, on the other hand, really had something wrong with her. She wouldn't need Gran making things worse.

Mr. Snodgrass nodded to Beckie. "You're all right," he murmured. Gran—surprise!—never noticed.

Beckie started trying to figure out how she felt herself. Was she warmer than she should have been? Did she need to sneeze? To cough? To do anything she wouldn't normally do? She knew that was silly . . . in a way. In another way, it wasn't. When you were with somebody who was all too likely to have a horrible disease, how could you *not* worry about coming down with it yourself?

She heard the ambulance's siren long before it got to the Snodgrasses' house. Sound carried amazingly far in Elizabeth. In Los Angeles, the constant background noise of cars and machinery and airplanes and everything else that went into a big city muffled and blunted distant sounds. Not here. Here, the background noise was birdsongs and the wind in the trees, and that was about it.

The ambulance screeched to a stop in front of the house. All up and down Prunty, people would be coming out to stare at it.

Beckie was as sure of that as if she could see them herself. What else did they have to do for excitement? And, like her, they had something real to worry about.

Mr. Snodgrass let the paramedics into the house. They were dressed in what looked like spacesuits. *A shame space travel never quite panned out,* Beckie thought. Satellites that relayed signals and kept an eye on the weather came in handy. Probes had flown all across the Solar System and men had gone to the moon and Mars. But there didn't seem to be much room for people anywhere but Earth.

All that went through Beckie's mind in less than a second. The lead paramedic hurried over to Mrs. Snodgrass, who'd got visibly sicker while everybody waited for the ambulance. "How do you feel, ma'am?" he asked. Coming from behind his respirator, his voice sounded all ghostly.

"Cold," she answered. "Cold and kind of purple. I mean . . . I don't know what I mean." Beckie shivered. That didn't sound good.

The paramedic stuck a thermometer tip in Mrs. Snodgrass' ear. "What's her temperature?" her husband asked anxiously.

"It's just over 104, sir," the paramedic said. Beckie translated that into the Celsius degrees she was used to. Over forty! That was a high fever. The man went on, "We'll have to take her in." He turned to his partner. "Give these people shots, George."

"Right," George said.

"What kind of shots?" Mr. Snodgrass said.

"Gamma globulin, made from the blood serum of people who've had this thing," the paramedic answered. "We don't know how much good it will do, but it won't hurt you. And you've sure as the devil been exposed."

Mr. Snodgrass took his shot without a word. So did Beckie,

but it wasn't easy—she didn't like needles, not even a little bit. Gran kicked up a fuss. Beckie might have known she would— she kicked up a fuss about everything. "They say gramma glofulin isn't good for you," she squawked. Beckie was sure she'd never heard of gamma globulin in her life before—if she had, she would have pronounced it better. But her mysterious *they* had something to say about everything.

"Look here, ma'am—if you want to get sick, that's your business," George said. "But if you get sick and spread it to other people like this pretty little girl here"—he pointed at Beckie with a gloved hand—"that's Virginia's business. So I'm going to give you this shot no matter what. It's the best hope for staying well you've got."

"They say—" Gran broke off with a yip, because the paramedic did what he'd said he would do. She let him put alcohol on the spot where he'd stuck her. If looks could have killed, though, George would have fallen over on the floor.

Instead, he and his partner put Mrs. Snodgrass on a stretcher and carried her out. The ambulance shrilled away. Gran watched avidly till it turned the corner on State Route 14 and disappeared. Other people's catastrophes were meat and drink to her.

Mr. Snodgrass watched, too, but not the same way. All at once, he looked shrunken and ancient. He'd been spry enough to seem much younger than his years. He suddenly didn't. They'd crashed down on him like a landslide, and his shoulders slumped under the weight of them. "Are you all right?" Beckie asked softly.

He shook himself like a man coming out of cold water. Every bit of his attention had been with the ambulance. Now he had to call himself back to the real world, and it wasn't easy for him. "Am I all right?" He might have been asking himself the same question. After some serious thought, he shook his head. "Well, now that you mention it, no. Ethel and me, we haven't spent more than a handful of nights apart the past forty-five years. It'll be powerful strange, lying down tonight and trying to sleep without her lying there next to me."

"I'm sorry," Beckie said. "I'm sorry about everything."

"I only wish I could have gone with her, but they weren't about to let me," he said. "I guess they worried I might come down with it myself. Like I care! If she's not with me, what difference does it make whether I live or die? But I suppose I might pass it on to other folks if I come down sick, and that wouldn't be right."

How am I supposed to answer him? Beckie wondered. She couldn't see any way at all. The ambulance siren faded into silence. Mr. Snodgrass still seemed old.

"Do you think we ought to be doing this?" Justin asked as he and Mr. Brooks walked toward the Snodgrasses' house. Then he answered his own question: "Well, why not? Way things are, it's about even money who's exposing whom to what."

Randolph Brooks nodded. "That's how I look at it, too. What with Irma breathing in our faces every day for who knows how long, we're not taking any big chances ourselves. And everybody there has already been up close to the virus. Besides, Ted Snodgrass is a friend of mine. These are the least I can do." He hefted the flowers he was carrying.

Justin nodded. Before coming to Elizabeth, he'd wondered if people from the home timeline really could make friends with the locals. Now that he'd got to know Beckie, he saw they could. People were people, no matter where they came from. And this alternate's breakpoint was only a little more than three hundred years old. Folks here still had a lot in common with those from his America.

The weather had everything in common with his America's. It was hot and humid. Walking just the few blocks from the motel to the house on Prunty made sweat stand out on his face and made his shirt stick to him as if it were glued to his hide. He wondered how people had lived, he wondered how they'd worked, before air-conditioning was invented. A lot of them hadn't, or not for very long—doing hard labor in weather like this really could lay you low.

That was one of the reasons the white colonists imported African slaves into the South. They thought the Negroes could stand the climate better than they could themselves—and if the Negroes were doing the hard work in the fields, *they* wouldn't have to. If you thought of people as chattels, as property of the same sort as cattle or sheep, it made good logical sense.

If.

African Americans weren't property any more in this alternate, of course. Even in the states that tried hardest to keep them as slaves, they'd been legally free for two centuries now. But the difference between legally free and legally equal—let alone socially equal—made a gulf as wide as the Grand Canyon. Blacks hadn't been able to cross it anywhere here—except in Mississippi, where they'd put whites on the wrong side of it. People here had a lot in common with those from his America, yes . . . but not enough.

"No wonder Charlie Clark carried a gun," Justin muttered.

"No wonder at all—but don't say that out loud," Mr. Brooks replied.

"Don't say this out loud. Don't say that out loud." Justin knew he was losing his temper, but couldn't seem to help it. "Sure is a wonderful place where we're staying. Oh, yeah."

"Do you want the VBI men knocking on our door again?" the coin and stamp dealer asked. "They will, if you make people in Elizabeth suspicious of you. And if they think you've got anything to do with a Negro uprising, all the gloves come off. Can you blame them for thinking like that?"

You bet I can. Justin started to say it, but a gesture from Mr. Brooks made him hold his tongue. The older man mouthed one word. *Bugs.* Was somebody aiming a parabolic mike at them right now? Had the VBI men planted tiny microphones in their hotel room? In the Snodgrasses' home? In their pockets? It could happen in the home timeline. Here? The technology here wasn't as good, but was it good enough? Justin wouldn't have been surprised.

So Mr. Brooks was talking as if other people were listening. And Justin knew he had to do the same—for now, anyway. "No, of course not," he said. "An uprising would be terrible." That was true . . . from a white Virginian's point of view. Justin's real opinion was better left unsaid if anyone here was listening.

Mr. Brooks knocked on the Snodgrasses' door. Mr. Snodgrass opened it a moment later. "You didn't need to do that," he said when he saw the flowers.

"I think I did," Mr. Brooks said. "And whether I needed to or not, I wanted to. How's she doing? Have you heard?"

"Well, that's right kind of you. Come on in." Ted Snodgrass stepped aside to make room. He didn't seem to want to answer Mr. Brooks' question, but finally he did: "I haven't heard anything really bad. They've got her in intensive care in Parkersburg, and they're doing everything they know how to do. Heaven only knows how I'm going to pay for it all, but I'll worry about that later. We'll see what the insurance covers."

Virginia didn't have government-paid health coverage, the way the U.S.A. in the home timeline did. You bought insurance yourself. If you couldn't afford to, you paid up front when you got sick. If you couldn't afford to do that, you went in hock up to your eyebrows—or you stayed away from doctors. To Justin, that wasn't a medical system. It was more like a bad joke.

Several other bouquets already perfumed the living room. *Neighbors,* Justin thought. He lived in a suburb in northern Virginia in the home timeline. If someone in his family got sick, the neighbors might not even know about it. This alternate had good points as well as bad.

Beckie came into the front room. "How are you?" Justin asked her.

"Worried," she said, which was a straight answer. "You?"

"Yeah, me, too. Still okay so far, though." As he had once before, Justin knocked on his head, as if to knock on wood. He had more confidence in the home timeline's immunity shots than in this alternate's gamma globulin, but he wasn't quite sure he ought to. "Shall we go out back and talk?" he asked.

"Sure. Why not?" she said.

The back yard wasn't likely to be bugged. Of course, if his own clothes were . . . He didn't think that was likely, either, but Mr. Brooks was right to worry. You never could tell. They grabbed a couple of fizzes from the refrigerator and went out. Justin laughed. "Maybe we should have stayed inside after all. It sure is nicer with the air conditioning."

"You grew up in Virginia, and you say that? The humidity here drives me nuts," Beckie said. "But out here we won't have Gran hovering around trying to listen to everything we say."

He laughed again. She wasn't worried about bugging—she was worried about being bugged. "Your grandmother seems nice enough," he said. He'd done that before, too. You had to stay polite about other people's relatives.

The people whose relatives they were didn't have to stay polite. That was part of what made having relatives fun. Beckie sure didn't bother. "Only goes to show you don't know her very well," she said. "She's . . ." She stopped, shaking her head.

"That bad?" Justin was thinking of an aunt of his who drank too much every once in a while. When she did, she liked to tell stories—endless stories—about him as a little boy. That made him awfully glad to have her around.

"Worse," Beckie said without the least hesitation. "Back home, I could put up with her—sort of, anyhow—because we could get away from each other. But we've been in each other's pockets ever since this miserable trip started, and I don't think I'm going to want to have much to do with her for the rest of my life. All she ever does is complain and blame other people. Nothing's ever her fault. If you don't believe me, just ask her."

Justin laughed. Then he realized Beckie wasn't kidding, not even a little bit. "I'm glad you made the trip," he said.

"*I'm* not!" she exclaimed. "I wish I were in California, thirty-five hundred kilometers away from bombs and missiles and uprisings and diseases and everything else."

"Oh," Justin said in a very small voice. He'd wanted to say he was glad she'd come to Virginia because he wouldn't have met her if she hadn't. That would have made a pretty speech. But it was also pretty selfish when you got right down to it, which he hadn't. Coming to Virginia made it a lot more likely that she would get killed. Had he thought about that before he stuck his foot in his mouth? No, not even a little bit.

She raised an eyebrow. He had the bad feeling she knew exactly what he was thinking. "I like you," she said. "Don't get me wrong. As long as I'm stuck here, it's nice that I've made a friend. But I'd still rather be home. If that hurts your feelings, I'm sorry."

"It's okay," he said, which was . . . half true, anyway. "I understand how you feel." He wasn't lying there. He wished he'd thought faster.

She changed the subject on him: "Remember how I was talking about the old United States a while ago?"

"Uh-huh." Justin wasn't likely to forget that, or how much it had scared him.

"If they hadn't fallen apart, this kind of stuff couldn't happen," she said. "States wouldn't go to war with each other whenever they felt like it, because there'd be something bigger to stop them."

She was right—if you ignored the Civil War. But this was one of those times when being right did no good at all. "You're only about three hundred years too late to worry about it now," he pointed out.

"I know." She nodded sadly. "Still, they should have been able to do *something* back then. Have you ever written a story or drawn a picture where you know exactly how you want it to turn out—you've got this image inside your head—but what you end up with isn't like that because you just aren't good enough to make it come out right?"

"Oh, sure." Justin nodded, too. "Who hasn't?"

"That's what the United States reminds me of," Beckie said. "It was a good idea—they were a good idea?—but the people in charge didn't know how to put them together so they'd stick. It's too bad."

"I guess." Justin was lucky enough to come from a timeline where the Constitution took care of the problems with the Articles of Confederation. Till coming here, he took that for granted. He didn't now.

Beckie sighed. "But you're right—it's too late now. Nothing

will make any of the states give up power to some bigger government. And so we'll have lots of stupid little wars. I just hope we don't have any big ones."

"Me, too," Justin said. "How many states have atomic bombs and missiles these days?"

"Most of them," Beckie said, which was answer enough.

"Well, we haven't blown ourselves up yet. They haven't blown themselves up in Europe yet, either," Justin said. "They may be luckier over there than we are, because they've come closer." This was an alternate where people talked about great powers, not superpowers. There were no superpowers here. But there were plenty of great powers, powers with bombs and missiles and know-how enough to ruin anyone who pushed them too far. Britain, France, Prussia, and Italy in Europe, Russia and Ukraine farther east, India, two or three Chinese states, Japan, California, Texas, New York, Brazil, Argentina, Chile . . . Nobody with any sense messed with them. Virginia and Ohio were down in the second rank. They could devastate each other, but couldn't really stand up against, say, Britain or California.

Alliances ran around this alternate like fault lines. Every so often, somebody shifted from one camp to another. When that happened, it was like an earthquake. This alternate had known about nuclear weapons almost as long as the home timeline. They'd been used a few times here, as they had there. But the Big One, the nuclear exchange with everyone throwing everything at everyone else, hadn't happened either place. Maybe that was luck. Maybe it was simply terror.

There were alternates where the missiles *did* fly. Crosstime Traffic didn't operate in many of them. What was the point? Crosstime Traffic needed to trade to stay in business, and those shattered alternates didn't have much worth trading. If this one blew itself to hell and gone, Crosstime Traffic would pull out of here, too. Nobody would have to worry about whether this alternate discovered crosstime travel on its own, not any more.

"Nobody messes with California. We're strong enough so nobody dares," Beckie said, which was just what Justin was thinking. She went on, "When I came east, I never thought I'd get stuck in the middle of this dumb, pointless war." Justin coughed. Under her California tan, Beckie turned pink. "I didn't mean it like *that*," she told him.

"Well, I didn't think you did." He had to act like a Virginia patriot in spite of what he thought about racial politics here. He didn't like that—he despised it, in fact—but he didn't see what he could do about it. How many people like Senior Agent Jefferson and Agents Madison and Tyler did Virginia have? Lots of them.

"Can I say something and not have you get mad?" Beckie asked. "I mean, I know I'm a foreigner and everything. Will you remember?"

"I'll try." Justin thought he knew what she'd come out with. He waited to see if he was right.

She took a deep breath and brought it out with a rush: "If you treated your Negroes the same as you treat other people, then other states couldn't use them to give you trouble."

She was right. She couldn't have been righter, as far as Justin was concerned. He wanted to sink into the ground because he couldn't just come out and say so—it would have been too far out of character. He had to sound the way an ordinary Virginian from this alternate would, even if that meant sounding like a jerk.

"I don't know," he said. "How much have they done to show they deserve to be treated like anybody else?"

"How much of a chance have you given them?" Beckie returned.

"Well, if we did give them a chance like that and they didn't take it, we'd be even worse off," Justin said. "We can't ship them anywhere else, after all." The trouble was, every bit of that was true. Not all problems came with neat, tidy solutions all tied up with a pink ribbon and a perky bow. When two groups hated each other and were stuck on the same land . . . In the home timeline, Palestine had been a disaster for a century and a half, and showed no signs of getting better.

"We don't have troubles like this in California," Beckie said.

"You don't have very many Negroes, either," Justin reminded her.

"No, but we have lots of people from the Mexican states," she said. "Some of them lived there all along. Others come over the border looking for work, because we pay better. We treat them like people. We aren't like Texas. Anybody who isn't white in Texas is down two goals with five minutes to play."

Somebody from the home timeline would probably have said, *Anybody who isn't white in Texas has two strikes against him.* Rounders here, which was close enough to baseball for government work, was most popular on the East Coast.

No matter how Beckie put it, she wasn't wrong. Whites did rule the roost in this Texas, which was bigger than the one in the home timeline. In state after state, people who were on top clung to power, and no bigger authority could make them change their ways. People in the home timeline grumbled about the things the U.S. government did, but North America without any kind of federal rule was no paradise, either.

Beckie probably would have agreed with Justin had he said that. After all, she was nostalgic for even the weak United States of the Articles of Confederation. But he changed the subject instead. He didn't want her to start wondering how he knew some of the things he was saying. What he did say was, "I hope Mrs. Snodgrass pulls through. She seems like good people."

"She can be snippy sometimes, but she's a lot nicer than Gran—that's for sure," Beckie said. "I wonder what her chances are."

"Don't know," Justin said. That sounded better than *not very good*. Mrs. Snodgrass wasn't young, and, if she had the military virus, it was specially designed to kill people. This alternate's bioengineering was thirty or forty years behind what they could do in the home timeline, but the viruses the home timeline was able to cook up thirty or forty years ago were plenty nasty. He went on, "I'm sure they're doing everything they can."

She could have taken that the wrong way—she might have thought he was sneering at this alternate's medicine. But she said, "Yeah, but how much do they know in Parkersburg? She might die there even if she'd get better in Los Angeles."

People from the home timeline often thought of each alternate as a unit. That was only natural. Compared to the people who'd lived in an alternate since birth, Crosstime Traffic workers couldn't help being superficial. But every alternate was as complicated as the home timeline. The locals understood that. People like Justin had to pick it up as they went along. This California was richer than this Virginia, and likely ahead of it in a lot of ways.

Or is that so? Justin wondered. Beckie thought it was, but she came from California. She wasn't . . . what was the term? An objective witness, that was it. What would Ted Snodgrass say about the quality of medicine in Parkersburg? Would he know better than she did? He wasn't objective, either.

The more you looked at things, the more complicated they got. That was one of the first really adult thoughts Justin had ever had, but he didn't even know it.

He said, "They could probably do better in Charleston or Richmond than in Parkersburg, too." Chances were that was true. Charleston was a real city, and Richmond was the state capital. Anybody who was anybody went there.

"Sure." Beckie nodded quickly. "I didn't mean to say Virginia was backward or anything, Justin."

"Okay," he said. Chances were she'd meant exactly that. This Virginia *was* backward in some ways. Only somebody who lived here would say anything different. Since Justin was supposed to live here, he had to act as if he did. He felt like a hypocrite a lot of the time.

But Beckie worried about hurting his feelings. That was worth knowing.

"I hope we don't get it," she said.

"Yeah. Me, too," Justin said. "Every time I sneeze or I itch or I . . . do anything, I guess, I start to wonder—*Is this it? Am I coming down with it?*"

"Oh, good!" Beckie said.

"Good?"

"Good," she said firmly, and nodded again. "Because I feel the same way. It's . . . a little scary." She paused, then added, "More than a little," and nodded one more time. That took nerve, admitting how scared you really were.

Justin gave her a hug. She hugged him back, but she still looked relieved when he didn't hold on real tight or get too grabby. "It'll be all right," he said as he let her go. Then, since she'd been honest, he felt he had to do the same: "I hope it'll be all right, anyway."

Every time Mr. Snodgrass' phone rang, Beckie jumped, afraid it would be the hospital in Parkersburg with bad news. Mr. Snodgrass flinched, afraid of the same thing. Gran didn't seem to act any different from the way she always had. Maybe that meant she was holding things inside. Maybe it meant she didn't feel anything much. Maybe it just meant she didn't hear the telephone ring. You never could tell with Gran.

So far, the hospital hadn't called with the worst news. Mrs. Snodgrass was still alive. But everybody in Elizabeth seemed to be calling to find out how she was. People from Palestine telephoned, too. Mr. Snodgrass seemed to think that was a wonder. "Most of the time, the folks down in Palestine don't care if we live or die, and we feel the same way about them," he said. "It's only a couple of miles, but it might as well be the other side of the moon."

Beckie thought that was strange. Back in Los Angeles, a lot of her friends lived farther from her than Palestine was from Elizabeth. Nobody there thought anything of it. The city stretched for kilometer after kilometer. Things were on a different scale here. Elizabeth and Palestine were rivals, each wanting to be the boss frog in a tiny pond. Elizabeth was the county seat, but Palestine had more shops.

She also thought she knew why people in Palestine were calling. It wasn't just because they felt like burying the hatchet with Elizabeth. They were scared, too. Mrs. Snodgrass and Gran had gone down there to shop. Had they brought the disease with them? Nobody knew, not yet.

When the ambulance came back to Elizabeth two days later, no one seemed much surprised. Hearing the siren screech, Beckie worried that it was coming for Justin or his uncle. Outside of the Snodgrasses, they were the people she knew best here. And she'd needed that hug Justin gave her. If he'd tried to make it into something more than she needed . . . But he hadn't, so she didn't need to worry about that—yet, anyhow. It wasn't as if she didn't have plenty of other things to worry about.

And the ambulance didn't stop at the motel up near the county courthouse. The siren kept right on coming, and the ambulance pulled up three doors away from the Snodgrasses' house. A middle-aged woman burst out of the house, calling, "Come quick! Fred's got it, sure as anything!"

The men in the biohazard suits raced into the house. When they came out a few minutes later, they had a man—presumably Fred—on a stretcher. An IV drip ran down into his arm. They put him into the ambulance and slammed the doors. The ambulance sped away, red lights flashing.

"Fred Mathewson," Mr. Snodgrass said glumly. "He's hardly been sick a day in his life till now."

How do you know? Beckie almost asked. But in a town like this, Mr. Snodgrass *would* know. She offered the most hope she could now: "Maybe he isn't sick with . . . this."

"Maybe." But Mr. Snodgrass didn't sound as if he believed it. "Bessie sure thinks he is, though. And why would they come out if they didn't?" That only proved he had good reasons not to believe.

"They could be wrong," Beckie said. "He could have the flu or something, and his wife could be panicking."

"Bessie Mathewson wouldn't panic if she found a baby rattler in her coffee cup," Mr. Snodgrass said. He knew the woman and Beckie didn't, so she shut up. He went on, "I just wonder why I haven't caught it yet."

"So do I," Gran said. "I thought I did a couple of times. I may yet." She couldn't stand having other people around who were sicker than she was. "I don't know how much longer I can go on."

Probably about another thirty years, Beckie thought. Even if Gran always complained that she was about to shuffle off this mortal coil, she seemed ready to outlast people half her age. Everybody could see it but her. Besides, her aches and pains gave her something else to grumble about.

"Well, we've all been exposed, that's for sure," Mr. Snodgrass said. "The one I worry about is Rebecca here. I've pretty much lived my life, and so have you, Myrtle. Rebecca's got hers all out in front of her. Cryin' shame to see that go to waste."

Gran only sniffed. She might have lived a long time, but she wasn't ready to check out yet. Beckie didn't suppose she could blame her. Who *was* ready to up and die, when you got right down to it? Terminally ill patients in a lot of pain, sure. Their time really was up. Anybody else? No.

Mr. Snodgrass looked in the direction of Parkersburg. "I wonder when we're going to give Ohio something to remember us by," he said.

"Maybe you already have," Beckie said. "Ohio would keep it quiet if you did." Virginia wasn't *we* to her, and never would be. She'd stay a Californian all her life. If you lived in California, why would you want to move anywhere else?

"I don't reckon we've done anything," Mr. Snodgrass said. "You're right—Ohio wouldn't blab, not unless they found a way to lick it. But the consul'd be all over the TV and the radio and the papers and the Net. He'd want people to know we were hitting back."

That made more sense than Beckie wished it did. "I just wish the war would stop so we can go home," she said.

"Don't hold your breath, even after it does stop," Mr. Snodgrass said.

"Huh?" Beckie said brilliantly. Even Gran looked surprised.

"Don't hold your breath," he repeated. "Don't you reckon they'll stick you in quarantine before they let you go home? Even if you don't come down sick—and I hope to heaven you don't—you've sure enough been exposed."

Gran let out a horrible squawk. It had no words. Had it had any, it would have meant something like, *Oh, no!* Beckie felt the same way. And, again, Ted Snodgrass was bound to be right. California wouldn't want to see her and Gran again till it was sure they weren't carrying the latest bioplague. How long would her home state need to decide? She imagined a glass cage with an air filter about three meters thick at one corner and an air lock for passing in food. It wouldn't be just like that—she hoped—but that was the picture that came to mind.

For that matter, what airline would let her and Gran on a plane? Half the passengers—more than half—might be infected by the time they got off.

She wanted to cry. *If you lived in California, why would you want to move anywhere else?* Suddenly, she had an answer. Because your own state wouldn't let you back in, that was why.

"I wish I never came back here," Gran said. By the way she scowled at Beckie, it might have been her granddaughter's fault. Before long, Gran likely would think it was. She wouldn't blame herself, that was for sure.

Before Beckie could ask who'd wanted to see her relatives before she died, thunder rumbled off in the west. For a moment, Beckie took that for granted. You hardly ever saw rain in the summertime in L.A., but it happened all the time here. But even in Virginia, you didn't see rain on a bright summer day.

If it wasn't rain . . . "Is that . . . guns?" Beckie hesitated before the last word, as if she didn't want to bring it out. And she didn't. The deep rising and falling roar went on and on.

"Don't be silly," Gran said.

But Mr. Snodgrass was nodding. "That's guns, all right. Now— are we giving the dirty Ohioans what-for, or are they invading us?"

"Turn on the TV," Beckie said.

He did, but slowly. "I wonder if I really want to know," he said. "If those . . . people are in Parkersburg, they'll grab the hospital— either that or they'll blow it sky-high. My poor Ethel." He sat in front of the screen with his head in his hands, the picture of misery.

Eight

The artillery fire was getting closer. Justin was sure it was louder than it had been the day before. Virginia didn't want to admit that Parkersburg was lost, but it seemed to be.

"What do we do when somebody else gets sick?" he asked Mr. Brooks. One of the things he most hoped was that the coin and stamp dealer would stay healthy. The last thing he wanted was to be stuck in this little town on his own. For one thing, he would start going hungry unless his mother could transfer him some money—the credit cards belonged to Mr. Brooks. Justin was supposed to be nothing but a kid along for the ride. He wanted that supposition to stay true.

"Maybe they haul them down to Charleston," the older man answered. "Or maybe they decide the Ohioans are going to take Elizabeth, too, and so they're welcome to all the diseased people in it."

"That's—disgusting," Justin said. It also sounded a lot like the way governments thought, especially during wartime. Then something else occurred to him. "If we're occupied and Charleston isn't, how do we get back to the home timeline?" *How do I get back to Mom?* was part of what he was thinking. The way he said it, though, sounded much more grown-up.

"Good question," Mr. Brooks said. "If you don't have any other good questions, class is dismissed."

What did that mean? Justin saw only one thing it *could* mean: Mr. Brooks had no idea how they'd get back to Charleston, which meant getting back to a transposition chamber. Justin sent him a resentful look. What good were adults if they didn't have the answers when you really needed them?

Sometimes there weren't any good answers. Was this one of those? *It better not be,* Justin thought, not that he saw anything he could do about it. He didn't want to get stuck here the rest of his life. Oh, it wouldn't be horrible, not the way getting stuck in a low-tech alternate that had never heard of antibiotics or anesthesia would be. But it still seemed backward next to the home timeline. And he would be a foreigner wherever he went, a foreigner with a tremendous secret he could never tell.

Maybe I could settle down with Beckie in California, he thought, and then laughed at himself. How many conclusions was he jumping to with that? Enough to set an Olympic record, probably.

If he talked about such records with her, she'd give him a funny look. They'd never revived the Olympics in this alternate.

"Why aren't there any Virginia soldiers here?" he asked.

"They're coming up Highway 77 from Charleston to Parkersburg—the highway we turned off of to get here," Mr. Brooks answered. "That's the easiest road they can come up—and almost the only road the Ohio soldiers can go down if they want to get anywhere worth having. Nobody cares about Elizabeth, not one bit."

"I guess not," Justin said. "If I weren't stuck here, I wouldn't care about Elizabeth, either."

"You're not the only one," Mr. Brooks said with more feeling than he usually showed about anything. "At least you've got a pretty girl to keep you company. Ted Snodgrass is a nice man—don't get me wrong. But he's not the most exciting company in the world. And he doesn't care about anything now with his wife sick—who can blame him?"

"There's always Beckie's grandmother," Justin said. Mr. Brooks didn't dignify that with an answer. Had he suggested it to Justin, Justin wouldn't have dignified it, either. Some people were just natural-born pains in the neck, and Beckie's grandmother fit the bill.

Something made itself heard over the hum of the air conditioner: a deep diesel growl and the rattle and clank of tracks. While Justin was still trying to figure out where it was coming from, Mr. Brooks said, "Unless we've been invaded by a herd of bulldozers, those are armored fighting vehicles."

"Armored . . . ?" That was a mouthful for Justin.

"Tanks," the older man translated. Before Justin could say, *You're welcome*, Mr. Brooks went on, "Armored personnel carriers. Mobile antiaircraft guns or missile launchers. Self-propelled artillery. Engineering vehicles. That kind of thing."

"Oh," Justin said in a hollow voice, and then, "Oh, boy. How'd they get here, anyway, if they didn't come up from Charleston?"

"Well, they could belong to Ohio," Mr. Brooks said, which was certainly true. "Or they could have come up Route 14 to get here. It's the long way around and not a good road, but they could have done it. They might think they can hit the Ohioans in a flanking attack."

"Flanking attacks. Armored fighting vehicles. All this stuff," Justin said. "How come you talk like a general?"

The mild-mannered, bald coin and stamp dealer looked at

him over the tops of his glasses. "When I was just a little older than you are now, I did a hitch near Qom in the Second Iranian Intervention. When something can mean you keep breathing, it sticks with you."

"Oh," Justin said again, this time hardly above a whisper. For him, the Second Iranian Intervention was like the first one: something he had to remember for an AP test. The books said it hadn't worked out the way the U.S.A. and the European Union wished it would have. He tried to imagine Mr. Brooks in a camouflage uniform with a gas mask and an assault rifle. It wasn't easy.

Then the armored vehicles rumbled past the motel, and he was too busy staring at them to imagine much of anything. "They're Virginian, all right," Mr. Brooks said.

"How do you know?" Justin answered his own question: "Oh— because they're heading west, toward Parkersburg."

"Well, that, too," Mr. Brooks allowed. Justin must have made a questioning noise, because the older man—the veteran— explained, "They've all got *Sic semper tyrannis* painted on their sides, and that's Virginia's motto. *Thus always to tyrants,* you know."

"Right." To Justin, it was what John Wilkes Booth yelled after he shot Abraham Lincoln—one more bit of trivia from an AP class. But was *Sic semper tyrannis* Virginia's motto in the home timeline, too? Probably. Was that *why* Booth shouted it? Till this moment, Justin had never thought about why.

He could figure out which machines were the armored personnel carriers: the ones with soldiers sitting in them. *Brilliant, Justin—brilliant,* he thought sourly. As for the rest of the large, snorting, purposeful machines, he would have thought of all of them as tanks. And he would have been wrong. By Mr. Brooks' expression, he knew each one for what it was. As a—mobile anti-aircraft gun?—clanked past, the coin and stamp dealer murmured, "That's a good design—as good as we've got, except maybe the radar."

"What makes it good?" Justin asked. "How can you tell?"

He found out. "It's got a strong engine, well-shaped armor, and hard-hitting guns," Mr. Brooks answered.

When Justin thought of well-shaped things, he thought of girls and maybe cars. "How can armor be well-shaped?"

"See how it's sloped?" Mr. Brooks seemed eager to explain. "If a shell or a missile hits it, it's liable to bounce off instead of going through. The guys inside appreciate that, believe me."

"I guess they would," Justin said. *They're glad they aren't getting killed*—that was what he meant.

The tail end of the column rumbled past. Mr. Brooks went on, "They'd better get under cover pretty darn quick, that's all I've got to say. Ohio's aerial recon is bound to have picked them up by now."

So many things Justin hadn't thought about. He wasn't sorry to be ignorant of them, either. The home timeline had stayed fairly peaceful the past hundred years, not least because so many countries could create so much havoc that most of them were afraid of starting trouble with their neighbors.

A few minutes later, artillery started booming, close enough to make windows rattle. After a pause, the guns started up again somewhere else. Mr. Brooks nodded approval. "Shoot and scoot," he murmured, like someone reciting a lesson he hadn't thought about for a long time.

The only trouble was, the lesson didn't mean anything to Justin. "Huh?" he said.

"Shoot and scoot," Mr. Brooks repeated, louder this time.

"They fire. The guys they're shooting at pick up the incoming rounds on radar and shoot back. You don't want to be there when the other fellow's shells come down. Trust me—you don't, even if you've got armor around you. So as soon as you fire, you scoot away and send off your next barrage from somewhere else."

Like any other game, this one had rules. Justin had never had to learn them. Mr. Brooks had never given any sign of knowing them. In civilian life, he could put them away because he didn't need them. But when he found himself in the middle of a war, he knew what was going on. Justin wouldn't have worried that *he* didn't—except that his ignorance might get him killed.

He heard high-pitched whines in the air. They swiftly got louder, and were followed by more window-rattling explosions. Mr. Brooks nodded to himself once more. "The Ohioans are plastering the place where the gun bunnies were. I'm pretty sure the guys from Virginia were gone before that stuff came down." He cocked his head to one side and nodded yet again. "Sounds that way. I don't hear any secondary explosions."

Justin knew what those were. He'd run into the term on the news. If something blowing up made something else blow up, that was a secondary explosion. "What happens if shells start coming down in town?" he asked.

"Get flat," Mr. Brooks answered. "If you can find a hole, jump in it. If you've got anything to dig a hole with, dig one. Keep your head down. Pray."

That all sounded practical, even the praying. Just the same, Justin almost wished he hadn't asked the question.

On the TV screen, talking heads blathered about Virginia's brilliant counterattack. Beckie watched Mr. Snodgrass watching as much as she watched the TV herself. He looked much less happy than she'd thought he would. Then an announcer said, "Damage to Parkersburg is believed to be minimal," and she understood. He didn't care about Parkersburg for its own sake. He just didn't want the fighting to hurt Mrs. Snodgrass.

The phone rang. Mr. Snodgrass jumped. He took it off his belt. "Hello?" he said, and then he jumped again. "Oh, hello, Doctor! How is she?" The Ohioans were jamming cell-phone calls, but evidently not all of them. And then Mr. Snodgrass' shoulders slumped. He looked as if he'd been kicked in the face. "Thank you . . . Thank you for letting me know, sir. You stay safe now, you hear?" He clicked off. He didn't really need to say what he said next, but he did anyway: "She's . . . gone." He didn't sound as if he believed it.

"I'm so sorry," Beckie said.

"God will take care of her," Gran said. She got to her feet and pointed at Ted Snodgrass. "You stay there." She went into the kitchen with a more determined stride than Beckie could remember seeing from her.

Where would he go? Beckie wondered. He took off his glasses and pulled out a pocket handkerchief to wipe his streaming eyes. "What am I going to do without her?" he asked, which was a question without an answer. Then he said, "How can I even bury her? I'm on the wrong side of a stinking battle line." That was probably another question without a good answer—maybe without any answer at all.

"I'm sorry," Beckie repeated, feeling how useless words were. "She was a nice lady," she added, which was also true and also inadequate.

"She was . . . everything to me," Mr. Snodgrass said. "Now I've got nothing, and nothing left to live for."

"Here." Gran came back, carrying a glass half full of amber liquid. Ice cubes clinked inside. She thrust it at Mr. Snodgrass. "Drink this, Ted."

"What is it?" Beckie asked.

"A double," Gran answered briskly. Beckie's jaw dropped. Gran didn't usually approve of drinking. Her husband had drunk a lot when he was alive. (Beckie thought she would have drunk, too, if she were married to Gran.) But she went on, "Go on, Ted. It won't make you feel much better, but it'll put up a kind of a wall for a little while." She sounded like someone who knew what she was talking about.

And if she'd told Mr. Snodgrass to go up on the roof and flap his arms and crow like a rooster right then, chances were he would have done that, too. He finished the drink sooner than Beckie thought he could. She'd tasted whiskey before, and didn't like it. But when he got to the bottom of the glass, he said, "Thank you kindly, Myrtle. Most of the time, people who say they need a drink just want one. That one, I really needed."

"Drinks are for bad times more than they're for good ones, I think," Gran said.

"Wouldn't be surprised." Mr. Snodgrass blinked a couple of times. He still didn't look happy, or anything close to happy. But he didn't quite look as if he'd walked in front of a truck any more, either. He nodded to Gran. "I hope you stay well, you and Rebecca."

"And you," Beckie said before Gran could stick her foot in her mouth and spoil the moment. She didn't *know* Gran would do something like that, but it was the way to bet.

"Me?" Mr. Snodgrass shrugged. "Who cares about me at a time like this? I don't even care about me right now."

"Well, you should. You have to watch out for yourself," Beckie said.

"Nobody'll do it for you," Gran put in.

Sure as the devil, that was the wrong thing to say. Mr. Snodgrass clouded up. "Not now, anyway," he said.

Beckie gave her grandmother a look that Gran didn't even notice. *Of course she doesn't,* Beckie thought. She couldn't even come right out and say Gran was a jerk. Gran wouldn't listen. And even the truth got you a name for disrespecting your elders. You couldn't win.

More artillery boomed—off in the distance, yes, but not nearly far enough away. That was especially true because these were incoming rounds, not ones fired by the Virginians. Beckie could tell the difference now. There was one bit of knowledge she'd never imagined she would have. She wouldn't have been sorry to give it back, but life didn't work that way. Too bad.

Then she heard the rumble of diesel engines and the clatter of tracks. Route 14 was only about half a kilometer from the house, and the noise was easy to make out. "What's going on?" she said. "They just went through here a couple of days ago. Now it sounds like they're coming back."

"It does, doesn't it?" Mr. Snodgrass seemed eager to think about anything except what had just happened to him.

"Something will have gone wrong," Gran said. That was just about her favorite prophecy. And here it was much too likely to be true.

Watching the—the armored fighting vehicles, that was what Mr. Brooks called them—fall back through Elizabeth made Justin scratch his head. "Something's gone wrong," he said. "It must have."

"Pretty good bet," Mr. Brooks agreed. "But what? They weren't under what you'd call heavy pressure or anything. Why pull back?"

"Beats me," Justin said. "What do you want to do, ask them?"

To his amazement, the coin and stamp dealer headed for the door. "Why not? Maybe they'll tell us."

"Maybe they'll shoot us, you mean," Justin said. But he followed. He didn't want Mr. Brooks to think he was afraid, even if he was.

"Why should they?" the older man said as he walked outside. "We're just ordinary citizens of Virginia, going about our lawful business and trying to find out what our very own soldiers are doing. It's a free state, isn't it? Except for the sales tax, I mean."

"Funny," Justin said. "Fun*ny*."

Mr. Brooks ignored him. He waved to somebody standing up in the cupola of a tank—and yes, by now Justin recognized tanks and could tell them from the other armored behemoths that clanked through Elizabeth. "Where are you guys going?" Mr. Brooks yelled, pitching his voice to carry through the racket. "Y'all just got here." If he laid the accent on a little thicker than he might have, well, so what?

"We've got to pull back," the real Virginian said—sure enough, he didn't mind talking to a civilian.

"How come?" Mr. Brooks asked in a civilian-sounding way.

The soldier in the tank—they called them trackforts or mobile pillboxes in this alternate—cussed. *He swears like a trooper,* Justin thought. Then the fellow said, "Blacks went and rose up back in the cities. We've got to go and squash them before we can give those Ohio rats what they deserve."

Mr. Brooks swore, too, the way a real Virginian would have

when he got news like that. Justin was very impressed. "What are we supposed to do here?" Mr. Brooks asked.

"Best you can till we get back," the tankman answered.

Justin and Mr. Brooks trotted down the street to keep up with him. "What's going on in Charleston?" Justin called. If Mr. Brooks could do it, he could, too. "My mother's down there," he added, in case the soldier thought he was a spy. It was even true.

"Don't know much. There's some shooting—I've heard that," the soldier said. "Like I told you, just hang on. We'll be back." He waved as the tank clattered away. The pavement on Route 14 was taking a devil of a beating.

"Well, we might have known they'd play that card," Mr. Brooks said.

Justin hardly paid any attention to him. "There's fighting in Charleston!" he exclaimed.

Mr. Brooks nodded. "I heard what he said." He set a hand on Justin's shoulder. "Your mom's a smart woman. She'll know how to stay out of trouble."

"Sure she will—if she has the chance," Justin said. "But what if she was out shopping somewhere or something when the shooting started? She wouldn't have a chance then." Seeing everything that could go wrong was much too easy.

"Even when bullets start flying, they miss most of the time," Mr. Brooks said. "If that weren't so, I'd've been holding a lily for a long time now." He looked past Justin, probably looking back into another timeline a long time before.

"Can we get back to Charleston?" Justin asked.

The older man returned to here and now in a hurry. "We can try," he said, and Justin brightened—till he went on, "if you don't mind getting arrested somewhere south of Palestine or along whatever other highway we use. They're serious about not letting people move around."

Justin pointed to the armored vehicles pulling out of Elizabeth. "What about them?"

"They're soldiers. Soldiers always break the rules," Mr. Brooks said with a shrug. "I know what the consul was thinking when he ordered them to move, though. Maybe they're not infected. If they are, maybe they'll go someplace where other people are infected, too. But whether they're infected or not, he needs them to fight the uprising. And so—they're moving."

"If they're infected, they won't keep fighting long," Justin said.

"Mm, maybe not," the coin and stamp dealer allowed. "But if they're that sick, chances are they'll infect the Negroes they're shooting at. Do you think the consul's heart would break if they did? I sure don't."

"You've got a nasty way of looking at things, don't you?" Justin said.

"Thank you," Mr. Brooks answered, which left him with no comeback at all.

Explosions blossomed with a terrible beauty, there on the TV screen. The rattle and bang of small-arms fire blasted from the speakers. Bodies lay in the street, some white, some black. A white man and woman supported a reeling teenage boy. Blood ran down his face. "Why?" he said as he staggered past the camera.

A box in the corner of the screen said this was Charleston. But it might have been Richmond or Newport News or Alexandria or Roanoke. Uprisings crackled through the whole state—blacks murdering whites, whites savagely striking back.

Beckie watched with a special kind of horror. Every time somebody—who didn't matter—fired a burst from an automatic rifle, she flinched. Finally, she couldn't stand it any more. She put her hands up in front of her eyes. "Oh, my God!" she moaned. "Oh, my God!"

"See how bad it is?" Gran didn't mind when it was bad. If anything, she liked it that way—then everybody was complaining along with her. "Those people are getting what they deserve."

She hadn't talked about Negroes that way when she lived in California. Coming back to Virginia was bringing out all sorts of nasty things Beckie didn't know about and didn't want to know about.

But that wasn't why she couldn't bear to watch the TV right now. "Uncle Luke!" she said. By the way it came out, she couldn't have found anything nastier if she tried for a year.

"What about him?" Mr. Snodgrass asked. "He's the fellow who drove you here, isn't he?"

"My sister's husband," Gran said with a grimace that declared it wasn't her fault.

That would have been funny if the TV were showing something else. The way things were . . . "He was running guns," Beckie said.

"What?" Mr. Snodgrass and Gran said at the same time. No, her grandmother hadn't believed her when she said it before. She might have known Gran wouldn't.

"He *was*," Beckie said. "He dropped us off here, and then he went on to wherever he went to deliver them."

"I never heard anything so ridiculous in all my born days," Gran said. "Lord knows I don't love Luke, but—"

"Why do you say that, Rebecca?" Mr. Snodgrass broke in.

"Because I was in the back seat, and there was this blanket so I couldn't put my feet all the way down on the floor," Beckie said. "And I moved it back to see why I couldn't, and I found all these rifles."

"Why didn't you say something then?" Gran asked, which had to be in the running for dumbest question of all time.

"What was she supposed to say?" Mr. Snodgrass asked. "'Got any ammunition for these?'"

"I was just scared the customs people would find them when we crossed the bridge," Beckie said, remembering *how* scared she'd been and wishing she could forget it. "Wouldn't that have been great?"

A millimeter at a time, Gran got the idea that she wasn't crazy and she wasn't blowing smoke. She should have known that since they got out of Uncle Luke's Honda here in Elizabeth, but . . . As the realization sank in, her grandmother started to get angry. "Why, that low-down, no-good, trifling skunk!" she exclaimed. "I told my sister when she wanted to marry that man, I told her he was . . ."

She went on. Beckie stopped listening to her. Maybe she had told Great-Aunt Louise what a so-and-so Uncle Luke was. Or maybe she'd had a good time at the wedding and kept her mouth shut. That didn't seem like Gran, but it was possible. Either way, what difference did it make now? But Beckie knew the answer to that. Gran had to prove, to herself and to the world, that she was right all along.

"Maybe he wasn't sending the guns—selling the guns—to the Negroes," Mr. Snodgrass said. "Maybe they went . . . somewhere else, anyway." When you had to go that far to look for a bright side to things, weren't you better off leaving them dark? It looked that way to her.

On the television, meanwhile, planes dropped bombs on what was probably the Negro district in Roanoke. Virginia soldiers were herding prisoners—black men, most of them in jeans and undershirts—along a highway. "These fighters will receive the punishment they so richly deserve," the announcer said. He sounded happy about it.

One of the prisoners turned toward the camera and mouthed something. *I'm innocent, I didn't do anything.* Beckie was no great lip-reader, but she could figure that out. Figuring out whether to believe him was another story. There was a Negro rebellion here. Blacks were playing for keeps just as much as whites were. She would have bet anything that some of the men in that column, maybe most of them, were part of the uprising. She also would have bet not all of them were. The white soldiers would have grabbed anybody who looked as if he might be dangerous—if they left someone alone, he might get the chance to prove he was.

Mr. Snodgrass was watching, too. "What a mess," he said. "What a crazy mess." But he didn't seem to see that if white Virginians treated black Virginians better they might not have this kind of mess. He wasn't a bad man, but he just didn't see it—couldn't see it. Maybe that was the scariest thing of all.

Justin nodded to Beckie when she let him into the Snodgrasses' house. "How are you doing?" he asked.

"Not so good," she answered, her voice hardly above a whisper. "Mrs. Snodgrass died yesterday—a doctor in Parkersburg managed to get a call through to let Mr. Snodgrass know."

"Oh. I'm sorry." Justin wasn't just sorry, though—he was jealous. "I still can't reach Charleston."

"Charleston?" Then Beckie remembered. "Your mother's down there. I hope she's okay."

"You ain't the only one!" Justin exclaimed. "Somehow or other, I've got to get down there and find out."

"How?" Beckie asked reasonably. "Those aren't just roadblocks between here and there. Those are roadblocks with soldiers. Can you go sneaking through the woods?"

Justin wanted to say yes. He told the truth instead: "No, I'm a city kid." He wanted to add some pungent comments to that. In the home timeline, he would have; people there took swearing for granted. They weren't so free-and-easy about it here.

"Well, then, do what's smart," Beckie said. "Sit tight. Maybe your mom will be able to get through to you if you can't get through to her."

"Maybe." Justin didn't believe it. He couldn't reach her with his cell phone. Mail was shut down. Telegrams here were as dead as they were in the home timeline. E-mail was wireless, again like home. That was great—convenient as anything—when the system was up. When it went down . . . It was down now, in this part of Virginia, anyhow.

"What could you do there that you can't do here?" Beckie had to be able to tell he meant no even if he didn't say it.

"I could know she was all right. She could know I was all right, too." *Schrödinger's mom,* he thought. *Schrödinger's kid.* Just like the cat in the thought experiment, Justin and his mom weren't all right to each other till each one *knew* the other was all right . . . or wasn't. Uncertainty gnawed at him.

One thing he didn't say, or even think, was, *I could go back to the home timeline.* He couldn't. He knew too well he couldn't. There were too many genetically engineered viruses in the home timeline already. No transposition chamber would come to the room deep under Mr. Brooks' shop till somebody found a cure for this one. The quarantine methods the home timeline used were a

167

lot more effective than roadblocks, with or without soldiers. *Stuck.* The word resounded in his mind. *Stuck. Stuck. Stuck.*

"She'll be the way she is. And you *are* all right—as long as you don't come down sick." Beckie knocked wood. Justin wondered how old that superstition was. Plenty old enough to be in both this alternate and the home timeline. Older than the breakpoint, then. Thinking about things like that hurt a lot less than thinking about the disease or the war or what a mess this assignment turned out to be.

"I'm not the only one to worry about. You're in as much danger as I am," Justin said.

"Everybody in Elizabeth's in danger," Beckie said, which was bound to be true. She laughed. "If I didn't come with Gran, I could be lying on the beach right now, you know?"

"Sorry about that," Justin said.

"You want a fizz?" she asked.

"Sure," Justin said. They walked into the kitchen together. Before she opened the refrigerator, he put his arm around her. She gave him a surprised look—but not too surprised. "Thanks for listening to me," he told her. "Thank for putting up with me, you know?"

"No problem," she said. "It works both ways, believe me." She squeezed him for a second. Then she slipped away. "Fizzes."

He drank his in a hurry. It wasn't just like anything in the home timeline, but it was sweet and cold. It even had caffeine in it. What more could you want? He wondered if he should try something more with Beckie. Something about the set of her mouth told him it wouldn't be a good idea right this minute.

Then her grandmother walked into the kitchen. "Oh," she said. "The boy." By the way she eyed him, he might have been something she'd just cleaned off the floor with a wet paper towel.

"Gran!" Beckie said.

"What?" her grandmother said. "It is him, isn't it?"

Oh, yeah, Justin thought. *You stick in the knife and then you try to pretend you didn't mean anything by it.* And if he got mad—if he told her where to go and how to get there or even if he showed he was annoyed any way at all—she won. She was a sweet old lady, and he was just a punk kid. The very best he could do in the game was break even, and the only way he could do that was to make believe he didn't notice a thing. Kids had had to do stuff like that since Urk the australopithecine broke an antelope bone over Urk, Junior's, head for making a monkey out of himself when he shouldn't have. Nope, you couldn't win.

Beckie's grandmother took a pear out of the fridge, looked at it, breathed all over it, and then put it back and got out another one. She went away, munching. *You chew with your mouth open, too,* Justin thought.

Once her grandmother was gone, Beckie sighed. "I'm sorry," she said. "She's like that."

"What can you do?" Justin said. "My aunt's a world-class dingbat. People choose their friends. Your family? You're stuck with your family."

"Stuck with." Beckie looked in the direction her grandmother had gone. "Boy, you can say that again. I feel like she's my ball and chain."

"Yeah, well . . ." Justin kind of shrugged. "It's not like you're going anywhere much, not the way things are."

"Tell me about it." Beckie cocked her head to one side, listening. "What's that? That rumble, I mean?"

"Sounds like more trackforts and stuff," Justin answered. "But that's crazy. They pulled out to fight the uprising, and now they're coming back? Why would they do that?" Suddenly he

169

flashed on Mr. Brooks, and he knew just what the older man would say, right down to his tone of voice. "I bet the right hand doesn't know what the left hand's doing." He sounded cynical enough to alarm himself.

He made Beckie blink, too. But she said, "I bet you're right. Either that or"—she looked scared—"they're soldiers from Ohio instead."

She probably didn't care about Virginia or Ohio. She didn't want to get stuck in the middle of fighting, that was all. Since Justin felt the same way, he couldn't very well argue with her. Even so, he said, "I don't think they're Ohioans. The noise is coming from that way, not *that* way." He pointed first east, then west.

Beckie listened, then nodded. "It is, isn't it? That's a *little* better." No, she didn't care about either side. After a couple of seconds, she remembered he was supposed to. "I didn't mean—"

"Don't worry about it," he said. "To somebody from a rich state on the other side of the continent, this whole thing probably looks pretty silly."

"Nothing where you can die from a horrible disease or get blown to pieces looks silly when you're stuck in the middle of it." Beckie spoke with great conviction.

"You hit that nail right on the thumb," Justin said gravely.

Beckie started to nod, then gave him a peculiar look. "You come out with the weirdest stuff sometimes, you know?"

"Thanks," he said. This time, he knew exactly what kind of face she made at him. Before he could say anything more, he heard rising screeches in the air.

"What's that?" Beckie said again.

He didn't answer. He knocked her flat, and threw himself flat, too, even while she was squawking. He was dragging both of them toward the kitchen table—*get under something*, he told himself—when the first shells went off. Something slammed into the kitchen wall, and all at once the house started leaking air-conditioned air through a hole the size of his head.

"What was that?" Beckie's grandmother called. "Did anything break?"

Justin lost it. There with artillery raining down on Elizabeth, he started laughing like a loon. Half a second later, Beckie was doing the same thing. They clung to each other. Either they were both crazy or they were an island of sanity in a world gone mad. Part of it, probably, was simple fear of death. The rest was proof of just how far out of it Beckie's grandmother really was.

The shelling lasted only a few minutes. It sure seemed like forever while it was going on, though. When it finally stopped, Justin sat up—and banged his head on the underside of the kitchen table. The bombardment hadn't touched him. Banging his head hurt a lot—but only for a little while.

"Wow," he said in place of something stronger, "that was fun."

"Now that you mention it," Beckie said, "no." She wiggled out from under the table without trying to fracture her skull on it. Then she looked at the hole in the kitchen wall and slowly shook her head. When she muttered, "Wow," too, she seemed amazed. "If that hit one of us, or maybe both of us . . ."

"Yeah," Justin said. "I know."

That hole was about a meter—they would say three feet here—off the ground. Beckie looked at it some more. "Thanks for knocking me down," she said. "I didn't know what you were doing for a second, but—thanks. How did you know to do that?"

For that second, she likely thought he was attacking her. Well, he wasn't, not like that. "My uncle's a veteran," he answered. "He says you've got to get flat if they start shelling. He says a hole in the ground is better, but we didn't have one handy."

"I was trying to dig a hole in the linoleum for a while there." Beckie looked at her hands. So did Justin. She'd broken a couple of fingernails. She wasn't kidding. Justin had wanted to dig a hole and pull it in after himself, too. "Thanks," Beckie said again. She kissed him half on the cheek, half on the mouth.

"It's okay." Justin put a hand on her shoulder. "I mean, it's not okay, but I was glad to do it. I mean—you know."

"I think so." Beckie laughed—shakily this time, not the wild laughter that had kept them both from screaming. "You're all right, Justin. Better than all right."

"Am I?" He was stuck in Elizabeth. He was stuck in this whole alternate. He was liable to get blasted to hamburger or murdered by a plague. All things considered . . . He patted Beckie. "Could be worse, I guess."

Nine

Mr. Snodgrass stared at the hole in the wall. He'd been at the grocery when the Ohioans shelled Elizabeth. The store didn't get a scratch. "You were in the kitchen, you say?" he asked Beckie.

"That's right," she said. "Justin was over. We were getting fizzes, and . . ." Once terror was past, it didn't seem real. She'd been in a car crash once, when a drunk rearended her mother. This was like that, only more so.

He looked at the hole again. "You were lucky," he said.

"Tell me about it!" she exclaimed. That startled a smile out of him. But fair was fair. She had to give Justin his due: "It wasn't just luck. Justin kind of, uh, tackled me and got us both under the table."

"That was smart of him," Mr. Snodgrass said. Had he served in the army? Had he fought in one of Virginia's little wars? Beckie realized she didn't know. He nodded to himself. "That was right smart, matter of fact. Best he could've done with the two of you where you were, I reckon."

"It scared me when he did it," Beckie said. "Then things started blowing up, and I got scared worse."

"Yeah." Mr. Snodgrass' voice was dry. "Almost needed a new diaper myself." Beckie started to laugh, then cut it off when she realized he wasn't kidding. And she'd been about that scared,

173

too, when shells crashed down all around. For a little while, she'd had nothing to do with whether she lived or died. If that wasn't enough to scare somebody, she couldn't think what would be.

"What are we going to do?" she said, not so much because she thought Mr. Snodgrass had the answer as because she had to let it out or burst.

"Well, I'll tell you one thing I aim to do pretty darn quick," he said. Beckie made a questioning noise. He went on, "I'm going to get the spade out of the garage and dig me a good trench in the back yard. Maybe another one in the front yard. Cover over part of it with some corrugated sheet iron I've got and it'll make a tolerable shelter. Better'n ducking under the kitchen table, that's for sure."

"Sounds like a good idea," Beckie said, and then, "Can I help?"

He started to say no. She could tell. But she also watched him change his mind. "Well, maybe you can," he said. "I'm not as spry as I used to be. You don't mind getting dirty and sweaty, you don't mind blisters on your hands, I expect you'll do all right."

Beckie looked down at her palms. They were soft and smooth. Why not? What had she ever done that would toughen them up? She hadn't thought she would get stuck in the middle of—or even on the edges of—a war, though. "I don't care," she said firmly. "Better my hands than my neck."

"Now that's a sensible thing to say." Mr. Snodgrass looked around to make sure Gran was out of earshot. He didn't see her, but lowered his voice anyway: "You've come out with a good many sensible things lately, you have. Makes it hard for me to believe you're really Myrtle's granddaughter, no offense."

"I'm not mad—I know what you mean," Beckie said. They traded conspirator's grins. She went on, "Maybe I got it from my dad's side of the family—I don't know. But I'll tell you something: my mom doesn't get along with Gran, either."

"Can't say I'm surprised." Mr. Snodgrass looked around again. "Back when Myrtle lived here, nobody got along with her."

"Some things don't change, do they?" Beckie said.

"I reckon not," he answered. "Come on, then. Let's get to work."

It was just as hard as he said it would be. Digging a long, deep slit in the ground was no fun at all, not when the temperature and the humidity were both in the nineties. That was how Mr. Snodgrass put it, anyway. To Beckie, who was used to Celsius instead of Fahrenheit, it seemed about thirty-five. It was hot and sticky either way. One of them would dig for a while, then stop and pass the shovel to the other. Beckie didn't let Mr. Snodgrass be a hero—she didn't want him keeling over.

And she didn't feel much like a hero, either. Sweat made her clothes stick to her like glue. She figured she would have to wring out her blouse after she finally took it off. Antiperspirant or no antiperspirant, before long she could smell herself. She did get blisters. They stung. She could go on working in spite of them. She could, and she did.

Mr. Snodgrass got blisters, too. "Haven't tried anything like this in a while," he said while Beckie took a turn with the spade.

"It's tearing your lawn to pieces," she said.

"Well, I can set it to rights one of these days," he answered. "That'll give me something to do. And you notice we aren't the only folks digging in."

Beckie let fly with another shovelful of dirt. She had noticed. Several other people up and down Prunty Street were making shelters. One house had taken a direct hit. That made as good an argument for digging in as any she could think of.

Then Mr. Snodgrass said, "Don't know what we'll do if they start throwing poison gas at us. I couldn't begin to tell you where the gas masks're at. Have to dig 'em out, wherever they are."

"Why do you have gas masks?" Beckie asked.

He paused to wipe sweat off his forehead before answering, "Well, you never can tell." He seemed to think that was reason enough. In a place like this, not far from the border between two states that didn't like each other, maybe it was.

Travel was supposed to broaden you. It sure was teaching Beckie things she'd never known before. The main thing it was teaching her was how lucky she was to live in Los Angeles, a city far from any border, and in California, a state too strong for any of its neighbors to bother much. Before she left for this trip with Gran, she took all that for granted. As she started to dig again, she knew she never would again.

Most of the time, Justin and Mr. Brooks had been the only guests in Elizabeth's only motel. They weren't any more. Virginian soldiers filled the other rooms. They played the TVs in the rooms loud. They played what sounded to Justin like bluegrass music even louder. Being soldiers, they got up too early in the morning and made all kinds of ungodly noise right outside the window.

When Justin grumbled, Mr. Brooks gave him a crooked smile. "Go ahead," he said. "Bang on the walls. Go to their captain and complain."

Justin thought about that for a good microsecond, maybe even a microsecond and a half. "Yeah, right," he said sweetly.

Mr. Brooks laughed. "When I was your age, we said, 'And then you wake up.' Same thing either way."

"We say that, too, but it's not quite the same," Justin answered.

The coin and stamp dealer raised an eyebrow. "We *are* waking up—that's the problem," Justin explained.

"Oh. Well, you're not wrong. But I don't know what we can do about it," Mr. Brooks said. "Besides complain, I mean."

The last four words took away what Justin was about to say. Instead of giving the automatic answer, he had to think about what came out next. "The real problem isn't the soldiers," he said after a few seconds. "The real problem is that we're stuck in this miserable little place when we really need to be down in Charleston."

"That's a problem, all right," Mr. Brooks agreed. "I don't know what we can do about it right this minute, though. Sometimes you've got to sit tight and wait."

"I'm sick of doing that!" Justin said. "It's driving me up the wall."

"Have you got any better ideas?" the older man asked pointedly.

"If I did, I'd be using them, believe me," Justin said.

"Okay. That's fair enough. Just don't do anything dumb, that's all," Mr. Brooks said.

Big, growling trucks carried more soldiers west. Maybe the Negro revolt wasn't going as well as the white Virginians feared it would at first. Or maybe the powers that be in Richmond remembered they had a war on their hands, too. Justin thought leaving the first garrison west of Elizabeth would have been smarter, but he wasn't running things, which was bound to be just as well.

When he grumbled about how dumb the Virginian generals were—he was grumbling about everything these days—Mr. Brooks said, "You know what an oxymoron is, right?"

"Sure—two words you use together, but they don't really go together. Like 'jumbo shrimp' or 'recorded live.'"

"There you go." The coin and stamp dealer nodded. "Those are both good. Well, I've got another one for you—military intelligence.'"

"Uh-huh." Justin nodded. "That would be funnier if it didn't make me feel like crying at the same time."

"I'm sorry. Sometimes you're just stuck, and it looks like we are now," Mr. Brooks said.

Justin wished for some other word. "Stuck, as in permanently?" he asked.

"No, of course not," Mr. Brooks said. "Stuck, as in we can't do anything about it right this minute. Sooner or later, we'll be able to go back down to Charleston again. These crummy little wars between states don't usually last long—both sides get sick of them. And, sooner or later, we'll get back to the home timeline, too. Somebody here or somebody back there will work out an antidote for this virus, and they'll lift the quarantine." He made a sour face. "My guess is, somebody in Ohio already has the vaccine or antiviral or whatever it is. You don't put out what you can't control, not if you've got any brains you don't. Otherwise, you turn it loose on your own people, too. You lose friends doing that."

"I guess!" Justin said. "So how long do you figure we'll be cooped up in Elizabeth?"

"I don't know. Weeks? Months, tops." Mr. Brooks gave Justin a sidelong glance. "With all the soldiers in town, maybe you've got more competition for your girlfriend."

"I don't think so," Justin said. "Beckie doesn't like soldiers. Near as I can tell, she *really* doesn't like Virginia soldiers. She thinks they're a bunch of racist . . . well, you know. It's not like she's wrong, either."

"No, it's not," Mr. Brooks agreed. "But when the other guy has an assault rifle and you don't, telling him what you think of him isn't the smartest thing you can do. Which is why *you* were smart to keep your voice down here. The walls in this place are as thin as they can get away with, or five centimeters thinner."

"Yeah, I've noticed." Justin paused. "Do you really think we'll be stuck here for months?" If Mr. Brooks had said they'd have to stay in Elizabeth for the next twenty years, it could hardly have seemed worse. Justin's sense of what a long time was and the older man's were two very different things.

"I don't know for sure," Mr. Brooks answered. "I don't see how I can know for sure, or how anybody else can. I'm only guessing. But that's the best guess I've got. When we do get back to the home timeline, we ought to pick up a hazardous-duty bonus. Your mom, too."

"Oh, boy," Justin said in hollow tones.

"Don't knock it," Mr. Brooks told him. "Hazardous-duty pay . . . Well, when you think about how long we may be here, that could add up to a pile of benjamins. Maybe not as good as a college scholarship for you, but it'll sure pay a lot of bills once you're enrolled and everything."

"Oh, boy," Justin said again. What with this mess, it looked as if he'd have to start college a year later than he'd thought he would. If he had to go through applying again . . . *If I have to do that, I'll scream*, he thought. Going through it once was like going to the dentist for something nasty. Going through it twice would be like the dentist forgetting something and making you come back. Justin didn't even want to imagine that.

And what kind of hazards was his mother going through down in Charleston? The TV hadn't talked much lately about the fighting there. Was it petering out? Or was it so bad, the authorities didn't dare admit anything about it? He had no way to know. More than anything else, he wanted—he needed—to find out.

Beckie quickly decided that showing herself in Elizabeth wasn't a good idea. None of the soldiers in town gave her a hard time, exactly, but she didn't like the way the uniformed men followed her with their eyes. In California, men whistled at girls they thought were cute. They didn't do that here. Beckie didn't need long to figure out that a sharp, short cough meant the same thing. Those coughs were compliments she could have done without.

She was glad when Justin came over to visit. Gran and Mr. Snodgrass made dismal company. And she felt safer when Justin was around. She knew that made no sense. What could he do against somebody with a gun? What could he do against a bunch of somebodies with guns? Nothing, obviously, except maybe get shot. She was glad when he came anyway.

Even the back yard was ruined. The trench, and the sheet metal heaved over it, were a stark reminder of what could happen. She and Justin went out there with fizzes anyhow. It let her escape from Gran, and that felt more precious than rubies right now.

Something flashed on top of Jephany Knob. "What do you think that is?" Beckie asked. "Looked like . . . sun off glasses?"

"Where?" Justin hadn't seen it. Beckie pointed. *With my luck,* she thought, *it won't happen again, and he'll think I've gone nuts.* But it did.

"I bet the Virginians have observers up there," he said. "I bet they're watching whatever's going on farther west."

"I bet you're right," she said. "That sure makes more sense than anything I thought of. What are we going to do, anyway?" The question didn't exactly follow on what came before, but it didn't exactly *not* follow, either.

"Try to stay alive till this mess blows over. What else can we do?" Justin answered. "I only wish I were back in Charleston, or in Fredericksburg."

"I'm sorry," Beckie said. "I wish I were back in L.A., too, believe you me I do. But I'm here, in Elizabeth, with my grandmother. Happy day."

"And I'm here with my uncle. Happy day back atcha," Justin said. "And we kind of hang on to each other so we don't go quite as crazy together as we would by ourselves."

"That's about the size of it," Beckie said. "But I think I would have liked you even if we'd met without all this . . . stuff going on."

"Do you?" He smiled. "That's good."

"It really is," Beckie said seriously as she nodded. "You'll laugh or you'll get mad—or maybe you'll laugh *and* you'll get mad, I don't know—but I wasn't sure I *could* like anybody from Virginia. You people do things a lot different from the way we do in California. We wouldn't have some of our own people rising up against us because we don't treat them as well as the rest. . . . Are you blushing?"

"I don't know." Justin got redder still. "Am I?"

"You bet you are." Beckie thought about laughing, but she didn't think coming out and doing it would be a good idea. "Why are you blushing? Because of the way your state treats Negroes?" Justin had said he didn't like that, but she still wasn't sure she believed him.

"Well . . . partly," Justin said. "That's not all of it, though."

"Yeah?" Now Beckie was intrigued. "What's the rest of it?"

He *really* blushed then—red as a sunset. "I can't tell you," he muttered.

She poked him in the ribs. He jumped. "You can't say stuff

like that," she told him. "What is it? Why can't you tell me? What are you, a spy from Ohio or something?"

That got rid of the blush. Justin turned pale instead. "No!" he said. "Good Lord, no!" He sounded furious. And he was, because he went on, "And don't say anything like that out loud, for heaven's sake! It's not true, but it can get me shot anyway. There's a war on, in case you didn't notice."

"Sorry," she said. She was, too, but she could see how that might not do her much good—or Justin, either. "I *am* sorry," she repeated. "That was dumb of me."

"Uh-huh." He didn't try to tell her she was wrong. Instead, he pointed to a shell crater down the street. "They mean it here."

"I said I was sorry." Beckie started to get mad, too. But she knew she'd goofed, so she added, "I'll try not to do anything like that again."

"Okay." Justin nodded. "Fair enough."

"If you weren't acting like a mystery man . . ." Beckie said.

"I've got to get out of here," Justin muttered. She wondered what he meant. Away from her? *That would be great*, she thought, and really did get angry. Or did he mean away from Elizabeth? The way it sounded, he meant out of this world. But if he meant that, where did he aim to go?

She let out a little of her frustration—not much, but a little—by saying, "There's stuff you're not telling me, isn't there?"

"No," he said quickly: too quickly, in a way that couldn't mean anything but yes.

As if he did say yes, she went on, "It's okay. Who am I gonna tell it to? Gran?" Her own laugh came close to hysteria. Even she thought that was funny. "Sheriff Cochrane?" That wasn't funny—it was scary. "The soldiers?" That wasn't just scary—it was ridiculous.

"You've got it wrong," he said. She didn't believe him, even if he sounded a lot more convincing now than he did in his moment of surprise and dismay. He went on, "This is as silly as your idea about the United States holding together."

"I didn't say that was true. I just said it would've been neat." Beckie looked at him. "You're lying to me. I don't know why—maybe you've got reasons, even if I can't imagine what they are. But if you are, since you are, we're not going anywhere much, are we?"

"I guess not," he said sadly. "I'm sorry, Beckie." He didn't even bother pretending he wasn't lying any more. "You don't know what you're asking for, and I can't tell you. I wish I could, and I never thought I'd do that in a million years."

"You can," she said. "All you have to do is open your mouth and tell the truth."

"It's not that simple." He set his can of fizz on the grass not far from the trench. Then he started to walk away.

"Where are you going?" Beckie called after him.

"Back to the motel," he answered over his shoulder. "You called it—this isn't going anywhere. It's too bad, but it's not. Take care. I'll see you." By which he had to mean, *I won't see you.* He kept walking.

She couldn't even tell him he was wrong, because she knew he was right. Knowing that and liking it were two different critters. Beckie stared after him till ambush tears scalded her cheeks.

Justin sat on the edge of his bed in the motel room, his face buried in his hands. "It's not the end of the world," Mr. Brooks said. "You did the right thing, if it makes you feel any better."

"It doesn't," Justin said. "Chances are we weren't going anywhere anyway. That doesn't make me feel any better. Beckie

183

was—is—about the only nice thing here, and now that's ruined. What am I supposed to do, dance a jig?"

"This room isn't big enough," Mr. Brooks said. Justin looked up long enough to give him a dirty look, then submerged again. The older man went on, "I'm sorry—sort of. But one of the things you're *not* supposed to do is give away the Crosstime Traffic secret. California probably has the technology and the computer power to build transposition chambers if they get the idea that they can. And wouldn't that be fun?"

"Well, this California would be better than some of the other countries in different high-tech alternates," Justin said.

"Sure. But better isn't good, and you can't pretend it is." Mr. Brooks sighed. "Chances are we're fighting a losing battle. Sooner or later, somebody else *will* figure out how to go crosstime, and we'll have to deal with it. But later is better than sooner. We need to be in a stronger position ourselves. Look at the slavery scandal we just went through. How are we supposed to tell other people to play nice if we can't do it ourselves?"

"Beats me." Justin looked up again, a little longer this time. "Not easy for me to care right now."

"I know," Mr. Brooks said. "Breaking up always feels like the end of the world."

Justin started to ask him what he knew about it. He started to, but he didn't. Something in the coin and stamp dealer's expression told him it wouldn't be a good idea. Randolph Brooks didn't talk about himself a whole lot. That didn't mean he hadn't done things—more things than Justin had, plainly.

"It does get better eventually," Mr. Brooks went on. "You know what they say—time wounds all heels." Did they say that? If they did, did Beckie's grandmother know about it? Thinking about Beckie, or even her annoying grandmother, still hurt like anything. But Mr. Brooks still hadn't finished: "It's bad while it's going on, though. There's not much you can do about it. I'm sorry. I'm extra sorry 'cause she's a nice kid."

She's no kid! But that was one more thing Justin didn't say. Mr. Brooks was old enough to be his father, so Beckie probably did look like a kid to him. (Thinking about his real father, who had a new lady friend, also hurt.)

"What am I going to do?" Justin did ask. "I can't just stay cooped up in here 24/7."

"She doesn't hate you—or it doesn't sound like she does, anyway," Mr. Brooks said. "You can just be friends friends, if you know what I mean. Maybe that's better than nothing."

"Maybe." Justin didn't sound as if he believed it. The reason was simple: he didn't. "Seeing her is liable to hurt too much to stand."

"Chance you take," Mr. Brooks said with a shrug. "If it does, you don't do it anymore." He could afford to sound callous. He wasn't the one who'd just had things fall apart. Justin remembered reading something somewhere. *Nobody dies of a broken heart. You only wish you could.* Whoever said that hit it right on the button. Justin sure wished he could.

Before he could answer, the Virginia soldiers who'd taken over the rest of the motel started yelling and cussing a mile a minute, maybe faster. Some of them sounded furious. Others sounded scared. They were all shouting about somebody named Adrian. Whether that was a first name or a last, Justin had no idea.

Then someone said something he couldn't misunderstand: "He's got it!"

He and Mr. Brooks looked at each other. They both mouthed the same one-syllable word. It wasn't a big surprise that Adrian—or one of the soldiers, anyway—had come down with the disease. It was loose in Elizabeth. Everybody knew that. But knowing it didn't make this welcome news.

"Which one is Adrian?" Justin couldn't keep track of all the soldiers quartered here.

"I think he's the big guy, the one about your size," Mr. Brooks answered. When he said he thought something like that was so, it was, to about four decimal places. He wasn't a coin and stamp dealer for nothing. He remembered what things were worth, and all the technical details of why they were worth what they were worth, too. So why wouldn't he keep track of soldiers?

Men running in army boots outside the motel room sounded a lot like stampeding elephants. Elephants didn't shout and use foul language, though. Or if they did, people couldn't understand them, which amounted to the same thing.

"I think Millard's got it, too!" somebody yelled. That produced more cussing. Most people in this alternate swore less than they did in the home timeline, but the soldiers were an exception.

"Here comes the doc!" another soldier hollered. They were all carrying on at something above the tops of their lungs.

"What can you do for 'em, Doc?" Three or four people shouted the same question at once.

"If it is the plague, I can't do anything much," the military doctor answered. That was the meaning of what he said, anyhow. It came out a lot warmer. He also had unkind things to say about everyone who'd been born in Ohio for the past three hundred years. "And their dogs, too," he added.

"Can you give 'em that globby stuff?" a soldier asked.

"Gamma globulin, you mean? I can give the shots, but I don't know how much good they'll do, or if they'll do any," the doctor said. "That stuff is supposed to keep them from getting sick in the first place, not to cure them if they do. But I'll try it. I don't see how it can hurt them. And I'll tell you what y'all better do."

"What's that?" Again, several soldiers asked the question.

"Get away from this place," the doctor told them. "Go on— scoot. The less contact you have with infected people, the better your chances of staying well. And send Major Duncan close enough so I can shout at him. This cell-phone jamming is a pain in the. . . . Anyway, I need to talk to him. We have to figure out whether hanging on to this miserable little piddlepot of a town is worth the risk."

Some of the soldiers tried to volunteer to stay and help the military doctor take care of their buddies, but he wouldn't hear of it. He loudly and foully insisted it was his job, not theirs. Randolph Brooks nodded approval of the men for wanting to stay and of the doctor for not letting them. "He's got nerve, that one," the coin and stamp dealer said.

"Has he got any sense?" Justin asked.

Mr. Brooks shrugged. "He's already about as exposed as you can be. For that matter, so are we." Immunity shots or not, Justin could have done without the reminder.

Once given orders to leave, the soldiers didn't seem sorry to go. It got quieter than it had been since they took over most of the motel. It got so quiet, it made Justin nervous—he'd grown used to their racket, even if he didn't like it.

After a bit, someone—Justin supposed it was Major Duncan—came close enough to shout questions at the doctor. Justin had trouble making out what they were. The major didn't want to get real close, which was understandable enough. The doctor's answers were plain enough and then some. He knew how to project. Justin wondered if he'd done drama in high school or college.

"How are they?" he yelled. "They're sick, that's how they are. And they're getting sicker by the minute, too." A pause. A muffled question from the major. "Yes, the men lodged here are exposed," the doctor answered. "Everybody in this whole blinking village is exposed . . . sir." Another pause. Another question. "Yes, sir. That includes you."

This time, the major let out a very audible squawk. "Can we get them out without risking more people?" he asked, loud enough for Justin to hear him just fine.

"Won't be easy," the military doctor shouted back. "I'm not equipped for isolation cases. . . . Yes, I should have been. . . . Yes, those people are idiots, but what do you want me to do about it now?"

Justin glanced over at Mr. Brooks. The older man's face bore a small, tight smile. "Some things don't change from one alternate to another," he said in a low voice. "The people in the field, the people at the front, have to work around their stupid superiors. Law of nature, near enough."

"I guess," Justin said vaguely. He'd missed some of the back-and-forth between the doctor and the major.

"You can pull out if you want, sir," the doctor shouted. "I'll stay behind and take care of them. . . . No, I'm not afraid, or not too much. I don't go into combat, the way you do. I do this instead."

Justin thought he would rather go into combat. If you had a gun, at least you could shoot back. What could you do to a tailored virus?

The major said something. "Sir, I would have to disobey that order," the military doctor yelled back. "The patients come first. I'll stay here."

"He can play on my team any day," Mr. Brooks murmured. "Oh, yeah."

Another yell from the Virginia major. The doctor didn't answer. The major said something else. This time, Justin understood it perfectly. It made the officer's opinion very plain, even if it was on the earthy side. The doctor only laughed. "Thank you, sir. I love you, too," he said, and blew the major a loud, smacking kiss.

"Yeah," Mr. Brooks said. Justin found himself nodding. Whatever else you said about the doc, he had style. As for Justin . . . Justin had the beginnings of an idea.

Beckie had started to hope Ohio troops would occupy Elizabeth. Her passport and Gran's had Ohio visas that were just as good as their Virginia visas. Maybe the Ohioans could do something about the disease they'd turned loose, and wouldn't keep people in the area they occupied all cooped up. If Beckie and Gran could get back to Columbus, they could probably get back to California.

She knew better than to say anything about that where Mr. Snodgrass could hear it. He was, and had every right to be, a good citizen of Virginia. If he saw soldiers from Ohio on Prunty Street, he might take out a shotgun and bang away at them. If he did, the Ohioans would likely shoot him and another dozen people besides, but that might not be enough to stop him.

The soldiers from Virginia were pulling out of Elizabeth again. The disease had got its teeth into them. Beckie thanked heaven that she'd stayed well, and her grandmother, and Mr. Snodgrass. She wasn't so sure he was glad to be well. He might want to join his wife. He kept going on about how empty his days were without her. Beckie didn't know what to tell him. What *could* you tell somebody who said something like that?

Off to the west and northwest, Virginian guns still fired at the

Ohioans in Parkersburg. "How many shells come down on the enemy, and how many land on people who just happen to be in the way?" Beckie wondered after one especially noisy bombardment.

"Can't make an omelette without breaking eggs," Gran said. To her, nothing Virginia did in the war could be wrong. To Beckie, the cliché sounded like one of the things the mysterious *they* would say.

"It's a hard business, war," Mr. Snodgrass said. "A lot of the time, I think nobody comes out on top."

"I think you're right," Beckie said. Gran just sniffed. Beckie hadn't really expected anything else from her.

Somebody rang the doorbell. If that wasn't one of the soldiers wanting something, it was likely to be Mr. Brooks and Justin. Beckie couldn't very well tell Justin not to come over. This wasn't her house—it was Mr. Snodgrass'. And Justin hadn't done anything to make her hate him. He'd just . . . disappointed her. If he couldn't tell her whatever it was that he couldn't tell her, then they weren't going anywhere no matter what. She'd wondered if they might. Knowing they wouldn't—was too bad.

Even if they weren't, he still made better company than anybody else in Elizabeth. That was pleasant and annoying at the same time, because it reminded her of what might have been.

Today, though, Mr. Brooks beat him to the news: "The doctor who's treating the sick soldiers has come down with it himself. It's a shame—he was brave to stay with them."

"I haven't felt so good myself lately," Gran said. She was healthy as a horse, but she couldn't stand to let anybody upstage her.

"Are they sick, or are they dead?" Mr. Snodgrass asked.

"At least one of them is dead," Justin said before Mr. Brooks could answer.

Beckie sent him a sharp look. He didn't sound nervous or scared, the way he should have talking about something as nasty as germ warfare. He sounded excited. His eyes glowed. He was thinking about something, all right. What? Did Mr. Brooks notice? He didn't seem to. To Beckie, it stuck out like a sore thumb.

"That's a terrible business," Mr. Snodgrass said. "These Ohio people, you want to hunt 'em with coon hounds and tree 'em and shoot 'em right out of the blamed tree, is what you want to do." He didn't sound as if he was kidding. Would he have felt the same way if his wife hadn't got sick and died? He might have. Virginia was his state, and Ohio was giving it a hard time.

"It's pretty bad, all right," Mr. Brooks said. "I don't like it that our doctors haven't got a better handle on the disease by now."

Mr. Snodgrass' face had been angry. It went grim, which was scarier. "I don't like that, either, not even a little bit. What does it say about our state? Only two things I can think of, and neither one of 'em is good. Maybe our people are just asleep at the switch, and they'll get off the shilling and set to work in a spell. That's bad enough, but the other choice is worse. Maybe those Ohio, uh, so-and-so's"—he nodded to Beckie before he said that, so it would have been something juicier if she weren't around—"really are smarter than the best we've got. If they are, that means we're in deeper than anybody figured on when the war started."

"I hope not," Mr. Brooks said. "If people decide that's so, the consul won't get reelected, and you can take that to the bank."

"If it is so, he shouldn't be," Mr. Snodgrass said. "They ought to ride him out of town on a rail instead."

Listening to older people going on about Virginia politics was the last thing Beckie wanted to do. At least getting hit by a shell was a quick end—a lot quicker than getting bored to death. Any second now, Gran would jump in, and Beckie already knew all her opinions by heart. Gran's politics were a little to the right of Attila the Hun's.

"You want a fizz, Justin?" Beckie asked. "We can talk about stuff outside." She was still mad at him—how couldn't she be, when he was hiding things from her?—but talking with him had to be more interesting than what was happening in here.

His face lit up. "Sure!" Did he think she'd forgiven him already? If he did, he was dumber than she thought he was.

Going into the kitchen sobered her. Mr. Snodgrass had nailed a plywood square to the outside of the house to keep the bugs out and the air conditioning in till he could get proper repairs made. Every time Beckie saw the hole that square patched, she remembered the dreadful day she almost died. If not for Justin, she might have. She couldn't very well forget that, even if she was mad at him.

The half-roofed trench in the back yard was sobering, too. The cold fizz can felt wonderful against her blistered palm. Of all the things she'd never imagined herself doing, digging like a mole stood pretty high on the list.

"How you doing?" Justin asked her, maybe a little too casually.

"Fair to partly cloudy," she answered, which made him blink till he figured it out. She went on, "You've got something on your mind—something pretty big, I think. Can you tell me what it is?"

He looked alarmed. "How did you know? Uh, I mean, I do?"

She laughed at him. "Yeah, you do. And I know 'cause it's written all over your face. C'mon. Spill."

If he tried to deny it, she intended to push him into the trench and then maybe bury him in it. You could lie some, but you couldn't lie that much. He thought about it—she could tell. But then he must have decided it wouldn't work. He spoke in a low voice, to make sure nobody inside could hear: "I think I know how to get back to Charleston and make sure my mom's all right."

"Oh, yeah? How?" Beckie asked. He told her. She stared at him in admiration mixed with horror. "You're nuts!"

"I know," he answered, not without pride. "But I'm gonna try it anyhow."

Ten

Three minutes after four in the morning. That was what Justin's watch said as he got out of bed and slid into a pair of jeans. In the other bed, Mr. Brooks went on breathing smoothly and evenly. Justin tiptoed toward the door. If Mr. Brooks woke up and heard him go, the older man would stop him.

Don't let him hear you, then, Justin told himself. He opened the door and unlocked it so he could close it quietly. He slipped out. The latch bolt still clicked against the striker plate. Justin froze, waiting for Mr. Brooks to jump up and yell, *What was that?* But the coin and stamp dealer went right on sleeping.

The door to the room where the doctor had put Adrian and Millard stood open. Justin knew why: the doctor was sick, too, and couldn't close it. Nobody else—certainly not the motel manager—wanted to come near enough to take care of it.

Justin's thought was, *I haven't caught this thing yet, and I've had every chance in the world.* He hoped his immunity shots from the home timeline really were good for something. Going in there was risky for him, but a lot less than it would have been for other people. And he couldn't do what he wanted to do—*what I need to do,* was the way he put it to himself—without taking the risk.

Except for a distant barking dog and an even more distant

whip-poor-will, everything was quiet. *Quiet as the grave,* Justin thought, and wished like anything he hadn't. He slipped into the motel room. Millard and the doctor both lay unconscious, breathing harshly. Adrian wasn't breathing at all—he'd died the day before.

If he weren't more or less Justin's size, this scheme would have been worthless. Since he was . . . Justin hadn't thought he was squeamish, but stripping a dead body made his stomach twist. It also wasn't as easy as he'd thought it would be, since Adrian had started to stiffen.

Pants and shirt and service cap fit well enough. Justin worried more when he started putting on Adrian's socks and shoes. He had big feet, and he was still in trouble if the luckless soldier didn't. But the socks went on fine, and the heavy combat boots were, if anything, too long and too wide. He laced them as tight as he could. His feet still felt a bit floppy in them, but he could put up with it.

One of the packs against the wall was Adrian's. So was one of the assault rifles. When Justin slung on the pack with the longer straps, he gasped at how heavy it was. It had to weigh thirty kilos, easy. Were these Virginians soldiers or mules? The rifle added another four kilos or so. He'd thought he was in pretty good shape. Trying to lug all this stuff around made him wonder.

Dawn was painting the eastern sky pink when he tramped out of the motel room. From the outside, he was a Virginia soldier. On the inside, he felt half proud of his own cleverness, half nervous about what happened next. If things went the way they were supposed to, he'd be a hero. If they didn't . . . He hadn't thought much about that.

The extra weight he was carrying made the shoes start to rub. He trudged west anyway. If he got a blister on his heel, then he did, that was all. He remembered the blisters on Beckie's palms. She'd kept on digging after she got them. He could go on, too.

When the sun came up, he rummaged in Adrian's pack for something to eat. Canned ham and eggs wouldn't put Jack in the Box out of business any time soon. He ate the ration anyway. By the time he finished it, his stomach stopped growling. Not seeing anything else to do with the can, he tossed it into the bushes by the side of the road. He didn't like to litter, but sometimes you were just stuck.

Somewhere up ahead was the Virginia artillery unit that had been shooting at Parkersburg. He really was limping before he'd gone even a kilometer, though. He wouldn't get to them as fast as he'd hoped to.

Then he heard a rumble up ahead. A string of trucks and armored fighting vehicles was heading his way. He got off the road and onto the shoulder to let them by. Or maybe they wouldn't go by. Maybe they would . . .

One of the trucks stopped. The driver, a sergeant not far from Mr. Brooks' age, shouted to Justin: "What the devil you doin' there, son?"

"I was supposed to go out with the rest of the soldiers in Elizabeth," Justin answered, "but I was on patrol in the woods and I twisted my ankle. They went and left without me." He put his limp to good use.

"Some people just use their heads to hang their hats on," the sergeant observed. "Maybe you were lucky you were off in the woods. They've had people die from that disease." He used ten or fifteen seconds describing the plague in profane detail.

"Tell me about it," Justin said, "Millard's a buddy of mine. I think Doc has it, too." He figured he could earn points by knowing what was going on in Elizabeth.

"If Doc makes it, there isn't a medal fancy enough to pin on his chest," the noncom said. "Anyway, pile on in. We can sort out all this stuff"—he used a word something like *stuff*, anyway—"when we get back to Charleston."

"Will do!" Justin said joyously. They were heading just where he wanted to go. He'd hoped they would be. He limped around to the back of the truck. One of the men inside held out a hand to help him up and in. "Thanks," he told the local, who nodded.

Everybody already in the truck kind of squeezed together to give him just enough room to perch his behind on one of the benches against the side of the rear compartment. It was a hard, cramped seat, but he couldn't complain. He was in the same boat as all the other soldiers there. *All the other soldiers,* he told himself.

With a growl from its diesel engine, the truck rolled forward again. It ran right through the exhaust fumes of the vehicles in front of it. Justin coughed. A couple of soldiers lit cigarettes. He coughed some more. But nobody else grumbled about it, so he kept quiet. Lots more people smoked in this alternate than in the home timeline. Virginia raised tobacco. He tried to tell himself this one brief exposure to secondhand smoke wouldn't do him in. He hoped he was right.

And the truck was heading for Charleston! Once he got there, all he had to do was ditch his uniform, put on the regular clothes he'd stashed in his pack, and find Mr. Brooks' coin and stamp shop. Mom would be there, and everything would be fine. He nodded happily. He had it all figured out.

Somebody knocked—pounded, really—on the door to Mr. Snodgrass' house. "I'll get it," Beckie called.

"Thank you kindly," Mr. Snodgrass said from his bedroom.

In Los Angeles, the door would have had a little gizmo that let her look out and see who was there. No one in Elizabeth bothered with such things. Living in a small town did have a few advantages. She opened the door. "Hello, Mr. Brooks," she said, and then, after taking a second look at him, "Are you okay?"

"Well, I don't exactly know." He was usually a calm, quiet, self-possessed man. He seemed anything but self-possessed now. "Have you seen Justin? Is he with you?"

"No, he's not here," Beckie said. "I haven't seen him since the last time the two of you came over."

"Then I'm not okay." Mr. Brooks' voice went hard and flat. "He's gone and done something dumb. I wondered if the two of you had gone and done something dumb together." A beat too late, he realized how that had to sound and added, "No offense."

"But of course," Beckie murmured, and the coin and stamp dealer winced. She went on, "Whatever he's doing, he's doing without me, thank you very much." And then she realized she had a better notion of what Justin was up to than his uncle did.

Her face must have given her away, because Mr. Brooks said, "You know something."

"I'm not sure. Maybe I do." *What am I supposed to say?* Beckie wondered. Justin had told her, but he plainly hadn't told Mr. Brooks. But shouldn't Mr. Brooks know what he was doing? He was Justin's uncle, and as close to a parent as Justin had here.

Yeah, and Gran is as close to a parent as I've got here. Beckie knew that wasn't fair. Unlike Gran, Mr. Brooks had a clue. Even so . . .

"What's he gone and done?" the coin and stamp dealer asked, sounding like somebody braced for the worst.

"Well, I'm not exactly sure." Beckie was stalling for time,

but she wasn't quite lying. Justin hadn't known exactly what he would do, because he didn't know how things would break. *I'll just have to play it by ear,* he'd said.

"He's figured out some kind of scheme to get back to Charleston, hasn't he?" Mr. Brooks said. "I told him that wasn't a good idea, but I could see he didn't want to listen. Is that what's going on?"

Beckie didn't say yes. But she didn't have to. Once Mr. Brooks got hold of the ball, he didn't have any trouble running with it.

He clapped a hand to his forehead. "Oh, for the love of . . . Mike. Does he think he can con the soldiers into giving him a lift? They won't do that, not unless . . ." He hit himself in the head again, harder this time—so hard, in fact, it was a wonder he didn't knock himself flat. He'd done his best not to cuss before. What he said now almost peeled the paint off the walls in the front hall. "I'm sorry," he told Beckie when he ran down, though he obviously didn't mean it.

"It's okay," she said. "I want to remember some of that for later, though."

Mr. Brooks smiled a crooked smile. "Hope you never get mad enough to need it, that's all I've got to say. One of the soldiers who got sick was about his size. Did he tell you that?"

Again, Beckie didn't say yes. Again, she didn't need to.

"Okay, the good news is, he didn't go off somewhere and then come down with the disease. The gypsies didn't steal him, either—though right now they're welcome to him." Mr. Brooks didn't sound as if he was joking. "The bad news is, he doesn't know thing one about what being a soldier means."

"And you do?" Beckie asked.

She regretted the question as soon as the words were out of

her mouth. The ordinary-seeming bald man looked at her—looked through her, really. All of a sudden, she had no trouble at all imagining him much younger, and very tired, and scared to death. "Oh, yeah," he said softly, his eyes still a million kilometers— or maybe twenty or twenty-five years—away. "Yeah, as a matter of fact, I do."

"I'm sorry," she whispered. Then she wondered what she was sorry for. That she'd doubted him? Or that, a long time ago, he'd seen and done some things he'd likely tried to forget ever since? Both, maybe.

He shook himself, almost like a dog coming out of cold water. "Well, as a matter of fact, so am I," he said. "But I'm afraid I'm not half as sorry as Justin's going to be. The question is, will he be sorry because he did something dumb and got caught, or will he be sorry 'cause he did something dumb and got killed?"

"K-Killed?" Beckie had trouble getting the word out.

"Killed," Mr. Brooks repeated. "If he's going back to Charleston . . . Well, there's still fighting there. Those soldiers weren't doing much up here. The powers that be might have decided to get some use out of them after all. You learn to fight same as you learn anything else: you practice, and then you do it for real. Justin's never had any training. He knows how to load a gun, and that's about it. If he doesn't give himself away, he's liable to stop a bullet because he doesn't know how *not* to."

"What can you do?" Beckie asked.

"Good question. If I had a good answer, I'd give it to you, I promise," Mr. Brooks said bleakly. "He's been gone since some time in the night. I don't know when—I was asleep. He could be in Charleston already. Or he could be in the stockade already, if they figure out he's no more a soldier than the man in the moon. I hope he is. If he's in the stockade, I have time to figure out what happens next. If they just throw him into a firefight . . . Nobody can do anything about that."

"Why would they even think he was only pretending to be a soldier?" Beckie asked. "Nobody would look for anyone to try something like that. Most people don't want to be soldiers, and the ones who do join their state's army for real."

"Right the first time. Right the second time, too. You're a smart kid, Beckie. Only thing is, I wish you weren't," Mr. Brooks said. "Because if you are right—and I'm afraid you are—Justin's in a lot more trouble than if you're wrong."

"We've got to be able to do . . . something." Beckie wished she hadn't faltered there at the end. It showed she didn't know what that something might be.

"Yeah," Mr. Brooks said. "Something." His tone of voice and the worried look on his face said he didn't know what, either.

The convoy of trucks and armored fighting vehicles from around Elizabeth was getting close to Charleston. They'd already been waved through two checkpoints outside of town. The sergeant in charge of this—squad?—was listening on an earpiece and talking into a throat mike. He wore three chevrons on his sleeve, the way a U.S. Army sergeant would have. So what if they were upside down? Justin still knew what they meant. Virginia officers' rank badges were a different story. But if an officer told him what to do, he knew he had to do it.

"Okay, guys—here's what's going on," the noncom said. Everybody leaned toward him. "Those miserable people are still making trouble in Charleston. We're going to help make sure they stop."

He didn't really say *people*. The word he used was one nobody in the U.S.A. in the home timeline could say without proving he was a disgusting racist. People in the home timeline cussed a lot more casually than they did here. But words that showed you were a racist or a religious bigot or a homophobe . . . Nobody in the home timeline, not even people who really were racists or fanatics or homophobes, used those words in public. The taboos were different, but they were still taboos.

That thought was interesting enough to make Justin stop paying attention to the sergeant for a few seconds. If he were a real soldier, he didn't suppose he would have done that. *Then I can't do it now,* he told himself.

"We're going down to Florida," the sergeant said. That confused Justin till he remembered it was the name of a street in Charleston. The Virginian went on, "Stinking people have a barricade there." Again, *people* wasn't the word he used. "We'll be part of the infantry force that flanks 'em out, and the guns with us'll help blow 'em to kingdom come. Any questions?"

Justin had about a million, but nobody else said anything, so he didn't see how he could. The real soldiers probably knew the answers to most of them. One of those real soldiers, a guy named Eddie, tapped Justin on the leg and said, "Stick close to Smitty and me. I know you're out of your unit and everything. We'll watch your back, and you watch ours. Deal?"

"Deal." Justin didn't know exactly what kind of deal it was, but he'd find out. Any kind of deal seemed better than getting ignored.

Was he supposed to be excited now or scared? The other guys in the truck just seemed to be doing a job. Were they hiding nerves? How could they help having them?

They got into Charleston a few minutes later. The town, as Justin remembered from his brief acquaintance with it, had a funny shape. It stretched for several miles along the northern bank of the Kanawha River, but it never got very far from the stream. It didn't seem as big as the Charleston of the home timeline. It probably wasn't. That Charleston was a state capital, and the center of all the bureaucracy that went with being one. *This* Charleston was just a back-country town.

And it was, right this minute, a back-country town in trouble. Automatic weapons sounded cheerful. *Pop! Pop! Pop!* That brisk crackle might have been firecrackers on the Fourth of July. It might have been, but it wasn't. The occasional boom of cannon fire had no counterpart in the civilian world.

Whump! Justin wondered what that was, but not for long. A hole appeared, as if by magic, in the canvas cover over his truck's rear compartment. No, two holes—one on each side, less than a meter above soldiers' heads. Those were—couldn't be anything but—bullet holes.

He wanted to yelp, but nobody else did, so he kept quiet, too. How much of courage was being afraid to embarrass yourself in front of your buddies? A lot, unless he missed his guess.

"Hope one of the bad guys fired that," Smitty said. Justin stared at him, wondering if he'd heard straight. Smitty went on, "You feel like such a jerk if you get hit by a round from your own side."

"Hurts just as much either way," somebody else said. The soldiers' helmeted heads bobbed up and down.

The sergeant had the earpiece in one ear again, and a finger jammed in the other to keep out background noise. "Listen up," he said when he heard whatever he needed to hear. "When we get out, we go right two blocks. Then we turn left and go down five or six blocks—something like that, depending on what things look like. Then we turn left again, and we come in behind the people's position. Got it?"

"Right, left, left," Eddie said. "We got it, Sarge."

"Okay. Don't foul it up, then," the noncom said, or words to that effect. The truck stopped—stopped short, so that Justin got heaved against the guy in front of him. "Out!" the sergeant screamed. "Out! Out! Out! Move! Move! Move!"

Justin jumped out. So did the other soldiers. They all started running as soon as their boots hit the asphalt. The crackle of gunfire was a lot closer now, and didn't sound nearly so cheerful. *Those are real bullets*, Justin thought as he pounded after Eddie and Smitty. *If one of them hits me, it'll really mess me up.*

The African Americans firing those bullets had a genuine grievance against Virginia. The state *did* treat them badly. Were Justin an African American from this Virginia himself, chances were he would have been shooting at the white men in camouflage uniforms himself. He understood the fury and desperation that sparked the uprising.

All of which meant zilch to him now. However good their reasons for picking up a gun might be, those African Americans were trying to maim him or kill him. He didn't want them to do that.

Some of the other Virginia soldiers fired back. Most of them squeezed off a few rounds from the hip as they ran. They couldn't have expected to hit anybody, except by luck. But if they made the rebels keep their heads down, the ammunition wouldn't go to waste.

"*Aii!*" A soldier toppled, clutching at his leg.

Two of his buddies grabbed him and dragged him into a sheltered doorway. He howled and cursed all the way there. He left a trail of blood all the way there, too. It shone in the sun, red as red could be.

Something cracked past Justin's face. Automatically, he ducked. Then he looked around. Would Eddie and Smitty and the other soldiers think he was a coward because he flinched? He didn't need long to figure out that they wouldn't. They were ducking, too.

He saw a muzzle flash up ahead. *Somebody there is trying to kill me.* It wasn't a thought, not really. He felt it in his bones as much as anything else. He flopped down behind a trash can and fired a few shots at . . . at what? He tried to think of it as shooting at the flash. That way, it seemed like a video game. If those flashes stopped, he wouldn't be in danger any more—from there, anyhow.

But part of him knew this was no game, and he wasn't shooting just at a flash. A man held that assault rifle, a living, breathing, sweating man. What was that living, breathing, sweating man thinking as bullets cracked past *him*? What would he think if bullets slammed into him?

Justin wondered if he really wanted to know. All he wanted was to stay alive. If that meant he had to kill somebody else . . . He wished he'd done more thinking about that before he decided to put on Adrian's uniform.

Much too late to worry about it now.

"Come on!" Smitty yelled. Justin couldn't stay behind the trash can forever, even if it would have been nice. He scrambled to his feet and ran on.

He wasn't more than a few blocks from Mr. Brooks' shop. That meant he wasn't more than a few blocks from Mom. If he could slip away . . . But he couldn't. He was caught in the middle of something much bigger than he was. People were watching him to make sure he stayed caught in it, too. What would they do if he tried to duck out? Arrest him if he was lucky, he supposed. Shoot him if he wasn't.

Down toward the river for a few blocks. Then turn left and swing in on the Negro rebels. It all sounded easy when the sergeant laid it out in the truck. But the sergeant went down with a worse leg wound than the first one Justin had seen.

Another soldier went down, too, shot through the face. The back of his head exploded, blown to red mist. He couldn't have known what hit him—he had to be dead before he finished crumpling to the pavement. That didn't make watching it any easier.

And when the Virginia soldiers turned in, they found black rebels banging away at them from behind a barricade of rubble. Several Virginians fell then. Eddie went down, clutching at his arm. Justin dragged him into a doorway before he really thought about what he was doing. "How bad is it?" he asked.

"I'll live." Eddie's face was gray. "Right now, I'm not so sure I want to. Give me a pain shot, will you?"

"Sure." But Justin didn't know where to find the syringe, not till Eddie groped for it with his good hand. Then, awkwardly, he stuck the soldier. Even more awkwardly, he dusted antibiotic powder onto the wound and bandaged it. Eddie would need more work than that—Justin could see as much. He was no doc himself, though. All he could do was all he could do.

"Thanks, man. You did good." Eddie sounded much better than he had a few minutes earlier. The pain shot—morphine? something like it, anyway—kicked in fast. The wounded man went on, "You were on the ball, getting me out of the line of fire."

"You would have done the same for me." And Justin didn't just say it—he believed it. You didn't show you were scared so you wouldn't look bad in front of your buddies. And you didn't let them down so they wouldn't let you down, either. He hadn't needed long to figure out some of what made soldiers tick.

"Get moving!" somebody yelled from the street. "We'll do pickup on the wounded pretty soon."

Justin didn't want to get moving, any more than he'd wanted

to get up from behind the trash can. But Eddie was watching him, and so was the soldier—officer?—with the loud voice, and Smitty would be. This wasn't good, but what could he do? He ran out and got moving.

The first thing he ran past was a body. His ill-fitting boots splashed in the blood. Soldiers were scrambling over the barricade. Someone got hit climbing over it and fell back. That didn't make Justin enthusiastic about trying it himself. He couldn't stay here, though—again, too many people were watching him. Up he went, and thudded down on the other side. Bullets cracked past him. The blacks might have been driven from the barricade, but they hadn't given up.

He found out how true that was a few seconds later. A skinny African American kid who didn't look more than fourteen leaned out of a second-story window and aimed an assault rifle at him. Justin fired first, more because his finger was on the trigger and the gun pointed in the right direction than for any other reason. The kid dropped the rifle and fell out of the window, *splat!* on the sidewalk. Half his head was blown away.

Justin stopped and stared and threw up. How he missed his own shoes he never knew, but he did. *He would have killed me,* he thought as he spat and retched and spat some more. *He would have killed me if I didn't shoot him.* It was true. He knew it was true. And it did not a dollar's worth of good.

Somebody thumped him on the back—Smitty. "First one you know you scragged yourself?" he asked.

"Yeah," Justin choked out.

Smitty thumped him again. "That's never easy. You reckon he would have cared a rat's patootie if he nailed you?"

"No," Justin managed. The Negro kid was doing everything he could to kill him. He'd never had any doubts about that.

"Well, come on, then, before somebody else is luckier than that guy was," Smitty said. "It gets easier, believe me. After a while, you don't hardly feel a thing."

"Terrific," Justin said. Smitty smacked him on the back one more time, as if he really meant it. Maybe the genuine Virginia soldier thought he did. *After a while, you don't hardly feel a thing.* The scary part was, it was likely to be true. And he was liable to get shot if he just stood here.

Mr. Brooks hadn't talked about this. You probably *couldn't* talk about this, not unless you were talking to somebody else who already knew what you were talking about. Now Justin did, even if he wished he didn't. Wishing did him as much good as it usually does—none at all. He ran on, past the corpse of the kid he'd killed. He felt as if it were the corpse of his own childhood lying there in a spreading pool of blood.

Without Justin around, Elizabeth felt even more like Nowhere to Beckie than it had before. She had nothing to do except read and watch TV. Virginia TV mostly wasn't worth watching. She got into a screaming fight with Gran over nothing in particular. The two of them sulked around each other for the next several days.

She didn't realize till much, much later that her grandmother was worried about her. Seeing that Gran showed worry by snapping at people, Beckie's not noticing wasn't the hottest headline in the world.

She was sorry afterwards, but not sorry enough to apologize. Gran wouldn't have said she was sorry if torturers started pulling her toenails out with rusty pliers. The next time Gran admitted a mistake would be the first.

Beckie almost hoped . . . She shook her head, appalled at

herself. How could she wish—*almost* wish—the disease on somebody she was supposed to love? Never mind that her grandmother
was maybe the least lovable human being she'd ever known. She
hoped it just meant she was stir-crazy, not that she was some kind
of monster.

She wished she could talk it over with Justin. He would have
understood. But he was down in Charleston, doing . . . what?
Whatever a soldier had to do. Whatever they told a soldier to do.
What would that be? Beckie didn't know, not exactly, and she
was glad she didn't. Whatever it was, she suspected it wouldn't
be so easy to get out from under as Justin had thought.

I should have told him. She sighed and scowled and shook
her head. Would he have listened? She laughed, not that it was
funny. Justin was the sort of person who listened only to himself.
He sure hadn't paid any attention to his uncle, and Mr. Brooks
had more sense in his big toe than Justin did all over.

Of course, who didn't think he had sense? Or she, for that
matter? Gran was convinced she knew what was what and Beckie
was the one who needed to rent a clue if she couldn't buy one.
And if that wasn't crazy, Beckie had never run into anything that
was.

What about me? Beckie wondered. *Am I sure I'm right when
I really don't have any idea what's going on?* It didn't look that
way to her, anyhow. Here they were in Elizabeth, and here they
were, stuck. You didn't need to be Sir Isaac Newton or Benjamin
Franklin to figure that out.

What did Franklin say about the United States? *We must all
hang together, or assuredly we shall all hang separately*—that
was it. Actually, he was talking about the people who signed the
Declaration of Independence, but these days people remembered
the quote as a kind of early epitaph for the country that couldn't

stay united. Now all the states were separate, and all of them positive they were better off because of it.

"Penny for 'em, Rebecca," Mr. Snodgrass said from behind her.

She jumped. She hadn't known he was there. When somebody asked her something like that, she felt obliged to tell the truth. "You'll laugh at me," she said, and spelled it out.

He didn't laugh, but he did smile. "You ought to start a movement," he said. "Bring back the United States!"

"Oh, I know it wouldn't work," Beckie said. "None of the consuls and presidents and governors and what have you would want their power cut. No state would want people from any other state telling it what to do, or soldiers from another state on its land. But if things didn't break down in the first place, maybe we'd all be Americans now, not Virginians or Californians or what all else. Maybe we wouldn't fight these stupid little wars all the time. One's always bubbling somewhere."

She studied the expression on his wrinkled, lived-in face. It was the strangest blend of amusement and sorrow she'd ever seen. He knew much better than she did how dead the United States were. But if by some miracle they weren't . . . then what? His wife would still be alive. There wouldn't be shell holes down the street. He wouldn't have healing blisters on his hands from digging trenches. Beckie wouldn't, either.

"It would be nice," he said slowly, his voice—wistful? "Or it might be, if you could make states get along with each other like you say. I don't know how you'd do that, though. They couldn't figure it out three hundred years ago, and we are what we are now on account of they couldn't. Maybe you ought to write a book about what things would be like if we still had united states here."

Had he said that in a different tone of voice—and not a *very* different tone, either—he would have been mocking her. But he meant it. She could tell. "I never thought about writing anything longer than e-mail and school papers," she said.

"I bet you could if you set your mind to it," he said, and he still sounded serious. "You've got a way with words."

Beckie suspected a way with words wasn't enough to get her a book. The idea might be worth thinking about, though. Writing was a better job than plenty of others she could think of.

"I don't reckon we want any writers in the family," Gran said. Beckie didn't know she'd been listening. Her grandmother went on, "We go in for things that are a lot more ordinary, a lot more reputable."

If anything could make Beckie bound and determined to try to write a book, a crack like that was it. But before she could give Gran the hot answer she deserved, somebody rang the doorbell. "Who's that?" Mr. Snodgrass said. He went off to take a look. Beckie followed him so she wouldn't have to talk to Gran. Her grandmother followed, too, so she could go on giving Beckie what she imagined was good advice.

"Hello, Ted," Mr. Brooks said when Mr. Snodgrass opened the door. "And good-bye, too, I'm afraid."

"What's up?" Mr. Snodgrass asked. "Why do you think you can get out of here? Why do you want to try?"

"Because Ohio soldiers are coming up the road from Parkersburg," Mr. Brooks answered. "They're not coming very fast. I think the Virginians mined the road before they pulled out. But I don't want to get occupied, thank you very much. I'm going to try to get back to Charleston. I have a chance, I think."

"Take me with you," Gran said.

"What? Why? I can't do that!" Mr. Brooks yelped.

"Because I'm not about to let my sister lord it over me on account of her state's stolen the part of my state where I'm staying," Gran said. That probably made perfect sense to her. It didn't make much to Beckie, and she would have bet it didn't make any to Mr. Brooks.

She would have won her bet, too. He said, "I'm sorry, Mrs., uh, Bentley, but I don't see how I can take you."

But then Beckie said, "Maybe you'll need help finding Justin."

Mr. Brooks looked at Mr. Snodgrass. "Will you tell them they're crazy, Ted? I don't think they're paying any attention to me."

"Well, maybe they are and maybe they aren't," Mr. Snodgrass said. Mr. Brooks looked as if he'd been stabbed. Mr. Snodgrass went on, "When the Virginians come back—and they will—there's liable to be a big old fight around these parts. Can't blame a couple of furriners 'cause they don't care to get stuck in the gears."

"I'm no furriner!" Gran said indignantly. Beckie stepped on her foot. Gran was too dumb to see Mr. Snodgrass was doing their work for them.

"I suppose you want to come along, too," Mr. Brooks said sarcastically.

"Nope—not me. Don't want anything to do with the big city," Mr. Snodgrass said. "If a fight rolls by here, I'll take my chances. Don't mind a bit."

That flummoxed Mr. Brooks. He looked at Gran and Beckie. "You sure? I'll find you a hotel or something when we get there. With Justin and his mother in town, my place is crowded like you wouldn't believe."

Did he think that would stop Gran? "My credit card still works, I expect," she said. And if she ever ran low, Mom and Dad back home would pump more money into her account. Maybe cell phones in Charleston weren't jammed. *If they aren't*, Beckie thought, *I can talk to California again. My folks must be going out of their minds.* Then something else occurred to her. *Maybe they're worried about Gran, too.* That wasn't kind, which didn't mean it wasn't true.

Mr. Brooks opened and closed his mouth several times. He looked like a freshly caught fish. He didn't want to take them— that was as plain as the nose on his face. But he wasn't rude enough to say no. "How soon can you be ready?" he asked. "I want to get out of here, and I'm not kidding."

"Twenty minutes?" Gran said.

"Be at my motel at"—Mr. Brooks looked at his watch—"half past, then."

Most of the time, you could count on Gran to take too long to get ready to go wherever she was going—and to complain that everyone else was making her late. Here, she seemed to see that Mr. Brooks wasn't kidding and would leave if she didn't show up on time. She threw things into her suitcase as fast as she could. Beckie didn't pay a whole lot of attention to her, because she was busy doing the same thing.

"Thank you for taking care of us and putting up with us for so long," she told Mr. Snodgrass. Gran might have waltzed out the door without saying good-bye.

"I was glad to have you here, especially after. . . ." He didn't finish that, but Beckie knew what he meant. He went on, "Are you sure you're doing the right thing?" He answered the question himself before she could: "But you want to find out about your young man, don't you?"

"He's not exactly mine," Beckie said, which wasn't exactly a

denial. She added, "Besides, I've got to keep an eye on Gran."
That was all too true. Mr. Snodgrass nodded, understanding as
much.

Gran had already started trudging up the walk to the street.
Pulling her wheeled suitcase along by the handle, Beckie hurried after her. Mr. Snodgrass closed the door behind them. It
seemed very final, like the end of a chapter. What lay ahead?

Eleven

Justin wore a dead man's uniform. He ate from a dead man's ration cans, plus whatever else he could scrounge. The real soldiers called it liberating or foraging, depending on whether they smiled when they said it or not. A lot of it was just plain stealing. They didn't seem to care. Once Justin's belly started growling, neither did he.

The real soldiers . . . Justin grimaced. If he wasn't a real soldier himself by now, he never would be. He'd helped a wounded buddy. He'd shot somebody. He'd *killed* somebody. He might have killed other people, too, but he was sure of that one kid. He expected to have nightmares about it, maybe for the rest of his life. The only thing he'd missed was getting shot himself. Even if the Negro rebels had a better cause than the Commonwealth of Virginia, he couldn't make himself sorry about that.

"Smitty," the sergeant said.

"Yeah, Sarge?" said Justin's newfound friend—comrade, anyway.

"Take the new guy here and go on over to that sandbag revetment on the corner for first watch. Cal and Sam will relieve you in three hours."

"Right, Sarge," Smitty said, which was the kind of thing you said when a sergeant told you to do something. He nudged Justin.

"C'mon, man. If they couldn't shoot us out in the open, they won't shoot us when we got sandbags in front of us, right?"

"I guess," Justin said. "I hope." Smitty laughed, for all the world as if he were joking. He'd proved himself, so Smitty must have thought he was. Oh, joy.

"Safer here than back there," Smitty said when they got to the revetment. He kicked a sandbag. "Bulletproof as anything."

He was bound to be right about that. The sandbags were two and three deep, and piled up to shoulder height—a little less on Justin, because he was tall. "Yeah, it'd take a rocket to punch through this stuff," he said, and then, "Have they got rockets?" He wondered if Beckie's uncle had smuggled in some along with the rifles she'd had her feet on.

"I reckon they do," Smitty answered, and then said something rude about Ohioans' personal habits. "But they've got a lot more small arms. We came up against everything from the stuff we carry down to .22s and shotguns. Must give them nightmares about keeping everybody in cartridges."

"Yeah." Justin hadn't worried about such things. If you had an empty gun, though, what could you do with it? Hit somebody over the head—that was about all. He looked west through the smoke. "Sun's finally going down. I don't think I've ever been through a longer day."

"Not over yet. Some of those people"—again, not the exact word Smitty used—"will be sneaking around at night. IR goggles are good, but they aren't as good as the real eyeball."

"Uh-huh." Justin hoped his voice didn't sound too hollow. He didn't know how to use his goggles. Adrian had been trained with them. Justin hadn't. *I'll turn them on and hope for the best,* he thought. *That should be better than nothing, anyhow.*

With all the smoke in the air, it got dark fast. Justin flipped down the goggles, then fumbled till he found a switch. Now he watched the world in shades of black and green. Night-vision goggles in the home timeline gave much better images. A fire a couple of hundred meters away seemed bright as the sun. Justin didn't know how to turn down the gain.

He wished Smitty would fall asleep. Then he could put on his own clothes and find the coin shop . . . find his mother.

Smitty seemed much too wide awake. What did they do to sentries who fell asleep at their posts here? Shoot them, the way they had in lots of places (including the U.S.A.) in the home timeline? Justin wouldn't have been surprised. One thing he'd already found out about war: both sides played for keeps.

When Justin yawned enormously, Smitty reached into a pocket and pulled out a little plastic bottle. "Want a pill? You won't worry about sleeping for the next two days."

"I'll be okay." Improvising, Justin went on, "I don't like to use 'em unless I really have to. I'm liable to run down just when I ought to keep going."

"Then you take another one." But Smitty didn't push it. "You've got a point, I guess. Take too many and they'll mess you up. Every once in a while, though, you gotta."

"Sure," Justin said, and then, "What was that?" Was it an imaginary noise, a noise that came from nerves stretched too tight? He wouldn't have been surprised. Still, better to think you heard a noise that wasn't really there than to miss one that was.

"Where?" Smitty's voice was the tiniest thread of whisper.

"Over that way," Justin whispered back, pointing in the general direction of the fire. "Can't see anything much."

To his surprise, Smitty slipped off his goggles. When he did, he started to laugh. "Those sneaky so-and-so's," he said. "They know we'll be using the IR gear, and the fire masks them. But when you just look that way . . ."

Justin raised his goggles, too. The fire lit up three men crawling toward the revetment. They were almost close enough to chuck a grenade. That would have been no laughing matter. Smitty started shooting: neat bursts of three or four rounds, so his assault rifle's muzzle didn't climb too high. The advancing Negroes never had a chance. Justin fired a few rounds, too, not aiming at them, so he'd seem to be doing something. It hardly mattered—inside of a few seconds, the blacks were all dead or dying.

"Good thing you had your ears open," Smitty said. Killing people didn't bother him much. Yes, they would have blown him up if they got the chance. Even so . . .

"Don't know how I can hear anything after all the gunfire." Justin's ears were ringing.

"Gun bunnies have it worse than we do," Smitty said. "Artilleryman's ear is no fun at all. It makes you deaf to people talking and lets you hear the stuff that doesn't matter half as much."

"Wonderful," Justin said, and Smitty nodded. Justin wished he had ear plugs. Maybe he did—he didn't know what all was in the pack or in the pouches on his belt. He couldn't very well start fumbling around to find out now. One thing did occur to him: "Why don't you leave your goggles on, and I'll take mine off? That way, one of us will be sure to spot any kind of trouble." *And I won't have to mess with what I don't understand.*

"Good thinking," Smitty said. "We'll do it."

Every time anything made any kind of noise, close or near, Justin flinched. Adrenaline rivered through him. "I don't need your little pills after all," he told Smitty. "Nothing like fear to wire you."

"*Wire* you?" Smitty frowned. Justin realized that wasn't slang in this alternate. After a second, though, Smitty got it. "Oh, I know what you mean. Yeah, being scared cranks me, too—you betcha." That made sense here and in the home timeline.

Nobody else came close to them while they were on watch. Justin supposed three corpses lying not far away discouraged visitors. He knew they would have discouraged him. After what seemed like forever, their reliefs came up. "Had company, did you?" one of the soldiers said, pointing to the bodies.

"Yeah. They got cute." Smitty explained the trick the Negroes had used. "Don't let 'em catch you the same way, or you'll be sorry." He also mentioned Justin's idea for having one soldier use goggles while the other went without. "He's pretty smart," he finished, and thumped Justin on the back. "Glad we brought him along."

"He got Eddie to cover when they shot him, too, didn't he?" one of the new men said. Eddie nodded. The other soldier turned to Justin. "You're good in my book, buddy."

"Thanks." How much that meant to Justin himself surprised him.

He and Smitty made it back to their company's encampment without any trouble. As he unrolled his sleeping bag, he thought about waking up in the middle of the night and sneaking away. He thought about it. . . . Then he lay down. Sleep clubbed him over the head. Whatever happened after that, he didn't know a thing about it.

One of the amusement parks in Southern California had something called Mr. Frog's Crazy Ride. It was—loosely—based on a famous children's book. Beckie had always liked *The Breeze in the Birches*. All she could think now, though, was that the fabulous Mr. Frog was only a polliwog when it came to crazy rides. Getting from Elizabeth to Charleston beat the pants off anything at Mortimer's World.

Mr. Brooks started going by the route he'd used to come up to Elizabeth: over side roads west to the main highway south. That probably would have worked it he were able to get to the main highway. But he wasn't. A couple of kilometers west of Elizabeth, the road stopped being a road. There was an enormous crater that stretched all the way across it, and something—a bulldozer?—had piled the rubble into a neat barricade.

"Well . . . fudge," Mr. Brooks said. "I guess they didn't want anybody from Ohio coming down this road. They know how to get what they want, don't they?"

"Can you go around?" Gran asked. As far as Beckie knew, that was her second dumbest question of all time, right behind *Did anything break?* when the shell put a hole in Mr. Snodgrass' kitchen wall. That topped the list, but this one gave it a run for its money.

"If I had an armored personnel carrier, I might try it," Mr. Brooks answered with what Beckie thought was commendable calm. "In a Hupmobile that's seen better days—thanks, but no thanks."

"What *will* you do, then?" Gran asked.

"Go back and try the long way around. What else can I do?" Mr. Brooks said. Even going back wasn't easy. He did some fancy driving to turn around on the narrow road, then started east towards Elizabeth again. "I hope we don't get there at the same time as the Ohio troops do."

They beat the Ohioans, but not by much. Somebody yelled at them through a bullhorn. Somebody else fired a couple of shots at them. Beckie thought the shots were aimed their way, anyhow. Mr. Brooks took two corners on two wheels and got away. Beckie would have been more impressed than she was if she hadn't been scared to death, too.

"Are you trying to kill all of us?" Gran squawked.

"No, ma'am," Mr. Brooks answered, polite as a preacher. "I'm trying *not* to." The Hupmobile's brakes squealed as he jerked the car around another corner.

"Well, now I know why we wear seat belts," Beckie said. Gran hadn't wanted to put hers on. Mr. Brooks had been polite then, too: he'd politely told her she could walk in that case. He wasn't kidding. Even Gran, who was stubborner than most cats, could figure that out for herself. She had the belt on. So did Beckie, without argument.

As they sped east, away from Elizabeth, Mr. Brooks said, "I hope the Virginians didn't mine this stretch of road after they went down it."

Gran found another smart question to ask: "What happens if they did?"

"We blow up." Mr. Brooks sounded remarkably lighthearted about it. Would that make Gran stop asking questions? Beckie would have quit a lot sooner herself, but her grandmother never had known how to take a hint.

"Do you think we can get there without blowing up?" No, Gran had no clue that she might be irritating.

"Not a chance. I came this way on purpose, just so I could go sky-high," Mr. Brooks answered, deadpan. "And when you and Beckie wanted to come along, I really looked forward to blasting a couple of innocent bystanders, too."

Beckie giggled. She couldn't help herself. Gran was *not* amused. "Young man, are you playing games with me?" she demanded. Her tones suggested she would take Mr. Brooks to the woodshed if he dared do such a thing.

He stopped wasting time being polite: "Mrs. Bentley, get out of my hair and let me drive. I didn't want to bring you. You wanted to come. Now pipe down."

Gran opened her mouth. Then she closed it again. Chances were nobody'd talked to her like that since Beckie's grandfather was alive. It didn't do him much good, not from what Beckie'd heard, but Mr. Brooks took Gran by surprise. The silence was chilly, but he didn't seem to care.

Then they came to a checkpoint. A soldier strode out from a sandbagged machine-gun nest and held up his right hand. "Where y'all think you're going?" he demanded. "There's not supposed to be any civilian traffic on the road."

"I know that, but we've got a medical emergency." Mr. Brooks pointed to Gran.

The soldier took a step back. He brought up his assault rifle. "If she's got the plague, you really can't take her anywhere."

"No, nothing to do with that. You can see for yourself—she'd look sicker if she did," Mr. Brooks said. He was right about that. Gran, as usual, looked healthy as an ox. She also looked surprised to hear she was sick. Usually, she complained about her health. It would be just like her to say she was fine now. To Beckie's relief, she didn't. Mr. Brooks went on, "She's been getting her therapy in Parkersburg. We can't go there now, so I have to take her down to Charleston for treatment. You don't want her to die, do you?"

By the look on the soldier's face, he couldn't have cared less. "Let me talk to my sergeant," he said at last. "You stay right there till I get back if you know what's good for you."

He walked back to the revetment. When he returned, he had an older man with him. "What the devil's going on here?" the noncom said.

Mr. Brooks went through his song and dance again. "She's a sweet old lady," he said—with a straight face, too, which proved he was a good actor. "I wouldn't do this if I didn't have to, believe me."

"Well . . ." The sergeant rubbed his chin. "All right. Go on. I hope your mother gets better."

"Uh, thanks." Mr. Brooks hadn't said anything about that. In his shoes, Beckie wouldn't have, either. But he rallied fast— maybe he *could* have been an actor. "Yeah, thanks. Twonk's Disease is treatable if you catch it in time." He drove away before the sergeant could change his mind.

"Twonk's Disease?" Beckie said.

He cast off his usual air of gloom to grin at her. "First name that popped into my mind."

"Is there such a thing as Twonk's Disease?"

"There is now. If you don't think so, ask that soldier."

Beckie thought it over. Mr. Brooks had something, no doubt about it. What people believed to be true often ended up as important as what really was true. "What would you have done if he told you to turn around?" she asked.

"I don't know. Maybe I could have taken out the whole checkpoint." He didn't sound as if he was kidding. He sounded more like someone weighing the odds. Beckie didn't know what kind of weapons he had. She hadn't *known* he had any, though she would have guessed he did.

"More to you than meets the eye, isn't there?" she said.

"Me?" He shook his head. "Nah. I'm about as ordinary as—"

"Somebody who talks about taking out a checkpoint full of soldiers," Beckie finished for him. Had he tried, she suspected he could have done it. He might look ordinary, but he wasn't.

Come to think of it, neither was Justin. *An interesting family. An unusual family,* Beckie thought. She wondered what Justin's mother was like.

Mr. Brooks looked faintly embarrassed. Embarrassed at talking that way, or embarrassed at showing too much of himself? Beckie wasn't sure. "Talk is cheap," he said. "I got mad at that guy, and so . . ."

"Sure," Beckie said. *Yeah, sure,* she thought.

"You know," Gran said, "I saw a TV show about Twonk's Disease once. I think I should go to the doctor and get looked at, because I may have it."

Beckie didn't say anything. There didn't seem to be anything to say. Mr. Brooks just kept driving. If his eyes twinkled a little, if his cheeks and even his ears turned pink, then they did, that was all. If he was laughing inside, nobody could prove it. And that was bound to be just as well.

Things weren't as simple as Justin wished they were. They weren't as simple as he'd expected them to be. That seemed to be how growing up worked. Once you got into the middle of something, it usually turned out to be more complicated than you figured it would when you started.

With most things, that was annoying, but you dealt with it and went on. When you were pretending to be a soldier, complications were liable to get you killed.

Justin hadn't thought he would have to go on pretending very long. He hadn't thought he would have to go into combat, either. He had thought he would be able to slip away from the real soldiers as soon as he got into Charleston. He turned out to be wrong, wrong, and wrong, respectively.

Gunfire started up again well before sunup. He didn't hear it, not at first. Even if he was sleeping on the ground, he was sleeping hard. He didn't want to wake up even when Smitty shook him. "Come on, man—move," Smitty said. "You want to get shot?"

"Huh?" All Justin wanted to do was close his eyes again.

"Come *on.*" Smitty shook him some more. Then a bullet cracked by overhead. That got Justin moving. It got him moving faster than Smitty was, in fact. His lifelong buddy of not quite twenty-four hours laughed at him. "There you go," Smitty said. "See? I knew you could do it."

"Thanks a lot," Justin said as he dove into a hole a shell had torn in the ground.

Smitty went on laughing, but not for long. "Hey, man," he said, "you better pile some of that dirt in front of you. You'd rather have a bullet or a fragment get stopped there. That way, it won't tear you up."

"Uh, yeah." Justin pulled an entrenching tool—halfway between a big trowel and a small shovel—off his belt and started work. He dug some more dirt out of the hole and piled that in front of him, too. The deeper he dug, the thicker the rampart got, the safer he felt. Maybe some of that safety lay only in his mind, but he'd take it any which way.

Would he have thought to dig in if Smitty didn't suggest it? He hoped so, but he wasn't sure. Soldiering seemed like any other job—it came with tricks of the trade. Smitty knew them. He'd probably learned them in basic training, or whatever they called it here. Justin . . . didn't.

In an ordinary job, knowing the tricks let you work better, work faster. Maybe it kept you from getting hurt if you worked with machinery. Here, knowing what was what helped keep you alive. Justin had seen a lot of dead bodies since he got to Charleston. He could smell more that he couldn't see. It was another hot, sticky day, and corpses went bad in a hurry. The sickly-sweet stink made him want to puke.

He could smell himself, too, and the other soldiers. He'd been in this uniform for more than a day, and done plenty of sweating. How long before he could shower or change clothes? He had no idea. Nobody'd told him anything about stuff like that. People told you what to do. They didn't bother with why. You were supposed to know, or else not to care. That didn't strike Justin as the best way to do things, but nobody cared what he thought. Getting ignored by the people set over you also seemed to be part of soldiering.

An officer came forward with a white flag on a stick. He stood out in the open and waited to be noticed. Justin wouldn't have wanted that job for anything in the world. Little by little, though, the firing petered out.

Along with the flag of truce, the Virginia officer carried a bullhorn. He raised it to his mouth. "You people!" wasn't quite what he shouted. Hearing the hateful word he did use made Justin grit his teeth. It wasn't *as* bad a word in this alternate. He understood that. But understanding it didn't take the sick feeling out of his belly. And that word was no endearment here, either. The officer used it again: "You people! You want to listen to me or what?"

"We'll listen. Say your say," a Negro called from the rubble ahead. He didn't show himself.

The Virginia officer didn't seem to expect him to. "Okay," he boomed. "You better pay attention, on account of this is your last chance. You surrender now, you come out of your holes with your hands high, we'll let y'all live. You keep fighting, we won't answer for what happens after that. You're whupped. No matter what the fancy talkers from Ohio told you, you are whupped. Give up now and keep breathing. Otherwise . . ." He paused ominously. Looking at his watch, he went on, "You've got fifteen minutes to make up your minds. You make us come and get you, that's all she wrote."

"You'll get your answer," the black man shouted back. "Hang on."

No rebels showed themselves. They had to scurry back and forth somewhere out of sight, deciding what to do. Was the officer even telling the truth? Would Virginia authorities spare the Negroes' lives? Probably, Justin judged. If they didn't, and other bands found out, it would make them fight to the death. But would you want to go on living with what the authorities were likely to do to you? Justin wasn't so sure about that.

"Time's up!" the officer blared. "What's it gonna be?"

"Reckon we'd sooner die on our feet than on our knees," the rebel answered. "You want us, come an' get us."

"Your funeral," the officer said. "And it will be. You asked for it."

He turned and walked away. Some self-propelled guns like the ones west of Elizabeth—maybe they were the same ones—rumbled into place. Instead of hurling their shells twenty kilometers, they blasted away at point-blank range, smashing the buildings in which the Negro rebels were hiding.

After they finished wrecking one block, they ground forward to start on the next. The foot soldiers went with them. They got rid of the men the bombardment didn't kill or maim. They also kept the rebels from harming the guns. Justin wondered why they needed to do that—the guns seemed plenty able to take care of themselves.

Then a Negro jumped up on top of one. Justin didn't see where he came from. He yanked open a hatch and threw a burning bottle of gasoline into the fighting compartment. Somebody shot him before he could leap down again. But horrible black smoke poured from the hatch. Shells started cooking off in there. So did machine-gun ammo, which went *pop! pop! pop!* happy as you please.

Nobody got out of the self-propelled gun. One Molotov cocktail—not that they called them that in this alternate—took out an expensive machine and several highly trained soldiers. *One Molotov cocktail and one brave man,* Justin reminded himself.

Even Smitty said, "That took guts." Then he swore at the Negro who did it. Was he angry because the man hurt his comrades? Or was he angry because the black showed himself to be a man? Justin didn't know and couldn't ask without giving himself away. He wondered if Smitty knew.

Another Negro with a Molotov cocktail got gunned down before he could come close enough to a self-propelled gun to use it. The flaming gasoline set him on fire. He screamed for much too long before he died.

Justin was pretty sure he shot somebody else. The black man popped up from behind a bus bench, just like a target in a video game. Justin aimed and squeezed the trigger. The rebel went down, and didn't do anything else after that. It bothered Justin much less than shooting the first kid had. That it bothered him much less bothered him much more. He didn't want to get hardened to killing people.

He didn't want to do any of what he was doing. The people he was doing it with were no prizes, either. They didn't bother taking many prisoners. The rebels didn't try to surrender. They fought till they couldn't fight any more, and then, grimly, they died.

"They've risen up before. They've got squashed every time," he said to Smitty as they both crouched in a doorway. "They must have known they couldn't win this time, too. So why try?"

"Some folks are natural-born fools," Smitty answered. "And the Ohioans sent 'em guns and filled their heads with moonshine." He spat. "Look what it got 'em."

"Maybe if we'd treated them better beforehand, they wouldn't have wanted to rebel no matter what the Ohioans did," Justin said.

Smitty looked at him as if he were nuts. "Don't let an officer catch you talking that way," the real soldier warned. "You'll get in more trouble than you know what to do with." He wouldn't say any more than that. Plainly, though, Justin had disappointed him. You couldn't even talk about racial equality here. If you so much as opened your mouth, they thought you came from some other world.

And Justin did.

By the time evening came, there weren't many rebels left to kill. There wasn't much still standing in the part of Charleston they'd held, either. *They make a desert and call it peace.* Some Roman historian said that. It was just as true now as it had been back in the days of the Empire. The Romans had actually got peace—for a while—by winning their wars like that. Maybe the Virginians would, too . . . for a while.

And will I ever find any? Justin wondered. The chances didn't look good.

No Virginia soldiers arrested Beckie and her grandmother and Mr. Brooks. No suspicious military doctor asked him about how to treat Twonk's Disease. All that made getting to Charleston a little easier, but not much. The real problem was the road itself. It kept disappearing, usually at spots where going around involved something interesting—falling off a cliff, for instance.

"Cruise missiles. Terrain-mapping technology." Mr. Brooks sounded as if he admired the fancy technology that was causing him endless delays. Maybe he did. It wouldn't have surprised Beckie. He seemed a man who admired competence wherever he found it, because he didn't think he'd find it very often.

As Mr. Brooks admired the Ohioans who'd wrecked the road, so he also admired the Virginian military engineers who repaired it and let him go forward again. Beckie also couldn't help admiring them. They were busy with hard, dangerous work. They had no guarantee more cruise missiles wouldn't fly in and wreck everything they were doing—and maybe blow them up, too. But they kept at it.

Gran admired nothing and nobody. She complained whenever the road was blocked. And she complained that the military engineers weren't fixing it fast enough. When Mr. Brooks drove over one of the newly repaired stretches, she complained it was bumpy. When it wasn't bumpy, and saying it was would only make her look silly, she complained he was driving too fast instead.

Mr. Brooks took it all in stride. At one point, when Gran was going even better than usual, he looked over at Beckie and said, "This is fun, isn't it?"

She started to laugh. She couldn't help herself. Then Gran complained she wasn't taking things seriously enough. She only laughed harder.

Whenever the military engineers did finish a stretch, they waved the civilian car through. After about the third time it happened, Mr. Brooks said, "Maybe it's just as well you two came along after all."

"What do you mean?" Beckie asked.

"They see a car with a guy in it, they're going to wonder what he's doing here. They see a car with a guy and his 'mother'"—

Mr. Brooks made a face—"and his 'daughter' in it, they don't worry so much. Probably doesn't hurt that his 'daughter' is a pretty girl, either."

Beckie didn't think she was anything special. But he didn't sound as if he were praising her just to butter her up. And she'd seen the way the soldiers looked at her. Of course, how fussy were soldiers likely to be?

"Did Justin come this way?" Beckie asked, not least so she wouldn't have to think about things like that. "If he did, was the road smashed up for him, too?"

Mr. Brooks only shrugged. "Maybe this happened after he went through. Or maybe the convoy he's with is five miles ahead of us, waiting for the military engineers to fix another hole in the highway. But if he went to Charleston, he either went this way or the other way we couldn't get through, because there aren't any more."

"Oh." Beckie thought about that, then nodded. "What if he didn't go to Charleston?"

"In that case, we're up the well-known creek without a paddle," Mr. Brooks answered. "And so is he."

"Which creek?" It wasn't well-known to Gran. "What are you talking about?"

"I'm just being metaphorical, Mrs. Bentley," Mr. Brooks said.

"Well, cut it out and talk so a person can understand you."

He sighed. "If all writers did that, chances are it would improve ninety percent of them. But it would ruin the rest—and those are the ones we need most."

Gran only sniffed. After a few seconds, Beckie said, "You say *interesting* things."

"Who, me?" Mr. Brooks shrugged. "The only thing I want to say is, 'And they all lived happily ever after.' But I don't know if

I'll be able to manage that. Looks like the sun's about to go down, and we aren't there yet."

"Well? Turn on your lights and keep going," Gran said.

"I would do that, Mrs. Bentley, but I'm not sure it's a good idea," Mr. Brooks said. "Missiles may home on our lights. Or the Virginians may shoot us because they think we're trying to make missiles home on us. Which would you rather?"

"What? I don't want either one! Are you crazy?" Gran sounded sure he was.

"He's trying to tell you he doesn't want to keep driving after dark, Gran," Beckie said, working hard not to laugh.

"See? I told you he should just talk sense." Nothing got through to Gran, even the things that should have.

They stopped for the night in a town called Clendenin, which was even smaller than Elizabeth. Once upon a time, it had been an oil town. Now the derricks stood silent and rusting. The town did have a motel. It looked shabbier than the one in Elizabeth, and was full of soldiers. Clendenin also had a gas station. The travelers used the restrooms there. They also bought snacks—no diner there.

Then they went out and slept in the car, or tried to. Beckie couldn't remember a more uncomfortable night. Gran had the back seat to herself. She soon started snoring. Even with her front seat reclined, Beckie couldn't doze off. She usually slept on her stomach. She leaned back and did her best to keep quiet—Mr. Brooks was breathing deeply and steadily, too.

She tried counting sheep. She tried counting boulders— plenty of them all around the road they'd been traveling. She felt herself getting sleepy . . . till a mosquito started buzzing. She was so tired, she could hardly see straight. But her eyes wouldn't stay closed no matter what.

And then gray predawn light streamed through the windshield, and she had no idea how it had got there. She looked around in surprise. Mr. Brooks nodded to her. "Your grandmother is still out," he whispered.

She sure was. She was snoring louder than ever. "I guess I did sleep," Beckie said. "I didn't think I could."

"You get tired enough, you can do almost anything." Mr. Brooks sounded like a man who knew what he was talking about.

"How long have you been awake?" Beckie asked.

"A while now." He looked at what they'd bought the night before. "We've got some warm fizzes, and some chocolate Supersnax cakes, and some pork rinds. Sounds like a great breakfast, doesn't it?"

"Makes my mouth water," Beckie said solemnly. He laughed softly. She ate one of the cakes and drank a fizz. Then she hoped the fellow who ran the gas station would come back and open up, because she needed to make a pit stop.

He did, so she didn't have to go into the bushes behind the station. At least there were bushes to go back to. In Los Angeles, there wouldn't have been.

Gran crunched pork rinds as if she ate them for breakfast every morning. Beckie didn't want to think about what that meant. Had there been a time when Gran . . . ? Beckie shook her head. She *didn't* want to think about it.

She heard booms off in the distance. Before she came to Virginia, she would have thought they were thunder. Now she knew better—more knowledge she wished she didn't have. But she did, and so she said, "That's artillery."

"Sure is," Mr. Brooks agreed. "Sounds like it's coming from Charleston. They're blowing the place up to save it." That went right by Gran. The cynicism made Beckie wince.

"Will there be anywhere to stay?" Beckie asked.

"I expect there will," Mr. Brooks answered. "Charleston's a good-sized city. To wreck it all, you'd need a nuke or two great big armies fighting a no-holds-barred battle there—like, uh, Tsaritsyn in the War of the Three Emperors a hundred and fifty years ago. An uprising? An uprising's just a nuisance."

"Unless you get shot in it," Beckie said.

"There is that," he agreed. "You're just as dead if you get shot in an uprising as you are any other time. Shall we go find out how bad things are?" Neither Beckie nor Gran said no. He drove southwest toward Charleston.

He passed several military checkpoints coming into the city. Two things got him through: everybody in the car was white, and he had a genuine Virginia driver's license. Soldiers checked it with their laptops. It came up green every time.

"Oh, my," Beckie said when they got into Charleston.

"It wasn't like this when I left," Mr. Brooks said.

"I sure hope not," she told him.

"It's not this bad on the news," Gran said, looking around in disbelief. This was without a doubt a city that had been fought over, and fought over hard. Buildings were knocked flat. Bullet holes scarred wooden fences and walls. The stink of smoke filled the air and stung Beckie's eyes. Under it lay another, nastier stink: the stink of death.

"On the news, Gran, they don't want you to think it's bad," Beckie said, as gently as she could.

"But the news is supposed to show you what's what," Gran said.

Beckie wondered how Gran could have got to be an old lady while staying so innocent. Mr. Brooks said, "The news shows what the people in charge want you to think is what." No, he didn't come to town on a load of turnips.

He passed up a couple of motels and hotels that had taken battle damage, and a couple of more that hadn't. "What's wrong with this one?" Beckie asked when he drove past yet another.

"Didn't look good," he answered, and left it there. "Ah, here we go," he said a minute or so later, and pulled up at one across the street from a police station. "You ought to be safe here. I'll come back and check on you later today."

"Thank you very much," Beckie said.

"I want a room with a TV with better news," Gran said. When you got right down to it, that didn't sound like such a bad idea.

Twelve

Justin had been wondering how to get away from his squad. Once he decided to risk it, it turned out to be the easiest thing in the world. He just walked off, looking as if he knew where he was going and what he was doing.

He'd come a couple of blocks when he got to a checkpoint. "What's up?" one of the soldiers there asked him.

He pointed ahead. "I'm supposed to patrol down that way."

"Okay." The soldier didn't ask any more questions. Justin was white and he was in uniform, so the fellow figured he had to be all right. He'd counted on that. The soldier at the checkpoint did say, "Keep your eyes peeled. Still may be a few holdouts running around loose."

"Thanks. I will." That was the last thing Justin wanted to hear. He tramped on. Other soldiers went here and there, sometimes singly, sometimes in groups. Except for that one sentry, nobody challenged him. If you seemed legit, people assumed you were. Most of the time, they were right. Every once in a while, you could take advantage of them.

He heard scattered gunshots, but none very close. The civilians on the street were all white. African Americans were lying low. How much good would that do them? Sooner or later—likely sooner—the white Virginians would take their revenge for the uprising. That would make the Negroes hate them even more, and would light some sparks to help kindle the next revolt.

How could Virginia break the cycle? The only way Justin saw was for whites to treat blacks the same way they treated each other. He also saw that that was something no local whites wanted to do. They feared, and with some justice, equality wouldn't seem like enough. They looked fearfully toward black-ruled Mississippi, the way slaveowners in the home timeline once looked fearfully toward black-ruled Haiti.

That wasn't his worry, for which he thanked heaven. It might be Crosstime Traffic's worry one of these days. The company would have to figure out what to do here, and whether it could do anything. Sometimes slipping the right idea to the right people at the right moment made all the difference in the world. Sometimes it didn't change a thing. You never could tell till you tried.

He turned on to the street on which Mr. Brooks' coin and stamp shop lay. His heart pounded in his chest. Was everything all right? Was anything left? He didn't want to think anything bad could happen to his mother. But he'd seen enough horror the past couple of days to know anything *could* happen to any-body.

There'd been fighting here. Several buildings had bites taken out of them. Bullets pocked walls and shattered windows. The donut house across the street from the shop, the one where he'd seen the car pull up when he first got into Charleston, was noth-ing but a pile of rubble. Did somebody make a point of knocking it flat, or was it just unlucky? He'd probably never know.

But the coin and stamp shop was still standing. Even if it weren't, the room in the subbasement where the transposition chamber came and went wouldn't be damaged. But could Mom have got down there fast enough? Even if she could have, would

Crosstime Traffic have let her leave this alternate with a genetically engineered disease on the loose? It seemed unlikely.

Justin hoped that was all wasted worry. He looked up and down the street. No other soldiers in sight. Nobody to notice if he went in here. He pulled at the door. It was locked. He muttered—he should have known it would be. He still had a key. He put it in the lock and turned, then tried the door. It opened.

Nobody stood behind the counter. Justin took a couple of steps forward into the shop, letting the door click shut behind him. The sharp little noise brought his mother out from the back room. She looked alarmed—she looked terrified—at seeing a large soldier with an assault rifle in the shop. But her voice was brisk and didn't wobble as she asked, "What do you want, Private?"

She didn't recognize him. He was wearing a grimy uniform she didn't expect, a helmet that changed the shape of his face, and a couple of days' worth of filth and stubble. He grinned. "Hi, Mom," he said.

Her jaw dropped. "Justin?" she whispered. Then she said, "Justin!" at something not far from a scream and threw her arms around him. When she finally let go, she said, "I never thought I'd hug anybody carrying a gun."

That reminded him of what he'd seen and done while he wore the uniform and the helmet and the dirt and stubble. With a shudder, he set the rifle down and said, "If I never see this . . . this *thing* again, it'll be too soon."

"Oh." She looked at him again—for real this time. "You weren't just carrying ME! You used it, didn't you?"

"Yeah." He grimaced. "If I didn't, one of the rebels would have used one on me. I lost my lunch right after that."

"I believe you," his mother said. "How come you had it in the first place?"

"It was the only way I saw to get back here from Elizabeth," Justin answered. "It worked, too." He wasn't exactly thrilled that it had. People said you could buy something at too high a price. He'd understood that with money before, but no other way. He did now.

Mom must have seen as much on his face. "Well, you *are* here," she said. "That may not be the only thing that matters, but I'm awful glad to see you—now that I'm not scared to death any more, I mean. Is Randy all right?"

"He was fine the last time I saw him, a couple of days ago," Justin said. "But how have *you* been? You were in the middle of everything."

"More like on the edges," Mom said. "If this place were in the middle, it wouldn't still be standing."

She was right about that. "Can they cure the disease the Ohioans turned loose?" he asked. "Can they get us out of here?"

"They already have a vaccine. They're getting close to a cure," his mother answered.

"A vaccine's just as good," Justin said, and then, remembering Irma and Mrs. Snodgrass, "Well, unless you've already got it, anyway."

"Unless," his mother agreed. "The problem now, the way I understand it, is getting the vaccine to the Virginians without making them suspicious. Last I heard, we were thinking of mailing it to Richmond as if it came from a lab in Pennsylvania or Wabash." The state of Wabash wasn't too different from Indiana in the home timeline. "The hope is they'll be so glad to get it, they won't ask many questions."

"What about getting us back to the home timeline?" Justin asked. That was the thing that was uppermost in his mind.

"They . . . aren't quite ready yet," Mom said. "We've been

exposed to the virus. The air the transposition chamber picks up when it opens for us may have the bug floating around in it, too. They don't want to bring it back to the home timeline."

"But they've got the vaccine! You said they're close to a cure!" Justin had come back to Charleston wanting to get home. If he couldn't, if he was still stuck in this alternate, he might almost have stayed in Elizabeth—though it *was* nice to be sure Mom was okay.

"They've got 'em, and they don't want to have to use 'em," she said. "That would be expensive, and if they start having cases anyway. . . . Well, can you imagine the lawsuits? They really— I mean *really*—don't want another black eye so soon after the slavery scandal."

Justin could see that. It made good sense in terms of what Crosstime Traffic needed. In terms of what he and his mother and Mr. Brooks needed, though, it wasn't so great. "They can't just strand us here . . . can they?"

"I don't think they'll do that," Mom said.

"If they do, *we'll* sue them," Justin said fiercely.

"Well, no." His mother shook his head. "We signed liability waivers before we came here. This isn't company negligence or anything. This is part of the risk we take when we come to a high-tech alternate. No lawyer will touch this one, and we'd get thrown out of court if we found one who would."

"Oh." Justin didn't think he'd ever made a gloomier noise.

"They're working on it," Mom said. "I don't know the details— they haven't told me. But they don't want to leave us here. That wouldn't look good, either."

"Well, hooray." Getting saved because it helped Crosstime Traffic's image wasn't exactly what Justin had in mind, either.

"You ought to be glad they've got some reason to want to bring us back," Mom said. "Otherwise, they wouldn't try so hard."

"How hard are they trying now?"

"I think *something* is happening. I hope so, anyway."

"It had better be," Justin said, though he had no idea what he could do if it weren't.

A car pulled up in front of the shop. Justin wasn't very surprised when Mr. Brooks got out. If he'd managed to get down to Charleston himself, that had to be the boot in the behind the coin and stamp dealer needed. Justin opened the door for him. Mr. Brooks greeted him with, "You dummy."

"I made it," Justin said.

"Oh, boy." He didn't impress the older man. Mr. Brooks pointed to the assault rifle leaning against the wall. "Did you have to use that?"

"Yeah," Justin admitted in a small voice.

"How did you like it?"

Justin didn't say anything. His face must have said it all, though, because Mr. Brooks set a hand on his shoulder. Justin managed a shaky nod. "Thanks," he muttered.

"It's okay," Mr. Brooks answered. "If you did like it, that would worry me. It's not a game out there. Whoever you shot, he was real. You always need to remember that. Sometimes it happens. If he's gonna shoot you, you take care of yourself and worry about it later. But you always have to take it seriously, because the other fellow wants to live just as much as you do."

"I . . . found that out." Justin wondered if finding it out would set him apart from everybody he knew back in the home timeline. Knowing things your friends didn't couldn't help but isolate you from them . . . could it?

"You've joined a club nobody wants to belong to." Mr. Brooks was scarily good at thinking along with him. The older man went on, "Chances are you'll meet more members than you know about, because the others won't talk about it any more than you will." He turned to Justin's mother. "What's going on here?"

"I'm still alive. Nobody's robbed the place," she answered. Then she filled him in on the bigger picture, the way she had with Justin.

He nodded. "Okay. Thanks. It could be worse. It could be better, too, but it could always be better."

He was asking Mom more questions when Justin went into the back room. He got out of Adrian's uniform as fast as he could and put on the clothes he had in the pack. They were wrinkled as anything, but he didn't care. He didn't care about going upstairs for a different outfit, either. He wanted to turn into himself again, as fast as he could, not a Virginia soldier any more. Anything but a Virginia soldier, in fact.

When he came out again, Mr. Brooks nodded to him. "Took the whammy off, did you?"

"Yeah!" Justin said.

"Don't blame you a bit."

Justin nodded now. He was glad the coin and stamp dealer didn't blame him. But, all things considered, how much difference did that make? He'd blame himself for the rest of his life. If he hadn't put on the uniform . . . what?

He started to think, *That African-American kid would still be alive then.* But was that true? Was it even likely? Wouldn't Smitty or one of the other real Virginia soldiers have shot him instead? Or, if they hadn't, wouldn't the self-propelled guns have killed him? How could you know? You couldn't, not for sure. He wondered if he was looking for an excuse to feel less guilty. He hoped not. He would stay a member of Mr. Brooks' unhappy club no matter what. He'd just have to figure out how to live with it, and that wouldn't happen overnight, either.

He had the rest of his life to worry about it. The kid he'd shot didn't, not anymore. And that was exactly the point.

"I don't feel good." Gran said it in a surprisingly matter-of-fact way. Most of the time, she was proud of her aches and pains. She used them to outdo other people around her who might have the nerve not to be well. But coming out and announcing something like this wasn't her usual style.

Because it wasn't, Beckie paid more attention than she would have otherwise. "What's the matter?" she asked.

"The light seems too bright. And I'm warm, even though I know the air conditioner is running," Gran said.

Beckie walked over to her and put a hand on her forehead. She almost jerked it back in alarm. Her grandmother wasn't just warm. She was hot, much too hot. It could have been a lot of things. Beckie feared she knew what it was.

"Can you get me some water?" Gran usually milked her symptoms for all they were worth, too.

This time, Beckie didn't mind. As she went to the sink, she wondered what to do. Call the local emergency number? With fighting still going on in the city, would anybody pay attention? A long burst of machine-gun fire underscored her fears. Somebody screamed—not a short, frightened scream like the ones in the movies, but a shriek that went on and on and on. Anybody who screamed that way was dying as fast as he could, but not fast enough.

But with people in Charleston making noises like that, how long would the emergency people take to get here if they came at all? What would they do when they did? *Will they stick me in quarantine somewhere? Will I ever get out again?* She and Gran were foreigners here. Did California even have a consulate in Charleston? She looked in the phone book and didn't find one. Especially during a rebellion, the Virginians could do anything they wanted.

"Let me have some more," Gran said, so Beckie did.

Then she looked in the phone book again. Sure enough, there it was: CHARLESTON COINS AND STAMP COMPANY. It gave an address along with the phone number. Beckie didn't know where that address was. She'd never expected to come to Charleston. But the room had a computer terminal. It was slow and clunky by California standards, but it worked.

As she'd hoped, the coin and stamp shop was just a few blocks away. She'd figured Mr. Brooks would put her and Gran somewhere close to his shop. He and Justin were the only people she knew here. They could tell her what to do.

Whatever it was, she needed to do it in a hurry. Gran was sitting there, sort of staring at the TV. She often watched without really knowing what was going on, but this was different. Her brain wasn't working right. She would have stared the same way if she were pointed in some other direction.

Beckie tried using her cell phone to call the coin and stamp shop. No luck—all she got was static. The hotel room had no phone, any more than one in California would have. Land lines were dead, dead, dead. She wished she were in some backward part of the world where they still used them—Russia, maybe, or central Africa. She'd never imagined low tech could be better than high, but she'd never been in a war before, either. Phone service was probably out all over western Virginia and eastern Ohio. What a mess.

If she couldn't call, she had to go. She didn't like leaving Gran by herself, but she couldn't see that she had much choice. Gran wasn't likely to wander off. If she got sicker . . . Beckie gnawed on the inside of her lower lip. She didn't like to think about that.

I'm going to get help, she told herself. *I won't be gone long. I hope I won't, anyway.*

Then she told Gran the same thing. Gran nodded vaguely. "I think the muffins are spoiled," she said, which meant she didn't hear or she was out of her head with fever or all of the above.

Three blocks over and two blocks down toward the river. That was what the terminal said. It didn't say anything about what might be going on between here and there. Beckie wished it would have. She wasn't brave—not even close. But she knew she had to go, and so she left the hotel room before she gave herself much of a chance to think about it.

The bellhops and porters were Negroes. So were the waiters and, she presumed, the cooks. In California, she wouldn't have paid much attention—and there would have been all kinds of people doing those jobs. Here, seeing black faces made her nervous. She knew it shouldn't have . . . or should it? How much did they hate whites? How many good reasons for hating whites did they have?

When a bellhop tipped his cap to her as she went out, she almost screamed. What was he thinking? How much did he despise himself—and her—because he had to make that servile gesture? How much did he wish he had a rifle in his hands and were fighting the soldiers from Virginia? Wouldn't paying them back almost be worth getting shot?

A lot of Negroes in Charleston sure seemed to think so.

Going out on the street, getting away from those people who wouldn't have been polite if they weren't getting paid, came as a relief . . . for a little while. Then she found out how much the hotel's soundproofing muffled the noise of gunfire. It was much louder, and much closer, than she'd thought.

"Let's see your papers!" a soldier barked at the first checkpoint she came to. She handed them over. His eyebrows jumped in surprise, almost disappearing under the brim of his helmet. "California passport! What in blazes are you doing here?"

"Visiting friends," Beckie said, which wasn't even a lie. "I didn't know I'd get stuck when the war started." That was also true.

"Who are these friends?" the soldier asked.

"Justin Monroe and his uncle, Randolph Brooks," Beckie answered. "Mr. Brooks runs a coin shop not far from here."

"He does, Everett," another soldier said. "I remember seeing the place."

"Okay." Everett looked at the passport again, shook his head, and gave the document back to Beckie. "You can go, I guess. But be careful. Things aren't exactly safe around here yet."

She found out what he meant when she walked around the corner. Two bodies lay there—one white, one black. Flies buzzed over them and settled in the blood that had pooled on the sidewalk. A mockingbird—a cheerful, sweet-voiced mockingbird—pecked at one of the corpses and swallowed . . . something. Stomach knotting, Beckie waved her arms. The bird screeched but flew away.

Those bodies were fresh. Something in the air told Beckie of others she couldn't see. The ones she smelled had been dead longer. How long would that stench last? How could anyone stand to live here till it went away?

People were on the streets. Some moved warily, as if afraid of what might happen next. Beckie moved that way herself. Who could tell when a wacko of any color might pop out of a doorway and start shooting? But others walked along as if things were normal. A man in his twenties smiled at Beckie the way he might have on any street in the world. She nodded, but couldn't make herself smile back.

Three blocks over then a left turn, then downhill toward the Kanawha. Lots of Charleston—lots of western Virginia—seemed to be uphill or downhill or sidehill or somethinghill. California had country more rugged than this, but hardly anybody lived in it. There were no towns in the Sierras with a couple of hundred thousand people in them.

On the way down toward the river, she had to go by one of the bodies she'd been smelling. There it lay, all bloated and stinking, a monument to . . . what? To stupidity. To man's inhumanity to man. But the Virginians wouldn't see it, neither the whites nor the blacks. Why not? It sure looked obvious to her.

Not even Justin and Mr. Brooks would admit it, and they seemed different from the other Virginians she'd met. The Snodgrasses couldn't even see the problem. Beckie had the feeling Justin and his uncle could, but they didn't want to look.

She wondered if she was imagining things. She didn't think so. That was probably a big part of why she was on her way to the coin and stamp shop. They were unusual people, and they might have unusual ways to help.

And there was the shop, across the street. Actually, first she saw the car in which Mr. Brooks drove her and Gran to Charleston. But COINS AND STAMPS was neatly lettered in gold on the plate-glass window closest to it. So was the street number. In Los Angeles, odd numbers were on the western and northern sides of the street, evens to the south and east. She hadn't needed long to see they didn't do things that way in Ohio and Virginia. The stamp and coin shop was on the west side of the street, but its address was 696. *Close to the number of the beast, but not quite,* Beckie thought.

There wasn't much traffic. Beckie didn't feel the least bit guilty about jaywalking. In Charleston right now, she was more likely to get hit by a sniper than by an oncoming car. She wished she hadn't thought of it like that. She especially wished she hadn't when a burst of automatic-weapons fire only a couple of blocks away made her jump in the air. A woman screamed, and went on screaming. She shuddered. One more noise you never wanted to hear.

She tried the door to the coin and stamp shop. It was locked, which wasn't the biggest surprise in the world. But she could see people in there, even if the sun film on the window kept her from telling who they were. She knocked. When nobody came to the door right away, she went on knocking.

Justin opened up. "Come on in," he said. "You're no looter." An assault rifle leaned against the far wall. He was dirty and needed a shave. "What's up?" he asked.

Beckie was glad to see him no matter how he looked. "Gran's got it," she said baldly.

"Ohhh." It was almost the noise Justin would have made if someone hit him in the belly. Behind the counter, Mr. Brooks made an almost identical sound. A tall woman Beckie hadn't met winced. Justin said, "This is my mom. Mom, this is Beckie Royer, who I've been telling you about."

"I'm glad to meet you," Mrs. Monroe said. "I'm not glad about your news, though, not even a little bit. We've already had too many cases in Charleston."

Picking his words with obvious care, Mr. Brooks asked, "What do you want us to do, Beckie?"

"Whatever you can," she said. "I'm a stranger here. I don't have any money, not on my own. The credit cards are all in Gran's name, and she's . . . not with it right now." She told him about the muffins, whatever that was supposed to mean. Then she took a deep breath and went on, "I don't know that I'll ever be able to stand her after spending all this time with her. You've seen what a pain she is. But that doesn't mean I want her to up and die on me." Tears stung her eyes. No, it didn't mean that at all.

"We could get her to a hospital for you," Justin's mother said slowly.

"They aren't having a whole lot of luck with this in hospitals," Justin said. "Either you get better on your own or you don't. Mostly you don't." He sent Beckie an apologetic look, but he wasn't saying anything she didn't already know. "Doctors here are kind of dim," he added.

Both his mother and Mr. Brooks coughed loudly. Under the dirt and stubble, Justin turned red. He didn't take it back, though.

"Hospital's still my best bet, isn't it?" Beckie said. "I want to do everything I can."

"Well . . ." Justin started. He got two more sharp coughs. Beckie wondered what was going on. Whatever it was, nobody seemed to want to come out and tell her. Justin said, "Let me see what I can do."

What was that supposed to mean? Whatever it meant, Justin's mom and Mr. Brooks didn't like it for beans. Beckie could see as much, even if she had no idea why they felt the way they did. "What exactly do you think that is?" Beckie spoke as carefully as Mr. Brooks had a few minutes before.

"I don't know yet. Give me till five o'clock," Justin said,

while the two older people in the shop looked daggers at him. He went on, "If she gets really, really sick, don't wait for me. I don't want her to die before I do . . . whatever I can do."

He still wouldn't say what that was. What could a coin and stamp dealer's nephew do that a hospital couldn't? But he sounded as if he thought he could do something, somehow. And Beckie knew the hospitals weren't having much luck with the disease. Would they have done better in California? How could she tell?

She made up her mind. "Okay, Justin. I'll see what happens, that's all. I hope you're not just trying to impress me or something. If you're blowing smoke on this, I never want to have anything to do with you any more. You hear me?"

"I hear you," he said soberly.

"All right, then." Without giving him a chance to answer, she turned and walked out of the shop and started back to the hotel. When she went past the stinking, swollen body in the street, she was reminded you didn't need a plague to die. Being in the wrong place at the wrong time could do the job every bit as well.

As soon as the door closed behind Beckie, both Justin's mother and Mr. Brooks turned on him. "What do you think you can do for her grandmother?" Mom asked, at the same time as Mr. Brooks was saying, "What do you think you're going to do for the old bat?" The only difference between them was that Mr. Brooks knew Mrs. Bentley while Justin's mom didn't.

"I don't know," he admitted. "If I talk with people back in the home timeline, maybe I'll come up with something. I do want to try."

"Because you're sweet on Beckie, that's why," Mr. Brooks said.

"*Are* you?" Justin's mother demanded.

Justin didn't like getting yelled at in stereo any more than anyone else would have. He couldn't do anything about it here. "Some," he said, because Mr. Brooks would have made him out to be a liar if he tried to deny it. But he went on, "Seems only fair we try to help her grandmother, though. She might have picked up the disease from one of us."

"Not likely, not when the immunity shots seem to be working," Mr. Brooks said.

"You didn't let me finish!" Justin said. Mr. Brooks blinked. Justin didn't talk back a whole lot. Most of the time, he was on the easygoing side. That seemed to make him more effective when he did lose it. He went on, "Or she might have caught it—probably did catch it—when she was coming down to Charleston with you. Any way you look at it, it's our fault. We ought to fix it if we can."

"Would you say the same thing if you didn't like this girl?" his mother asked.

"I hope so," Justin answered.

Mr. Brooks started to laugh. Justin stared at him. So did his mom. "Let him try, Cyndi," the coin and stamp dealer said. "Sometimes, if you're eighteen or so, you've got to lower your head and charge. If he can talk the people in the home timeline into doing something about it, more power to him. And if he can't—well, he gave it his best shot, and he won't be mad at *us* for stopping him."

"It won't work," Justin's mother said.

"I don't think it will, either." Mr. Brooks talked as if Justin weren't there, which annoyed him. But they did let him try, and that was all that really mattered.

He went down to a room in the basement he had to enter

through a palm lock. The wrong prints would have immovably locked the door and turned on self-destruct switches behind it. He had some of the right ones.

Inside, everything came from the home timeline: plastic chairs, desk, PowerBook. Any kind of communication between alternates was hard. You needed enormous bandwidth to send even old-fashioned e-mail. And Justin did exactly that.

If you have a cure for the disease Ohio has turned loose on Virginia ready, please send some doses as soon as you can, he typed.

He waited. And he waited. And he waited some more. After what seemed like forever but was nine minutes by the clock on the wall (also from the home timeline, even if local ones were just as good), he got an answer. *Who is ill, and how serious is it?* wrote the person on the other end of the line.

It's pretty serious, Justin answered. *An old lady we stayed with in Elizabeth is sick now. She came to Charleston with Mr. Brooks. She probably caught the disease riding in the car with him. Only fair for us to help out if we can.*

Another pause. The message crossed the timelines in an instant. Figuring out what to do about it—figuring out whether to do anything—took longer. After another eternity, this one of eleven minutes, a reply appeared on the PowerBook's screen. *Regret that the possibility of spreading disease across the alternates makes this impossible.*

Justin said something that had to do with manure. He'd had plenty of time to think about this, and he wasn't going to take *no* lying down. *You've got to have a quarantine center on some alternate with no people in it,* he wrote. *Send the transposition chamber there and decontaminate it before you use it again.*

There is a quarantine center, admitted whoever it was back in the home timeline. *But there is no opening for a transposition chamber at what matches your location. The chamber cannot materialize inside solid ground, not without an explosion.*

He talked about fertilizer some more. He already knew a chamber couldn't come out inside of something solid. The boom that followed if it tried wouldn't be small. *How far from here is the closest digging equipment?* he asked. If the person back in the home timeline said it was five hundred kilometers away, he knew he'd have to give up.

Another pause followed. He had a pretty good idea of what was going on this time. The person back in the home timeline was checking the answer to his question. As time stretched, Justin started to suspect that person was also checking to see whether to tell him the truth.

About 500 meters away, Justin knew it was crazy to think the response appeared on the screen reluctantly, but it felt that way to him. He had to read it twice to be sure no *kilo* lay in front of *meters.* When he was, he whooped and did a war dance in the bare little room.

They couldn't see the war dance back in the home timeline. So the quarantine alternate did have some kind of installation in what corresponded to Charleston, did it? He ran back to the laptop and wrote, *Then what are you waiting for?*

Authorization of the effort and expense. The answer came as a dash of cold water. It reminded him he was working for a big corporation. The people who ran Crosstime Traffic worried about right and wrong only as much as they had to. They thought about cost and trouble first.

We would be fixing a problem we helped cause, Justin typed. *We're not supposed to interfere here. Curing Mrs. Bentley would be fixing our interference.*

And would be an interference of its own, came the cold-blooded reply. It was followed by, *Wait. I'll get back to you.*

Justin wondered where the person back in the home timeline thought he would go. Out of the basement here? Not likely! He wanted that answer. And he wanted it to be what he wanted it to be. He tried to sort that out inside his head. He didn't have much luck, but he knew what he meant.

He waited, and kept on waiting. This time, a good half-hour went by before new words appeared on the PowerBook's screen. *Okay,* it said. *They're digging. As soon as the GPS says they're in just the right place, we'll send a transposition chamber from the home timeline to you. Go in, take what you find inside, and get out. The chamber will head for the quarantine alternate. Don't hang around, or you'll go with it. Do you understand?*

Oh, yes. I understand, Justin wrote. *Thank you!*

Don't thank me. It wasn't my idea, and I don't think it's a good one, said the person on the other end of the connection. *But they're going to do it anyway. This Mrs. Bentley will let them make sure the antiviral is as good as they think it is, and one more connection to the quarantine alternate may come in handy. Out.* The dismissal looked very final.

He didn't care how it looked. He punched his fist in the air and shouted, "Yes!" The secret basement room echoed with it. He had wrestled with the powers that be, and had prevailed.

He went back upstairs, first carefully closing the door behind him. As soon as he walked into the shop, his mother started, "Justin, honey, I'm sorry they wouldn't give you. . . ." Then she got a look at his face. She stared. "They didn't?" Behind his spectacle lenses, Mr. Brooks' eyes were enormous, too.

"They sure did!" Justin said.

"But how? Why?" His mother shook her head in disbelief.

"They told me—they told me over and over—they wouldn't, they couldn't, get me out even if I came down sick. They meant it, too. I was sure they meant it."

"Maybe that's it," Randolph Brooks said. "You believed them, so you didn't argue very hard. Justin wouldn't take no for an answer. He kept looking for angles, and I guess he found one. Congrats, kid." He stuck out his hand. Justin gravely shook it.

He pictured a bulldozer in the quarantine alternate, an alternate where men never evolved at all. He pictured a virgin forest full of passenger pigeons and other birds extinct for centuries in the home timeline. He pictured one humongous hole in the ground. When it was deep enough, they'd be able to send a transposition chamber there.

"What exactly is going on?" His mother's voice had something in it he'd never heard there before, not directed at him. She was asking the question the way she would have to another grown-up—and wasn't *that* something, as long as we were on the subject?

He explained. Then he said, "I'm going down to the subbasement to wait for the chamber to come through."

"Or for the *Robert E. Lee*," Mr. Brooks said, which didn't mean anything to Justin. The older man added, "You may have a long wait if they're digging."

"That's okay. I don't care." Justin all but flew down the stairs. He got past another palm lock to go down to the lowest level below the shop. Yellow lines showed where the chamber would materialize. He stayed behind them. He knew the drill.

An hour went by, then another one. Some of his enthusiasm disappeared. But he was too stubborn to go back up for a sandwich or a fizz or whatever. At last, after close to four hours, the transposition chamber appeared. It had no human backup operator.

Under the circumstances, that made sense. A package sat on one of the front seats. Justin grabbed it, then got out as fast as he could. Half a minute later, the chamber softly and silently vanished away.

He didn't care. He had the package. That was all that really mattered.

Thirteen

Beckie watched Gran and watched the clock and worried more with every few minutes that slid past. Justin was right—hospitals couldn't do much for this disease. But could he do anything at all? And would waiting to find out cost her—and Gran—too much?

Gran wasn't even pretending to watch TV any more. She just lay on the couch, as out of it as a yam. Beckie had made a cold compress from a hand towel in the bathroom and ice from the noisy machine down the hall. She'd bought aspirins with Virginia money from Gran's purse. She'd even got her grandmother to take them, which wasn't easy. But the fever stayed high.

A hospital could give her an IV, keep her from drying up like a raisin. Once the thought came to Beckie, it didn't want to go away. She kept looking over at Gran and trying to decide when bad turned to worse. The more she brooded, the more she doubted she would wait till five o'clock.

On the other hand, would an ambulance even come if she called one? She still heard spatters of gunfire, and sometimes gunfire that wasn't spatters. A firefight seemed to last forever. It really did go on for half an hour. Even after it ended, quiet didn't come—more spatters followed on its heels.

At half past two, somebody knocked on the door. Beckie all but flew to get there. One second, she was in the chair. The next, she was looking through the little eye-level spyglass. In between? She had no idea.

It was Justin, all right. She undid the dead bolts and slid the chains out of their grooves—Virginia hotels assumed bad things could happen to you if you weren't careful. Bad things could happen to you if you weren't careful out on the streets, too, or even if you were.

"You okay?" Beckie asked Justin.

"Yeah." He nodded. "I got stopped at one checkpoint, but I showed 'em my regular ID and they let me through." He made it sound easy.

"What if they recognized you?" Beckie said.

Justin laughed. "Fat chance. I didn't have a helmet on, I shaved, my face wasn't filthy, and I didn't smell bad. Boy, was I glad to take a shower."

"I believe you." She pointed to the brown paper bag in his left hand. "What have you got in there?"

"The cure for your grandmother. I hope." Justin started over to the couch. "How is she?"

"Like you see. Not good," Beckie answered. "I wasn't going to wait a whole lot longer, no matter what you said."

He felt Gran's forehead, then jerked his hand away the way she had earlier. "I don't blame you. She's hot, isn't she?" He opened the bag and took out something that looked like a syringe with a CO_2 cartridge riding shotgun.

"What's that thing?" Beckie pointed to it.

"Air-blast hypo," Justin answered. "They've been using them for a couple of years here. Don't you have 'em in California?"

"No." Beckie wouldn't have thought Virginia was ahead of her own state in anything, but you never could tell.

Justin rolled up the right sleeve of Gran's blouse and held

the air-blast hypo just above her biceps. When he pressed the button, the thing made a noise between a hiss and a sneeze. He straightened up. "Let me do you, too, in case you've got it."

"All right," she said warily. She hated shots. The air-blast hypo made that funny noise again. The thing stung, but less than a needle would have.

"There," Justin said. "That ought to do it."

"Thanks—I think." Beckie looked at her arm. She saw a red mark, but no blood. "Let me see your gadget." Plainly, Justin didn't want to, but he couldn't find any excuse not to. She took it from him. It said it was a Subskin Deluxe—said so in half a dozen languages, including one that looked like Chinese. It also said it was made in Slovenia. "Where's Slovenia?" Beckie'd never heard of it.

"Isn't it a province in Austria-Hungary?" Justin said.

"I don't know, but if it is . . ." Beckie shrugged. Austria-Hungary had been a mess for an awfully long time. The government treated some of its minorities as badly as Southern states treated Negroes. "Why would you buy your, uh, Subskin Deluxes from Slovenia?"

"Because they're cheap, probably," Justin answered, which did make a certain basic sense.

Even so, Beckie repeated, "Slovenia," in a way that suggested she had trouble believing it—which she did. And she found another question: "Why do you have medicine that may help Gran if the hospitals here don't?"

"They will, real soon now," Justin said.

Beckie started to get mad. "That doesn't answer what I asked you."

Before he could say anything, Gran stirred on the couch. "Get me some water, Beckie, will you?" she said. She didn't sound what you'd call strong, but that was the first time she'd made sense for hours.

"Wow," Justin said. "I didn't think it would work like *that*."

Beckie hurried into the bathroom. She filled a glass and brought it to her grandmother. "Here you go, Gran," she said. When she felt the old woman's forehead, she was amazed all over again. Gran still had a fever, but not the killing kind she'd been fighting a little while before.

She held out the glass when she'd emptied it. "Fetch me some more, would you? I'm mighty dry inside. And could you call down to room service for some food? Feels like I haven't eaten anything in ages." She suddenly noticed Justin was there. "Oh. The boy. Hello."

"Hello," Justin said. "I'm glad you're feeling better."

"Thank you," Beckie told him in a low voice as she went past him to get Gran another glass of water. He nodded. He really did seem as surprised as she was about how well the medicine was working. She called room service and ordered soft-boiled eggs and toast for Gran. Then she said, "Justin brought you the medicine that helped break your fever."

"Went to the drug store for you, did he?" Gran said. "That was nice of him. I've been sicker before—you'd better believe I have. Why, I remember a couple of times. . . ." And she was off. She never got tired of talking about her ailments, and she didn't realize *how* sick she'd been here. She was lucky, or it looked that way to Beckie.

Once Gran got going, you didn't have to listen to her. She was her own best company. Beckie talked under her drone: "Will you please answer my question? How come you've got this medicine before the hospitals do?"

"It's a secret," Justin said unhappily. "You really shouldn't look a gift horse in the mouth."

Listening to Gran, looking at her, told Beckie he had a point, and a good one. She was reviving right before their eyes. It was amazing to watch. Even so, Beckie said, "I want to know. I won't blab, honest. You know me pretty well by now. Do I break promises?"

Somebody knocked on the door. It was room service, with a tray for Gran. When Beckie found she was out of Virginia cash, Justin tipped the black man who brought it. He touched the brim of his cap with a forefinger. "Thank you kindly, suh," he said, and withdrew.

Gran started eating soft-boiled eggs as if she thought they'd be outlawed tomorrow. Sadly, Justin said, "I wonder what that waiter was really thinking about us. Nothing good, that's for sure."

Even though Beckie had wondered the same thing, hearing it from a Virginian was strange. She wanted to ask Justin about that, too. *One thing at a time,* she told herself. "*Do* I break promises?" she asked again.

"Nooo," he admitted, sounding as if he didn't want to. "Okay, then. Here." He reached into his pocket and pulled out something—a folded envelope. "Hang on to this. Don't open it till you get back home to California. Promise?"

"I promise," she said, and put it in her purse. "What do I do with it then?"

"That's the other half of the promise," Justin answered. "Look at it. Keep it. But don't do anything else with it. These are . . . good-bye promises, I guess you'd say. All right?"

"All right," Beckie said firmly. But then, not so firmly, she went on, "Good-bye promises?"

"Afraid so." Justin nodded. "Doesn't look like we're going to stick around here much longer."

"You're going back to Fredericksburg? You can do that?" Beckie asked.

"Sure. We're going back to Fredericksburg." Justin was lying through his teeth. Beckie knew it. She also knew he wanted her to know it. But before she could ask him any questions, he wagged a finger at her. "Don't. Don't even start, okay? This has to do with your promises. I can't tell you how, but you'll understand better— a little better, anyway—when you open the envelope."

Naturally, that made her want to open it right away. But she *was* somebody who kept promises, so she nodded and said, "I can hardly wait."

He smiled. She got the feeling she'd passed a test. "I'd better go," he said. "I'm awful glad the medicine worked so well for your grandmother. And . . ." He smiled a crooked smile and shook his head. "Nah. Even if things were different, I don't suppose it would have worked out."

"Neither do I, not really," Beckie said. "But even so, since you're going . . ." She took a step forward. So did Justin. Afterwards, she never did figure out who kissed whom first. His arms were tight around her, but not too tight. They felt good.

Behind her, Gran coughed.

Beckie pulled away just long enough to say, "Oh, hush," and went back to what she was doing. Finally, it was done. She took a deep breath. Then she asked, "Will I ever see you again?"

"Maybe. You never know for sure," Justin said. "But I wouldn't bet on it."

She nodded. "That's about what I thought. Take care of yourself . . . in Fredericksburg."

Justin's smile said he noticed the little pause and knew what it meant. "Thanks. You, too, when you get back to L.A. I don't think the war here will last a whole lot longer. You'll be able to go through quarantine or whatever and head for home. And now"—he bobbed his head, suddenly and surprisingly shy again—"so long." Faster than Beckie expected, he opened the door and was gone.

"So long." She hoped he heard it before the closing door cut it off. But she was never sure about that afterwards, either.

"The boy," Gran said, "he's a nice enough boy."

Beckie sighed. "More than nice enough," she said.

Down in the subbasement, Justin and his mother and Mr. Brooks waited for the transposition chamber. "Home!" Mom said. But it wouldn't be home, not yet. It would be a stretch in the quarantine alternate, while they and the chamber that carried them there got cleaned out. It wouldn't be much fun, but almost anything was better than staying in battered Charleston.

Mr. Brooks set a hand on Justin's shoulder. "Way to go," he said. "I'm not kidding, not even a little bit. You nudged Crosstime Traffic into doing things it didn't want to do, and that's not easy. If you hadn't, no telling how long we would've been stuck here, or whether they ever would have let us get away from this alternate."

"I couldn't get them to bend, that's for sure," Justin's mother said.

"You didn't think you'd be able to when you started," Mr. Brooks told her. "You settled for no. Justin didn't want to hear it, and he kept after them till he got what he did want. If you aim to get anywhere, that's what you need to do."

"I just want to get back to the home timeline," Justin said.

"Well, we'll only be one stop away," said Mr. Brooks. "And you won't have anybody shooting at you while you wait."

A few days earlier, it would have been a joke, and a tasteless joke at that. Now Justin understood how wonderful not getting shot at was. Most of the people of Charleston, white and black, probably appreciated it by now.

Silently and without any fuss, the transposition chamber appeared. The door slid open. Justin and his mother and Mr. Brooks got in. Justin expected the chamber to be on full remote control, the way the one that brought the antiviral for Beckie's grandmother was. But it had a human operator. Not only that, the man was smiling.

"Don't you know you're going into quarantine?" Justin asked.

"I know I'm going on vacation," the operator answered. "I'm a birder, and I'll be able to see things I never could back home." On the seat beside him were binoculars, spotting scope, camera, and two books: *Field Guide to Birds of Eastern North America* and *Guide to North American Birds Extinct in the Home Timeline*. He was ready for what he'd be doing in the quarantine alternate, all right.

Mr. Brooks laughed. "When life gives you lemons, make lemonade."

"No." The chamber operator shook his head. "Close, but not quite. When you want lemonade, go out and pick lemons. I volunteered for this run."

"I bet you didn't have much competition," Justin's mother said.

"Not a whole lot," the operator agreed. "But when I get back with my photos and the new birds on my life list, plenty of people will be jealous. Unless you're able to get out to the alternates, you'll never see these birds. Crosstime Traffic ought to run birding safaris into some of these alternates. Lots of people would pay to go."

"Don't tell us. Tell the company," Mr. Brooks said as the doors slid shut. "If they take you up on it, you'll get a suggestion bonus."

"Maybe," the operator said. Some of the lights on the board in front of him went from red to green. "Well, we're on our way." He came back to what Mr. Brooks said: "They might try to take the idea and do me out of the bonus. That would help their bottom line. But maybe not. You never can tell."

As usual, nothing seemed to happen in the chamber. Justin tried to guess how much subjective time they would need to get where they were going. However long it seemed, the sun wouldn't have moved in the sky from when they left here to when they got here. Ever since travel between alternates began, chronophysicists had been wrangling about the difference between time and duration. Justin didn't have the math to follow the argument in detail. *One of these days, maybe,* he thought.

This journey felt longer than the one from the home timeline to the alternate where the Constitution never replaced the Articles of Confederation. That meant the quarantine alternate had a much more distant breakpoint . . . if it meant anything at all. Chronophysicists were still writing papers about that in the learned journals, too.

Nothing to do but wait. Justin didn't like it. He wondered if he would go stir-crazy in the quarantine alternate. It wouldn't be very exciting there. He hoped they'd have game boxes and video players. Or maybe he could go birding with the chamber operator. Normally, he wouldn't have thought that was interesting. Seeing birds he couldn't find in the home timeline gave it a special kick, though.

More lights on the instrument panel went green. "We're here!" The operator sure sounded excited.

The doors slid open. "Passengers, please disembark," said a recorded voice coming out of a ceiling speaker.

Out Justin went. He expected to smell fresh air—not much pollution here. What he did smell was freshly dug earth. This hole in the ground hadn't been here very long. A hastily made set of wooden stairs offered a way up out of it.

Spoil from the digging ruined the look of the meadow by the Kanawha. The slab-sided prefab buildings a few hundred meters away did nothing to improve things. A Red Cross flag floated over them. Maybe that was meant to be reassuring. If it was, it didn't work, not for Justin. It struck him as wasted effort. People who showed up here would know this was a quarantine station, and the passenger pigeons and whatever else lived here wouldn't care.

Something fluttered in a tree a couple of hundred meters away, at the edge of the woods. The chamber operator—his name was Lonnie something—aimed his binoculars at it. "That's a passenger pigeon, all right!" he said. "There'll be billions of 'em in this alternate, and you can only seem 'em stuffed in a few museums back home." He held out the binoculars to Justin. "Want a look?"

"Okay." There were passenger pigeons in the alternate Justin had just left, too, but not billions of them. He couldn't remember seeing any. He pointed the binoculars at the tree. Not one but dozens of birds perched there. They were slimmer than the ordinary pigeons that scrounged for handouts in cities around the world—built more like mourning doves. They had salmon-pink bellies, gray backs, and eyes of a startling red. Justin handed the binoculars back. "Passenger pigeons, all right."

A noise came from deeper in the woods—a bear? a fox? a falling branch? Whatever it was, it spooked the birds. They erupted, not just from that oak but from all the oaks and elms and chestnuts and maples and hickories and other trees close by. As the flock zoomed past overhead, it was big enough to darken the sky. How many birds were in it? Not billions, not in this one group, but surely many, many thousands. The din of their wings was like the roar of the surf.

"Whoa!" Justin said.

"Whoa is right," Mr. Brooks said. "I've seen starlings in our Midwest and queleas in Africa, but I've never seen anything like this." He sent a wary glance up at the sky, where stragglers still whizzed past. "If you go anywhere around here, you'd better carry an umbrella."

"Let's see what kind of quarters we've got," Mom said.

They put Justin in mind of the motel room where he'd stayed in Elizabeth. They had all the basic conveniences: bed, sink, shower, soap, shampoo, computer, even a bare-bones fasarta. But they wouldn't make a home, not in a million years. Everything about them screamed, *People pen!* Well, he could put up with it till they decided he wouldn't come down sick and let him go back to the home timeline.

Food came out of a freezer and went into a microwave. There was also canned fruit, and plenty of soda. "The beer is Bud," Mr. Brooks said. He and Lonnie exchanged identical sighs. Justin thought any beer tasted nasty, so he wasn't as sympathetic as he might have been.

He let the fasarta pamper him for a little while—as much as it could, anyhow. Then he fired up the computer to find out what had gone on in the home timeline while he was stuck in Elizabeth. He hadn't had much of a chance to do that in Charleston—too many other things going on.

Getting it all in text, without video or even stills, made him feel he'd fallen back in time instead of going across it. The Russians had turned a tailored virus loose in Chechnya, and hadn't immunized enough people outside the borders to keep it from spreading. He shook his head, People had been wondering when the Russians would get their act together for hundreds of years. It hadn't happened yet. It didn't look as if it would happen any time soon, either. Russia was too big to conquer and too big to ignore, same as always.

In Iran, the Shah's secret police were executing ayatollahs again. And a suicide bomber tried to blow up the Shah's prime minister in revenge. That was also another verse of the same old song. So was the ecoterrorist outfit claiming responsibility for poisoning fifty kilometers of the Amazon to protest logging policies in Brazil. And the Scottish nationalists had blown up another British mail truck. It was as if Justin had never left the home timeline.

But getting his news like this left him strangely distant from it. He couldn't see and hear what was happening. All he could do was read about it. He had to make the pictures in his own mind, the way he would if he were reading a history book. He didn't even have any pictures to help, as he would in a book. He might have fallen back from the end of the twenty-first century to the end of the nineteenth.

Along with the usual hotel supplies were special soap and shampoo marked PLEASE USE ON YOUR FIRST DAY HERE. When Justin did, he found they smelled strongly medicinal. They probably killed a lot of the germs he'd brought from the alternate where he was staying. The shampoo wasn't easy on his hair—that was for sure.

Later, he wondered how Crosstime Traffic would know whether he used that soap and shampoo. Did transmitters in the packaging record that it was opened? Had he washed away a microchip on the surface of the soap that reacted when it got wet? Or did a camera in the shower stall send his image back to the main station in this alternate, wherever that was?

He didn't like the idea, not one bit. Probably no humans were involved—only a computer program that wouldn't squeal to a real, live person unless it caught him breaking the rules. He didn't like it anyway.

Mom squawked when he mentioned it at dinner that night. Mr. Brooks only shrugged. "With all the computer technology we've got these days, something or somebody is watching you all the time anyway. Either you get used to it or you go nuts."

"That's how it works, all right," Lonnie agreed. "I know they monitor transposition chambers." He shrugged. "What can you do?"

"There's a difference between monitoring a chamber and a shower." Justin's mother sounded like a cat with its dignity ruffled.

"To you, maybe. Not to Crosstime Traffic, especially not in a quarantine station," Lonnie said. "If you kick up a fuss, they'd say they had an interest in making sure you followed instructions. How would you convince a court they were wrong?"

What Mom said then didn't have much to do with convincing a court. It came from the heart, though. Mr. Brooks laughed. "That's telling 'em," he said.

He'd been through the army. You didn't have much privacy there. Sometimes you didn't have any. Justin had found that out himself, the hard way, when he put on Adrian's uniform. His mother had never had to do anything like that. She didn't know how lucky she was, which might be literally true.

The mattress on the bed was softer than Justin liked. That kept him awake . . . oh, an extra fifteen seconds or so. He was still catching up on sleep from his hectic couple of days of carrying a gun. He didn't have any nightmares about shooting the African-American kid. That was progress, too.

Sunshine sliding between slats of the Venetian blinds poked him in the eye and woke him up the next morning. He heated up some waffles and slathered them with syrup.

Mr. Brooks came into the kitchen as Justin was fixing himself seconds. The older man made a beeline for the espresso machine. He waited impatiently while it made rude noises. "Couldn't get a decent cup of coffee in that alternate, either," he grumbled, and then, "Waffles, eh? That doesn't look too bad."

"They're okay." Justin wouldn't give them any more than that.

Mr. Brooks laughed. "You can't expect Trump City food and service here." Justin nodded. The original Trump was many years dead, but his name remained a byword for extravagant luxury. Justin had seen pictures of him on the Net. He wore stiff, old-fashioned, uncomfortable-looking clothes, but he always had one very pretty girl or another on his arm. The girls probably didn't think the clothes were funny.

Justin—and Lonnie—spotted Carolina parakeets the next day. They heard them before they saw them. To Justin's ear, the squawks and chirps belonged to a tropical jungle, not these ordinary Eastern woods. But there they were: green birds with yellow heads and, some of them, reddish faces.

Lonnie was in seventh heaven. "They've been extinct in the home timeline about as long as passenger pigeons have," he said. "They never were as common, though. Of course, nothing was as common as passenger pigeons before the white man came. But Audubon, back in the first part of the nineteenth century, talks about Carolina parakeets all the way out past the Mississippi. We don't know what we're missing."

"We've got starlings instead," Justin said.

He wanted to hit a nerve with that, and he got what he wanted. Lonnie said some things about starlings that would have shocked the Audubon Society and the SPCA. Then he said something even less polite. Justin laughed, but he knew Lonnie was kidding on the square. Starlings were nothing but pests.

Lonnie went into the woods looking for ivory-bill woodpeckers. As far as Justin was concerned, the chamber operator was welcome to that kind of exploring. No cell-phone net here, wild animals that had never learned to fear people . . . He shook his head. If an ivory-bill happened to show up where he could see it, that would be great. And if not, he wouldn't lose any sleep over it.

But when Lonnie came back that night, he was even happier than he had been when he set out. He waved his video camera. "I've got 'em!" he said, as if he'd gone hunting with a shotgun instead of a lens and a flash drive.

"Way to go," Mr. Brooks said. "But now that you've seen the birds you wanted to see most, what will you do for the rest of the time you're here?"

The question didn't faze Lonnie. "Keep on watching them," he answered. "When will I have another chance?"

"Well, you've got me there," Mr. Brooks admitted.

They stayed in quarantine for three weeks. Once a week, a computerized lab system drew blood from their fingers and analyzed it for any trace of genetic material from the plague virus. The system did the same for breath they exhaled into plastic bags. After three negative readings in a row, the powers that be were . . . almost satisfied. More bars of the disinfectant soap and tubes of the disinfectant shampoo appeared, with instructions to use them as on the first day in quarantine.

As Justin washed, he wondered again if he was under surveillance. He went on washing. What else could he do? Maybe, when he got back to the home timeline, he would ask some questions. Or maybe he wouldn't. Maybe those weren't smart questions to ask.

The transposition chamber appeared in the hole in the ground the next morning. Justin and his mother and Mr. Brooks and Lonnie hurried down to it. Lonnie had color prints of some of the birds he'd seen. Birders in the home timeline would turn green when they saw them.

Going back to the home timeline seemed to take about as long as traveling from the alternate to the quarantine station had. But when the chamber's door slid open, it was still the same time as it had been when the machine set out. It was as if what happened inside the chamber while it was traveling between alternates didn't count.

When the doors opened, there was the room from which Justin and his mother had left the home timeline, bound for Mr. Brooks' coin and stamp shop in the alternate where the Constitution never became the law of the land.

"Welcome back," said a woman who had to be a Crosstime Traffic honcho. "You had quite a time, didn't you?"

Justin wondered if she was wearing nose filters to block any viruses quarantine didn't catch. Then he wondered how paranoid he was getting. Of course, you probably weren't fit to live in the home timeline if you weren't a little bit paranoid.

"*I* had quite a time." Lonnie gestured with his camera. "Pigeons and parakeets and woodpeckers and—"

"That's not what I meant." The way the woman cut him off said she was a wheel, all right.

"Just before we came back, I saw that Virginia and Ohio finally called a truce," Justin said.

She nodded briskly. "That's right. And maybe it will give us a chance to help Virginia change a little bit. A few people there *are* smart enough to see that mistreating their African-American minority only puts a KICK ME! sign on their own backs."

"Not many. Not nearly enough," Randolph Brooks said. Justin and his mother both nodded. The only person Justin had seen who was really appalled by the way Virginia treated African Americans was Beckie, and she was from California.

"No, not enough, not yet," the woman executive agreed. "But some. And an election to the House of Burgesses is coming up soon. We'll put money into the moderates' campaigns. Even if they win—and not all of them will—this isn't something we can change overnight. It'll be a start, though. We'll keep working on it, there and in some other states."

"Are you working in Mississippi in that alternate?" Justin asked.

The executive gave him a sharp look. "Not as hard as we are some other places," she admitted. "There's a feeling that the white minority there is getting what's coming to it."

"Why?" he said. "The revolt there happened more than a hundred years ago. There aren't any whites in Mississippi old enough to have oppressed African Americans. And they get it just as bad as blacks do other places in the South in that alternate. Fair's fair."

"Logically, I suppose you're right," she said. "Logic doesn't always have anything to do with feelings, though, and feelings are important, too. We've only got limited resources in any one alternate. We have to decide where the best place to use them is."

"Feelings are a funny thing to base policy on," Mr. Brooks remarked.

"Not necessarily," the executive said. "We back groups that think and feel closer to the way we do. We want to see them succeed. If we were still racists ourselves, we'd back the hardliners in Virginia, not the moderates. And we'd feel we were right to do it, because they'd be like us. We do a lot of the things we do just because we do them, not because they're logical. One thing the alternates have taught us is that there are lots and lots and lots of different ways to do things, and most of them work all right in their own context."

"Mm, you've got something there, but only something," Mr. Brooks said. "Virginia wouldn't be in such a mess if blacks there didn't want equality."

"And we think they ought to have it," the executive said. "A racist would say they ought to be educated so they don't even want it. That's logical, too—it just starts from a different premise. It could work. There are alternates where that kind of thing does work."

She seemed to think she had all the answers. Justin doubted that. People who were always sure often outsmarted themselves. But she did find interesting questions. He found an interesting question of his own: "Can we go now?"

"Yes," the executive said. "If you're not healthy, we need to do a lot more work with our quarantine alternate." Maybe she wasn't wearing nose filters, then. She went on, "It was an interesting discussion, I thought. But remember, freedom of speech is just a custom, too. It's a good one, but it's not a law of nature."

Right then, Justin wasn't thinking about laws of nature. After three weeks of bland quarantine rations, he was thinking about the biggest double burger in the world, with French fries—no, onion rings—on the side, and a chocolate shake to wash everything down. He headed for the stairs. Somewhere within a block or two, he'd be able to find just what he wanted.

Home. Beckie had started to wonder if she would ever see it again. She and Gran went through quarantine in Virginia. Then they went through quarantine in Ohio. And *then* they went through quarantine in California. It would have been bad enough if she were cooped up all by herself. Going through quarantine with her grandmother really made her want to stay away from Gran for the rest of her life.

But she didn't quite go looking for blunt instruments. It was over now. She had her own room, and she didn't feel like a guinea pig going in and out of it.

No plagues. No guns going off. No bodies stinking in the streets. No humidity. Back with her family and friends. It all seemed like heaven.

And everybody made a fuss over her, too. "We're so glad to have you back," her mother said over and over again. "We were so worried about you, and we couldn't find any way to get through. E-mail didn't work, phones didn't work, even letters came back. UNDELIVERABLE—WAR ZONE, they said."

Gran sniffed. "I don't suppose anybody worried about *me*."

"Of course we did," Beckie's father said loyally. Beckie didn't know how he put up with Mom's mother so well. Mom described it as the patience of Job. Beckie didn't know exactly what that meant till she found it in the Bible one day. When she was in a good mood, she thought her mother was exaggerating. When she was in a bad mood, she didn't. After going through quarantine with Gran, she was convinced Job didn't have it so bad.

"Well, you could have called and said so, then," Gran said.

"I just explained why we couldn't. The phones weren't working." Mom had been putting up with Gran much longer than Dad and Beckie had. If that wasn't heroism above and beyond the call of duty, Beckie didn't know what would be. And Mom, growing up with Gran for a mother, turned out nice, probably in reaction. If it wasn't in reaction, what was it? A miracle? Knowing Gran wouldn't pay attention, Mom just kept repeating herself till something eventually sank in.

"What was being in a war like?" Dad asked.

"Scary like you wouldn't believe," Beckie answered. "You didn't have any control over where the shells came down. If they hit you, even if you were in a trench, that was it. Just luck. Same with bullets." She shivered, remembering some of the things she'd heard and seen and smelled.

Gran went off to call some of her friends. Beckie's mother said, "It must have been awful, stuck with your grandmother and stuck in that little town with nothing to do. Virginia!" She rolled her eyes. "I shouldn't have let you go."

"It . . . could have been better." Beckie let it go there. Some of the things that had happened to her, she wondered if she would ever tell anybody. She doubted it.

"Did you make any friends at all while you were there?" her mother asked.

"There was a guy named Justin. He was up there from Charleston. He was nice," Beckie said. "He was . . . interesting, too. He could get things. When we went down to Charleston, he got Gran the medicine for when she came down sick. I swear that was before the Virginia hospitals had it."

"I wonder how," Mom said.

"So do—" Beckie stopped. She snapped her fingers. Then she ran for her bedroom.

"What's going on?" her mother called after her.

She didn't answer. "I almost forgot!" she said when she picked up her purse, but she'd closed the door by then. Her family—

except Gran some of the time—respected that as a privacy signal. She'd kept her promise to Justin: kept it so well, she nearly forgot about it. But she was home at last. She could finally find out what he'd given her.

She had to rummage to find the folded-up envelope. When she opened it, a brass-yellow coin fell into her hand. There were lots of different coins in North America, but she knew she'd never seen one like this before. Benjamin Franklin looked up at her—she recognized him right away. LIBERTY was written above his head. On one side of his bust were the words IN GOD WE TRUST, on the other the date 2091 and a small capital P.

Marveling, she flipped the coin over. The design on the reverse was an eagle with thirteen arrows in one claw and a branch—an olive branch?—with thirteen leaves in the other. Ice walked up her back when she read the words above it: UNITED STATES OF AMERICA. Below that, in smaller letters, were the words E PLURIBUS UNUM, which didn't mean anything to her right away. Under the eagle, the coin said, ONE HUNDRED DOLLARS.

"United States of America," she whispered, and turned the coin back to Franklin's portrait. Yes, it still said *2091* there. It was real. It *felt* real, not like some fake Justin had had made up. Why would he do that, anyway, and how could he? She'd asked him to explain, and he did. And if she spent the rest of her life wondering about the explanation . . . Well, wasn't that better than going through life never wondering about anything at all?

The
Disunited States
of America

by Harry Turtledove

Reader's Guide

About This Guide

The information, activities, and discussion questions that follow are intended to enhance your reading of *The Disunited States of America*. Please feel free to adapt these materials to suit your needs and interests.

Writing and Research Activities

1. Harry Turtledove starts readers in a moment of intense, dangerous action. With friends or classmates, make a list of novels with action-packed opening paragraphs. If desired, make another list of novels beginning in a slower manner, perhaps with description instead of action. Discuss how these different types of openings affect your reading of a novel.

2. What would you do if you found yourself riding in a car atop a pile of guns? Write 2–3 paragraphs describing your thoughts and actions. Or write the opening paragraphs of your own story, starting with an action scene.

3. Imagine you are an executive from Crosstime Traffic. Give a presentation to friends or classmates describing the alternate universes your company has discovered, listing some

benefits of crosstime travel, and noting some of the cautions that must be used when visiting alternates. If desired, include graphs or tables, PowerPoint, modified maps, or other visual aids to enhance your presentation.

4. In the character of Beckie, trapped at the Snodgrass house, or Justin, alone with Mr. Brooks at the motel in Elizabeth, write a journal entry beginning, "If I have to stay here another day . . ."

5. Go to the library or online to learn more about biological warfare throughout history. Use your research to create a short report or informational poster to present to friends or classmates.

6. In the character of Mr. Brooks, write a memo to the Crosstime Traffic corporation describing the war in which you find yourself and asking that Crosstime break its noninterference rules to help. Include a suggestion for the type of help Crosstime should provide and your argument for why this exception should be made.

7. Go to the library or online to find a definition for the political term "constitution." Use this information in an introduction to an essay discussing the value of a constitution. Be sure to point to moments in the novel where having a constitution might have meant the difference between war and peace.

8. In the novel, Harry Turtledove creates a bleak and disturbing world. Make a playlist of songs, a catalogue of artworks,

or another creative work which you feel reflects the chaos of Beckie Royer's America.

9. In the character of a newspaper reporter from Ohio or Virginia, write an article explaining how the war started and another describing the end of the conflict. If possible have friends or classmates write articles from differing points of view to share with the group.

10. Has reading this novel impacted your thoughts about racism in America today? Write an essay entitled "Things Crosstime Traffic Can Teach Us About Real-Time Racism." If desired, clip articles from current newspapers or magazines which deal with issues also explored in the novel to share and discuss with friends or classmates, or to consider in your essay.

11. Imagine you are Justin one year after he has returned from Beckie's alternate. Write a letter to Beckie explaining why you gave her the coin, what you hope she will do with it, and whether you still believe giving her the coin was the right thing to do. Read your letter aloud to friends or classmates, then debate whether or not you should try to somehow send the letter to Beckie in her world.

12. Imagine you are Beckie at age twenty-eight, attending your ten-year high school reunion. What is happening in California? Are you there? What is going on in the rest of your "disunited states"? What have you done with the coin Justin gave you? Answer these questions in a presentation to your reunion classmates.

Questions for Discussion

1. The novel opens as Beckie Royer finds herself an unwilling accomplice in a gun-running effort. Describe the life Beckie left behind in California. How are Ohio and Virginia different from her home state?

2. What is Crosstime Traffic? How does it bring Justin and his mother to Beckie's America? What are the critical differences between Justin's and Beckie's timelines?

3. As they discuss the issues of racial equality and freedom on page 72, Mr. Brooks says to Justin, "You may as well ask why terrorists in the home timeline don't get it. . . . They've got free countries for examples, too. But they worry more about being on top than being free." Do you think Mr. Brooks' thoughts about terrorists could be applied to our own timeline and international political situation? Explain your answer.

4. Describe the different ways in which Beckie and Justin feel like foreigners in Virginia. How might this feeling of foreignness contribute to their friendship with each other?

5. In chapter 4, Beckie discusses racism with Justin. How does Justin react? How might the conversation have gone differently had the two been in California? In Justin's home timeline?

6. Explain the troubles between Ohio and Virginia. How does this lead to the virus attack? Do you think that the use of a virus as a weapon should be allowed—even in warfare? Why

or why not? How might the risks of viral warfare be compared with the dynamics of nuclear warfare?

7. How does the death of Mrs. Snodgrass mark a critical moment in the novel? How does it affect the thoughts and actions of Mr. Snodgrass, Beckie, and Justin?

8. Do you agree with Beckie and Justin when, at various points in the action, they agree that theirs is a relationship unlikely to work out in the long run? Had you been Beckie or Justin, might you have approached the relationship differently? If so, how and why—or, why not?

9. What happens when Justin puts on the Virginia soldier's uniform? What does it teach him about loyalty? About the reality of Beckie's alternate? About the value of life?

10. What does Justin come to realize about Mr. Brooks' past at the end of the novel? To what "club" do both Justin and Mr. Brooks now belong? How do you think you would feel to be a part of that club?

11. Near the end of the novel, Justin persuades Crosstime Traffic to send a viral antidote to save Beckie's gran. Describe the argument Justin makes. Had you been the Crosstime staff member corresponding with Justin, would you have been persuaded to send the antidote? Why or why not?

12. Can reading *The Disunited States of America* offer us lessons in handling situations involving racial inequality or other problems in our world today? Explain your answer.